THE Darkest KING

BOOK ONE

BY JULIETTE N. BANKS

COPYRIGHT

ABOUT THE AUTHOR

Juliette is an indie romance author who has taken the romance genre by storm with her popular bestselling series The Moretti Blood Brothers and The Dufort Dynasty.
Juliette has a vast background in consumer marketing and was previously published by Random House. She lives in Auckland, New Zealand, with Tilly, her Mainecoon kitty, and all her book boyfriends.

Official Juliette N. Banks website:
www.juliettebanks.com

Instagram:
www.instagram.com/juliettebanksauthor

Facebook:
www.facebook.com/juliettenbanks
www.facebook.com/groups/authorjuliettebanksreaders

TikTok:
@juliettebanksauthor

ALSO BY JULIETTE N. BANKS

Go to www.juliettebanks.com to buy or download

The Dark Kings of NYC

The Darkest King

The Ruthless King

COMING SOON

COMING SOON

THE DUFORT DYNASTY

Sinful Duty (**FREE**)

Forbidden Touch

Total Possession

Desire Unbound

Dark Surrender

THE MORETTI BLOOD BROTHERS

The Vampire Prince (FREE)

The Vampire Protector

The Vampire Spy

The Vampire's Christmas

The Vampire Assassin

The Vampire Awoken

The Vampire Lover

The Vampire Wolf

The Vampire Warrior

The Vampire's Oath

The Vampire's Fate

THE MORETTI BLOOD WOLVES

Steamy paranormal shifter romance

The Alpha Wolf

The Unbound Wolf

The Protector Wolf

REALM OF THE IMMORTALS

The Archangels Battle

The Archangel's Heart

The Archangel's Star

THE
Darkest
KING

1

CONNOR

ere we fucking go again.

Another gala event. Another speech. Another night spent with strangers who schmooze me for my money and power.

It's all part of the charade I'm playing, I remind myself, tugging on the sleeve of my Armani jacket and adjusting my cufflinks before leaning back into the soft leather seats of my limousine. Nothing to prepare. My finance manager arranged the transfer of funds this afternoon, and my scriptwriter emailed me the same cut-and-paste version of the speech I've already given at least five times this year.

Only the name changes, with a modified reason why the cause is so important to Barrett Enterprises.

Except this one *is* important to me...personally.

The We Are Family Foundation is committed to the care of orphans in the U.S. and around the world—a cause I deem important. No one should be alone because they don't have parents or a family.

There are eight fucking billion people on the planet. Few of them with the sort of money I have to contribute, to make a difference. Still, I'd rather have sent a check and sat at home, sipping on my Macallan Gold, watching porn, and jacking off.

Or rather, ordering in.

I don't mean Chinese food.

Truth is, I don't watch porn. I have no need for it. If I want a woman spread before me, I can have one at any time.

I'm Connor Barrett, one of the wealthiest and most powerful men in New York City.

Yet, I'm not who I say I am.

I'm both a ghost and, ironically, one of the most visible men in America. Why hide in the shadows when you can hide out in the open? The opposite of what they trained me to do in the marines.

Even more ironic—I have skilled security protecting me, which even they know is unnecessary. I'm six foot four, broad and muscular. And I've been trained to kill.

I *have* killed.

Still, I can't look over my shoulder while running a billion-dollar empire, doing deals with politicians and untrustworthy businessmen who would love nothing more than to see me fail.

That happens when people owe you favors. They know I'll come knocking, and when I do, they won't say no.

No one says no.

I'm the founder and CEO of Barrett Enterprises. Entrepreneur, philanthropist, investor, and prolific businessman.

Men want to destroy me.

Women want to fuck me.

I reach for the crystal cut glass filled with whiskey in the console beside me and bring it to my lips, remembering the last woman who slid down my black silk sheets and wrapped her red-stained mouth around my cock.

God, I could do with round two.

It's been weeks since I've had a good release without using my fist. I should've booked someone for this evening, but I didn't think ahead.

Booked? Yes. They're not prostitutes—I'm paying for their discretion. I'm paying for control.

Something I never give away.

But I'm careful about the women I fuck. By the time they enter my penthouse, they've accepted payment and signed a confidentiality agreement—one no lawyer would ever let their client sign—which demands their silence and agreement to the terms of our time together.

One, should they break, that would destroy their lives.

So, not prostitutes, but they *are* escorts.

They're instructed to undress and blindfold themselves in my private elevator. I'm not fucking Batman—everyone in NYC knows my address—but it just sets the scene. One which makes it clear why they are here, and that intimacy is not welcome.

I'm not looking for a wife.

I need to stay a ghost.

If my enemies knew I was alive, I would be hunted.

The last words my father said to me...*Never tell anyone who you are, son. Run!*

The familiar grinding of my teeth, the pain slicing up the back of my neck from my fury, brings me back to the present, and I blink. I stretch one of my legs and check that the knife strapped just above my sock remains invisible. Just as all the other weapons on my body are.

I don't leave home without them.

"We're going to be a few minutes late, sir," Benson, my driver, says. I pulled him out of the military a few years ago. He knows how to scan for bombs, drive if we're attacked, and protect both of us if shit goes down. "The traffic was built up near Madison Square Gardens."

I'm silent, my body tensing, and my eyes slide over to Mack.

As if on cue, Mack Turner, my head of security, turns from the passenger seat and gives me a reassuring look. "It's an accident, Mr. Barrett. Turn up here, Benson. Then take 27th Street."

My body relaxes.

Mack is one of three men I trust with my life. He's by my side ninety percent of the time.

Not when I fuck.

That's not my kink.

While the We Are Family Foundation is important to me, I don't give a damn about being on time—I'm the VIP guest, and they'll wait for me. However, when you're hiding in broad daylight from the mafia—that's correct, *all* the mobsters and cartels—and are as powerful as I am, it would only take two minutes to go from being the *hunter* to the *hunted*.

Because I *am* hunting them.

They just don't fucking know it.

Glancing at my Rolex, I note I'm ten minutes late. I run my hand over my solid jaw, rubbing my dark scruff. I need to fuck. I've been agitated and impatient recently. As a dominant and controlling lover, the act helps me release built-up energy.

I nearly snort at the word *love*. There's no love in my life.

"Keep the car close when we arrive, Benson," I say darkly. "I'm only staying an hour."

"Yes, sir."

When the limo pulls up outside the Convention Center, I wait for Mack to open the door, then I climb out and stand, running my hands over my Armani tux and glancing around.

The red carpet is empty. Everyone inside is waiting for me.

In and out. That's the plan.

"Give Billy the night off tomorrow," I say to Mack without looking his way. When I take a few steps and he hasn't responded, I turn.

My dark eyes connect with his.

"You need a new location. It's not safe, Connor," Mack replies.

I nod.

He's not disagreeing with me. No one would. He'll have his reasons, and I trust him.

"Arrange it," I say, then step into the hotel lobby. The sign for the event points to the large conference rooms in the back.

To be honest, I'm surprised someone from the company organizing the event is not greeting me. I was told they would. But it's one less annoying person on this planet to deal with, so I couldn't care less.

I make my way through the space and find the room and the main door. As I reach for it, it flings open.

Ommph.

"Oh, shit!" the small body who just slammed into me whisper-yells, and the door closes behind her with a click.

Then I feel it...

Wet, cold, and seeping through the front of my tuxedo.

As I grip the petite brunette's arms and remove her from my chest, her eyes fly open wide, and I can't ignore the magnetic pull from the crystal blue globes.

Jesus, she's fucking gorgeous.

My cock wakes up and begins to swell. I imagine gripping all that long dark hair and wrapping it around my fist. Then, as panic fills her eyes, I'm tempted to smirk. But I never smile, and my hands, which have released her, want to touch her again, and that bothers me.

Who is this young woman?

"Connor Barrett," she gasps quietly, knowing who I am. Her eyes drift down over the dark liquid on my shirt, and she bites her lip, letting out a soft curse. Then those lids dip further down my body.

Don't look any lower, sweetheart, or...

Too late.

Her eyes shoot back to mine, and I say in a dark, thick voice, "You shouldn't have done that."

As she swallows, my lips curl up at the corners.

Tonight just got a whole lot more interesting.

2

MIA

Oh God! Donna is going to kill me. She'll have to hurry, as Connor Barrett looks like he's two steps ahead of her.

Then he smirks at me.

Holy fuck.

Connor Barrett doesn't smile. He was on the cover of *Forbes* once, and it was obvious the photographer had asked him to smile, but Connor just looked like he was snarling.

His smirk is different, and it just lights my panties on fire.

I stare up at those lopsided lips, square jaw, and deep chocolate eyes—full of thoughts I'm sure most women would give anything to experience—and realize Connor Barrett is a sex god.

Damn.

Until this week, I never thought I'd be standing in front of the dark-haired and ridiculously handsome man. When Donna asked who wanted to greet the billionaire when he arrived, all the girls on the team turned into something resembling a teen reality show.

I sighed and said I would do it.

"Thank you, Mia," Donna, my manager, had said. "I'm sure he won't bite."

Staring into his eyes, I'm pretty sure he does, and although I'm not in the market for a one-night stand, I think I'd be very okay with him biting me.

Anywhere.

Powerful men don't scare me. Okay, they *do* scare me, but just the right amount, according to the situation.

This isn't one of them.

Mr. Sex-God Barrett isn't a threat to me.

My panties? Oh yes.

I've grown up around much more dangerous men than Connor, and all of them would give their lives to save me. Or rather, save themselves.

My name is Mia Mancini. Daughter of Joseph, or Joe "The Rock", Mancini, head of the Italian mafia here in the United States. He's one of seven bosses affiliated with the global Italian mafia.

In other words, he's a big deal.

And yes, that makes me the mafia princess.

Unfortunately.

I'd rather be just an everyday girl, working and paying my taxes, dating and shopping at Walmart. Which I do, but it's a farce and very, very temporary.

When I left college two years ago, Father agreed, after a lot of crying and screaming, to let me go out into the world and get some work experience. My mother had died a few years earlier, and I played the card hard. You have to do what you can in the gangster world to survive. I might not like the world I grew up in, but I learned a thing or two.

I have my own apartment, a job at Bloom Events Management, friends...and no one knows who I am.

Not even Donna.

I'm just Mia.

Mia Mancini...but it's a common enough name.

Joe, my father, gave me two years, then I must return and work in the family—a.k.a. gangster—business. Or, and get this, I can marry and he will give me my trust fund.

A trust fund worth *two million dollars*.

Twenty-four years old and I have barely dated. I'm not a virgin, but dating the head of the mafia's daughter isn't on the top of any man's to-do list.

There's more.

It's likely the man I marry will be chosen by my family. Or rather, Joe. If there is a partnership to be made that benefits the family, it is expected of me. My mother primed me to be prepared, but it's not a given.

However, I have been kept out of the media's eyes and protected because of who I am.

A mafia asset.

But I have different plans. I love my family, but I don't want any part in the business they are involved with. Yes, it pays for my apartment and financed my education. I've not had the freedom of choice to do anything differently.

But that ends now.

When I marry, it will be for love.

I'm working toward freedom and independence. Or at the very least, not being involved with the soul-destroying business my family profits from.

I just haven't figured out how yet.

In around two weeks, this bubble I've been living in for nearly two years is about to burst, so my plan is to renegotiate with my father for more time.

I'm confident.

So, this mafia princess has some experience being around large and intimidating men. Just about every single one of my father's soldiers has run their eyes over my body and shown me they desire me.

I've slept with a few of my bodyguards—sorry, Papa—and enjoyed their broad chests and height compared to my petite frame, the dominant way they took me.

But the hunger I feel staring up into the rich brown eyes of

Connor Barrett is beyond any type of arousal a man has elicited from me before in my life.

My hands are clammy, and my throat nearly clunks as I swallow. Worse, it feels like my core is throbbing so loud the entire room can hear.

I can see in his eyes that dark knowing sparkle—he is enjoying the way he's affecting me. Connor's well aware of what he's doing.

I can smell whiskey on his breath, he's standing so close. Or maybe it's the bourbon I just poured down his tuxedo. All I want him to do is kiss me.

Irrational.

But I do.

Just one mind-blowing, wild kiss, then I can carry on with my life.

"I think the word you're looking for is 'sorry,'" Connor says slowly, darkly.

You assume I can form words right now, sir.

I cannot.

I'm also quite sure my panties are just as wet as his tux, so it feels like an equal swap, but I don't say that, of course. Instead, I do something even stupider. I run my hands over his jacket and shirt, feeling solid, ripped muscles as I go, and attempt to wipe the bourbon away.

Oh God, I'm insane.

"Mr. Barrett, I'm so sorry," I say as I keep touching him. Then he grabs my wrists and I freeze, drawing in a breath.

"Are you planning to brush the stain off?" Connor raises a single brow at me.

He's amused, but there's no hiding the desire, the lust, the wanting, written all over his face. I'm surprised he's not trying to hide it.

I find myself unable to look away.

A man standing several feet behind him lets out a quiet snort. My eyes dart to the man, and I'm suddenly embarrassed.

Connor smirks wider, and my shame turns to anger.

Does he think he can intimidate me with his size and money?

Wrong girl, buddy.

"No, of course not." I take a step away, and his hands begin to release my wrists, but not before they tighten for a moment. My body flares at the dominance.

God, I bet he's an incredible lover.

Too bad I'll never get to find out.

Connor watches me intently, and when I run my tongue over my lips—unintentionally, I might add—his eyes narrow darkly. I simply blink back. He tips his head an inch, curious why I'm not intimidated.

Keep wondering, Mr. Barrett. You won't guess.

However, I *am* impacted by his powerful height and size and the chemistry flowing between us. I want his hands back on me. I also want to run. Not from fear, but from the enormous amount of desire running through my body. It has the power to overwhelm me.

None of which matters because, despite this moment between us, I am Mia, the events coordinator, and Connor is a powerful billionaire desired by millions of women around the world.

I shake off my attraction—fail—and take in the golden stain on the front of his white shirt.

Damn, it's bad.

My job is important to me, and Donna is inside the conference, waiting for me to bring our VIP speaker—Connor Barrett—through to go on stage.

Like, now.

There might only be two weeks of my freedom left—or more —but I don't want to lose my job.

I bite my lip.

How the hell am I going to fix this?

We have contingencies for a lot of things, but destroying the guest speaker's designer tux is not one of them.

"I—"

Donna pushes through the door behind me, interrupting us.

"Mia, what...Oh, Mr. Barrett." She clears her throat. Then she glances at me in question.

Fuck.

"There's been an accident," I say, stating the obvious. My hands clench in front, and I hate how they give away my nerves.

Connor's eyes move from my hands and over to Donna, taking in the dynamics between us. He thinks I'm concerned about losing my job, and he's right, even though it's incredibly unlikely. His eyes drift across my face and meet mine.

I can barely breathe.

The ball is in his court, and he knows it. He needs to react. Is Connor going to go all prima donna on us, or brush it off?

A dangerous glint sends an icy chill down my spine.

Please don't, I want to say, but I will never beg. Whether I like it or not, I'm a mafia princess, and I know my worth and power.

I will never bow to any man.

Not even Connor Barrett.

"Oh." Donna gasps, noticing the stain and breaking the tension. "We have some spare white shirts in the back, but I doubt we will have one in your size. I'm so sorry about this. Mia, can you—"

"There's no need." Connor turns to the man behind him, who nods. In just under a minute, he's back and handing the billionaire a fresh new shirt. Connor thanks the man and then...begins to undress.

In front of us.

"Thanks, Mack," Connor says.

Donna and I stand there with our mouths open while he removes his jacket and shirt, baring his chest.

Sweet baby Jesus.

I was right. He's ripped, with those thick juicy pecs you just want to lick. His arms—*holy mother of mercy*—are smooth and powerful. But it's Connor's tattoos, hidden under his corporate attire, which surprise me.

They appear tribal.

I'm not an expert on ink, despite it being on every man in my family—and I have one of my own—but what I do know is whether they look hot or not.

And it absolutely is.

This dark swirly piece of art covers one of his pecs, and I spot another poking from the waistband of his pants. I want to nudge his pants down to see the rest.

He lifts his eyes, as if he can read my mind, and heat flares between us. I literally feel my cheeks warming.

Crap.

I know my nipples are hard, so I cross my arms over my black Bloom Events Management T-shirt and admit this man has tilted me off my axis.

I do not like it.

I need to remain professional and gain some control.

"I'm sorry, Mr. Barrett. That was clumsy of me," I say, and as Donna is taking his shirt and rolling it up, Connor Barrett fucking...winks...at me.

My eyes fly open.

Is he flirting with me? Openly?

People recognize Connor for his serious, powerful, and scrupulous nature. But he's no playboy. Nor is he charming. He's extremely discrete about his personal life. The media speculate, but he never has a woman on his arm at events and seems to be a solo creature.

I doubt it now that I've met him. As someone who comes from a powerful family, I know the lengths women will go to marry or trap a wealthy man. It's my guess he just doesn't have the time or inclination to be bothered with dating, so he's subtle about how he obtains his...pleasure.

If he thinks a night with me is an option, then I need to be clear it's not. It would be dangerous for both of us.

Not that he knows who I am.

And it must stay that way.

If my identity is revealed, there goes my freedom.

"The jacket is still wet, sir." Mack holds the black item up with two hands.

"I'll live," Connor replies, taking it and sliding it over his big shoulders. "Make sure we put a complete suit in the car as a backup."

As Mack nods and pulls out his phone, I cringe.

"So sorry. Again," I say, this time shooting a glance Donna's way so she knows how much I mean it.

"Mia, accidents happen. It's fine. I'm sure Mr. Barrett understands. We'll have it all dry cleaned." Donna looks his way. "Speak to Mia before you leave, and she can arrange it for you. We'll have it back to you in a few days."

I nod at them both. "Even tomorrow," I say eagerly. After all, it was my fault, and I want to show Donna I am going out of my way to fix this.

Because I believe in miracles, and if I can convince my father to extend my life outside the family, then I need this job.

Well, a girl can dream.

We watch as Connor tucks himself in because, honestly, we'd be stupid not to.

"Meet me out here after my speech, Mia." Connor's eyes meet mine for a brief second before he turns to the conference room door and nods at Donna. "Shall we?"

When the doors close behind the two of them, Mack clears his throat beside me, holding the door handle so I can't open it.

I turn my head.

He's clearly Connor's personal security.

"Take my advice and stay far away from him, sweetheart." His voice is rough.

Something in his warning irks me. He sees me as nothing but another adoring fan. A woman who wants his money and power.

Pfft.

I should've kept my mouth shut, but I don't.

"On the contrary," I reply, holding his stare, "it's *me* he should stay away from."

I am a mafia princess, after all.

I don't need his money or power. It's freedom I want.

It's love I long for.

Neither Connor nor my father offer either of those things, but I am determined, one day, to have both.

3

MIA

From the back of the room, I watch the tall, handsome billionaire speaking on stage. Mack stands several feet away from me, and Connor is holding every single person in the room hostage with his timbre, deep voice, and power.

Then again, who isn't intrigued by a billionaire?

As if the act of listening to them could make you richer or gain even a small percent of the power and success they have.

Pfft.

Not me. I've seen what power does to a man.

Still, as much as I'm trying to resist, Connor Barrett is drawing me in. I just can't look away.

In the flesh, he's so much more. Gorgeous? Yes. But people can be beautiful and not make an impact. There's an energy about this man unlike anyone I've met before.

Everybody has a unique energy signature. I learned that from my uncle. He said that's how you can tell the truth of a man. How dangerous they are. He said it's not the darkness of their eyes or how they hold themselves, or even their tattoos and piercings.

All of that is manufactured.

The essence of a man, my uncle Antonio said, could only be felt. And should be heeded.

"*Use your heart, Mia,*" he would say, "*not your head.*"

Power and control radiate from Connor Barrett—that's for sure—but when I close my eyes and listen to him speak, I begin to feel his truth.

And his lies.

He does care about this cause, but he doesn't want to be here.

In a wet tuxedo? I don't blame him.

The crowd breaks into loud applause, and I open my eyes. People stand to greet him and shake his hand as he steps down off the stage and networks the room. His eyes reach me through the crowd, and I'm filled with that same searing heat.

Why is he singling me out?

Is he *as* attracted to me as I am him, or does he just want to ensure his dry cleaning gets done?

I nearly snort.

He will have employees to do that.

I'm not going to pretend there isn't a chemistry between us, but I'm surprised he's acting on it. Even the simple glances across the room.

He's a powerful man and could have anyone he wants. Not a clumsy events coordinator.

In truth, I know I'm pretty. I have long dark hair, long eyelashes—*thank you, Italian genes*—and plump lips. But I'm five foot five, small-boned, and my hair is currently up in a messy bun. Along with my Bloom Events Management T-shirt, I'm wearing a boring black business skirt, which ends at my knees.

I don't even have lip gloss on, which is rare as I am usually pedantic about it. Pulling it out of the fanny pack tied around my waist, I slide some on. Vanilla. I have about a dozen different flavors, but this is my favorite.

Rubbing my lips together, I glance up. Connor is staring at me while talking to some people.

I look away.

I can't believe I poured bourbon on him. It was a glass I'd planned to take to our private room after a guest advised it had a crack. We hired crystal cut glasses for this event, so there was no way I was throwing it in the trash. Donna will want a refund. The cost per glass was insane.

Suddenly, I wonder if Connor has recognized me.

I don't recall him being at any family events, where I would've been dressed in a designer gown, with full make-up and sparkling jewels. Quite different to how I look today. Even if he had noticed my slim figure and unusual light blue eyes, back then I would've been far too young for him to find beautiful.

At twenty-four, I'm a decade younger than Connor.

Plus, if he'd been caught appreciating my beauty, he'd be swimming with the fishes by now. As my family would say.

Yeah, I know. Total cliché.

It would be funny if I hadn't grown up finding bloodstains in the backs of cars or in the basement. Or worse, witnessed men being dragged—screaming or with a bag over their heads—through the front door.

My mother used to yell at my father and tell him to keep the business out of the house. Like they were bringing home boxes of cookies or car parts.

Not murder.

It didn't matter. My father had ignored her wishes right up to the day she died, five years ago.

Rest in peace, Mama.

Just as my mind goes to that miserable place, Sienna comes skipping over and presses her shoulders up against mine. "OMG, Mia. One of my ovaries just exploded."

"What?" I ask, my eyes flying open.

Sienna is my best friend. I have friends from growing up and the university, but Sienna and I clicked on a whole different level. The day I started working at Bloom Events, she immediately took a dislike to me. Donna put us to work on a project together, which seemed counterintuitive, but by the end of the week, we were best friends.

Sienna said she didn't like me because of my beautiful icy blue eyes. I was too pretty, she said, and in her experience, pretty girls were always bitches.

While not a statistical truth, I had an inkling it was because Sienna had spent her life believing she was a wallflower. After telling me how boring-looking she was—and that her parents had repeatedly told her she needed to do well at school because "ugly kids needed to work harder in life"—I was ready to send one of my father's men over to off them.

Momentarily.

I felt very protective of Sienna.

What irked me the most was she was gorgeous.

If only she would believe it.

That's the thing about belief patterns—you almost created them when you bought into them.

One night, soon after we'd become close, I went to Sienna's and did her hair and makeup, taking a couple of dresses with me for her to wear.

She nearly fainted when I let her look in the mirror.

Talk about sex goddess.

But she hadn't felt comfortable, so we had toned it down, and she still got hit on all night when we finally left the house.

Slowly over the last two years, she has grown more comfortable in her skin and started to see how unfair her parents' comments were. I can't judge. My family is the furthest from perfect, but I still hate what her parents did to her.

I love Sienna completely. She is the first real best friend I've ever had. The only thing I haven't shared with her is my real identity.

Okay, so that is a *huge* thing.

Sienna doesn't know who I am, and it needs to stay that way for her safety.

What I will do if Joe makes me go home, I don't know.

I'll deal with that issue if it arises.

Sienna giggles, drawing my attention back to her. She nudges her chin in Connor's direction.

"Don't *what* me. Connor Barrett. Are you broken? Please tell me you noticed how hot that man is. Seriously, I know you're picky, Mia, but that man is a ten going on twenty." She laughed.

Oh, I noticed. Too damn much.

"Fine, yes, he's a ten," I reply, shooting Mack a glance and hoping he can't hear us. My pride would die a quick death if he had.

"What I wouldn't give for a night with a man like him." Sienna sighs. "Do you think he'd be as good as all the books and movies make billionaires out to be? All dark and broody, making you come just by looking at him."

I snort.

Sienna reads way too many steamy novels. Her sense of reality is a little unhinged. Twelve-inch cocks could wound a woman, and not in the *have a bath and I'll be fine for round two in a moment* kind of way.

Not that I'd know.

I've slept with only two men.

"Just with a glance? No." I laugh. "A bank balance doesn't make someone a good lover."

Except she is sure Connor Barrett has an offer every night of the week here in Manhattan to do all the practice he needs to be a very good lover.

She isn't offering. Maybe in another life.

"Maybe they take lessons," Sienna muses, holding her tablet up to her chest while she watches Connor.

His eyes find mine and hold for a moment, before drifting back to the man he's speaking with.

Damn, now he's going to think we're talking about him. Which we are. But the last thing I need is for him to think I'm interested in anything except his dry cleaning.

I'm not.

I press my thighs together. Fine, yes, if he threw me against the wall and kissed me passionately, I wouldn't be able to stand afterward, and I'd like a lot more.

But he's Connor Barrett, and I'm Mia Mancini.

He donates to good causes, and my family destroys societies. Plus, if I have only two weeks left of freedom, spending a night of it tasting the sweet pleasure of a man like Connor would be bittersweet.

Call it self-preservation.

I just can't.

"Lessons? I think they call those *teachers* prostitutes," I say, and we share a giggle. "Connor Barrett doesn't need to pay for sex, I can tell you that."

"I'm suddenly considering a change in career." Sienna smirks, then nudges me.

I shake my head and laugh.

"Gotta go," Sienna says when Donna instructs the teams through our comms earpieces. She shadows Connor around the room as he glides from group to group, cleverly making his way to the exit.

"Hey," I call out to Sienna, "see you tomorrow night."

The event is close to finishing, and it's possible we won't see each other during the pack-up of a function this size.

Every Sunday night, after the mandatory weekly lunch with my family, Sienna and I go to Toast Bar for drinks and dinner. Her friends, Duncan and Isabelle, quickly adopted me into their group, and they're like a salve to my soul after being back in the mafia world.

Normal and full of hope and optimism about life.

"See you there. Oh, and can you bring my silver shoes?" Sienna says, referring to the pair I recently borrowed, and I nod as she disappears.

There are a dozen things I could be doing, but instead, I remain by the exit, waiting for Connor to leave, as he requested.

Bloom Events is Donna's baby. She creates some of the biggest and most notable events in NYC. Tonight's is not as big as some of the more lavish events we put on; however, the people in attendance are dripping in money. A man like Connor Barrett is important, so I'm not moving an inch.

"Excuse me, Ms. Mancini," one of the conference employees says. "We've increased the heat in the room, so it should be okay now. Also, can I get your signature on this form?"

A request that took way too long to be actioned.

I take note to give Donna feedback so we can consider it when looking at this venue in the future.

"Thank you," I reply, receiving the folder and scribbling my initials.

As she walks away, two things happen.

Mack takes a couple of steps toward me and I stiffen, feeling a body behind me. I've had a bodyguard all my life. I know the signs, I know who it is, but more than that...

I can feel him in my veins.

I swallow, hating the way my body has reacted to Connor, heating, without even seeing him.

I turn. "Mr. Barrett—"

Oomph.

"Lucky I put my drink down." Connor's dark chocolate eyes sparkle as he takes hold of my arms, keeping me upright after I faceplanted his chest.

Jesus, could he stand any closer?

I stare up at him, trying to suppress my scowl, knowing he did it on purpose. When our eyes lock, we both drop the act and chemistry explodes.

His gaze follows my tongue, which sweeps nervously over my lip. Nervous because this man is so masculine, so powerful, and so much more than any other man who has touched me before.

I need to get away from him as soon as I can.

I know my father has men checking on me. Someone could be

in this room, and I'd not know. I've seen people in the shadows. Cars parked across from my apartment.

Less these days, but they are still there.

He wouldn't leave me unguarded.

I'm the mafia princess, after all.

4

CONNOR

I haven't been able to take my eyes off her all night.

It's pissing me off.

Who the hell is she? Mia from Bloom Events Management.

Jesus, I'm losing my mind. No disrespect—she's a beautiful young woman—but events assistants aren't exactly my type.

Don't go believing the escorts I fuck are common sex workers. They aren't. Many are lawyers, for example, during the day, looking for a way to spice up their lives. Women living in a man's world, wanting to submit and be controlled, instead of having to be in control.

Control I desire.

A young girl like Mia wouldn't understand or crave what I need and want to give. I would terrify her.

My cock jumps.

Apparently, I like that idea.

Mia's eyes grow wide when I let out a groan.

I shouldn't, but I'm going to. She *did* pour liquor all over me. The least she can do is let me come over her little tits.

"I believe you need to follow me," I say, releasing her arms.

"Yes, of course. Your tuxedo." Mia nods.

Mack opens the door, and we walk through the lobby. She's tiny beside me, and my hand itches to be placed in the small of her back. Instead, I stay close, as if concerned she'll try to escape.

That's one thing she won't do.

Benson greets us, opening the car door when we step outside.

"If you want, I can just wait—" Mia begins.

"Get in, Mia," I order, and her mouth falls open.

I'M NOT USED to people ignoring my orders, or disregarding them, but as Mia stands shaking her head, I'm a mix of amused and irritated.

"I said, get in the car," I growl, taking a step closer.

The truth is, I want to breathe in her scent again. Whatever it is, she smells like cinnamon and honey. It's most alluring and comforting. A memory knocking at my door, wanting to get in from long ago. A feeling of belonging.

Mia's fingers curl as I remove my jacket. She's fighting her attraction to me, which is unusual. Most women would be clambering to get inside my car, offering me their bodies.

And asking when the wedding is.

Fuck that.

Not Mia. She's fighting it, while I want to own her body.

At least for a few hours.

"No thanks. I can just wait out here while you..." Mia swirls her finger in the air.

I raise both my brows and nearly laugh.

She has got to be kidding. Does she really think I'm going to strip and hand her my laundry?

I break my own rule, once again, as Mack shoots me a look. He already has the passenger door open and is ready to climb in. Lingering makes him nervous, and I respect that.

He's a former marine, like me.

All my men are.

"Three seconds, Mia. Get in the car," I repeat. "Or should I ask Donna to send someone else to assist?"

An asshole move, but I never said I was a gentleman.

This job is important to her. I could see her nerves when Donna discovered the unfortunate incident earlier.

Her eyes narrow.

"I'm not coming home with you," Mia almost growls, and my lips twitch.

Yes, you are.

She has far more fire than I anticipated, and that excites me. Breaking tigers is much more arousing.

I nod to Mack, who begins to walk back inside.

"Wait," she calls out, and Mack—who knew as well as I did he wouldn't get more than two steps—halts.

I raise another brow.

"I'm not stripping outside the fucking convention center, Mia. You've been instructed to take my dry cleaning. I will undress at home, and then you can take it with you," I say. "So, get in the goddamn car."

She glares at me, then finally nods.

As she climbs in, I hear a faint mumble, something about baring my stupid chest earlier, and I grin.

"Let's go," I say, my smile disappearing, then I climb in after her.

MIA HAS POSITIONED herself in the furthest spot from me in the limo. When the car pulls away, she removes a device from her ear and the god-awful fanny pack wrapped around her body and drops them on the seat beside her.

Only then does she lift her eyes to mine.

Neither of us speak during the fifteen-minute drive. Instead, Mia fidgets, blushes, slides on a lip gloss, swallows repeatedly, and lowers her eyes to my crotch as I undo my sleeves and roll them up.

I wonder if she noticed my cock twitch.

If my observations are right, she's currently counting her breaths, trying to lower her heart rate.

Adorable.

I wonder what she's thinking while I focus on whether I'll fuck her over the sofa, in my bedroom, or on the sweeping balcony of my penthouse.

The kitchen bench wins.

I want to lick her pussy, taste her, then tie her up on my bed and see which of my toys her body likes the most. Though I'm not a betting man, I won't be putting my money on a butt plug. She's way too innocent.

God, she better not be a virgin.

I won't take her virginity.

"I could've picked it up in the morning," Mia finally says, shaking her head as if kicking herself.

Yes, she could've.

If I'd let her. Which I hadn't.

As we pull up outside my building, I lean my arms onto my knees and lock eyes with hers. Electricity shoots through me, and I swear the temperature skyrockets to about a thousand degrees inside the car. She's lucky I'm not pulling her onto my lap—I really fucking want to touch her.

"Come upstairs, Mia. You can take it when you leave. What we do between now and then is up to you," I say darkly, leaving no question about what I'm offering. What I'm wanting.

Her lips part and she licks them, causing my dick to jerk in my pants.

Fuck me.

"I should wait here," she says, looking indecisive.

I give her a long moment, until finally her eyes slide to mine, and the sexual tension is so thick you could cut it like a knife.

Definitely not used to working so hard for this.

"You should come with me," I say, and as if rehearsed, Mack

chooses that exact moment to open the door. I sit back and sweep my hand out.

Bravely, Mia shuffles along the seat, then climbs out, and my cock does a little happy dance.

I smile privately.

Tonight, I get to taste this young woman. There's something about her that's caught my attention. Those icy blue eyes, the way she holds herself with attitude but seems vulnerable. I want her wide and begging, those glossy lips around my cock.

After I arrange my pants, I join her on the sidewalk and do everything in my power to stop from placing my hand on the small of her back.

Again.

We walk inside, and my private elevator opens. Mack shoots me a questioning look. I know what he's asking, so I nod.

"Bring me a copy."

Like all the women I fuck, Mia will need to sign the contract. She's not an escort, but the same rules apply.

Tomorrow, I have an important meeting with Nathan, one of the Dark Kings. I'm eager for news inside the Italian mafia. Nathan has not been successful in reaching the upper level of the mob, and there have been no new leads in months.

Tonight, I play.

5

MIA

What am I doing?

The elevator door closes, and we're standing in a soft ambient light, rising to what I know is the luxurious penthouse owned by Connor Barrett. The man himself is across from me, eyeing me, like I'm his prey. He slides his hands into his pant pockets, his jacket draped over his arm, and watches me.

That's all he seems to do.

Watch me.

"Not one for conversation, huh?" I ask because direct is my middle name.

Unperturbed, he replies, "It's usually unnecessary."

Jesus, he's arrogant.

And correct. Connor Barrett is wealthy beyond imagination, even compared to my family. Gorgeous women would rip their panties off and beg to be with him.

I'm not going to be one of them.

If he wants me, he will have to work a bit harder.

Says the girl who got out of the car and all but said, "yes, please fuck me."

Don't judge. He's utterly gorgeous. There's a darkness about him, but he also has that Superman jaw, moody eyes, and a lazy scruff that makes you want to slide your fingers over it.

I want to touch him.

Desperately.

The need is growing the more I'm near him. My panties are wet, my nipples hard as fuck and pressing painfully against my bra. My core is throbbing, and I swear not even my fingers would relieve me at this point.

I want to slide my fingers into the curl of hair flicking along his collar and slam my mouth over his. I want him to ravage me. I want his cock inside me as I scream...and then run away as fast as I can.

But I really shouldn't.

I need to grab his laundry and get the hell out of here.

There is a chance they followed me, and then I'd have to explain what I was doing in Connor Barrett's penthouse at eleven o'clock at night.

I hope I haven't put him in danger.

He might be rich and powerful, but when you're dealing with a family who lives outside of society's rules, no one is safe.

I don't want a man's blood on my hands.

Also, more selfishly, I don't want to taste heaven before I go back to hell. A night with Connor would be incredible, but the memories would taunt me for the rest of my life.

"How old are you?" he suddenly asks.

"Twenty-four," I reply. "Old enough to pick up dry cleaning."

Connor smirks, and the elevator doors open.

He moves closer to me as I step out and take in the gorgeous view of his forty-fifth-floor penthouse. It overlooks a section of Central Park—a similar view to one of my father's homes.

Connor walks past me, his eyes dipping to take in my reaction. I catch myself, knowing I should be far more impressed than I am.

"Wow, what a view," I lie.

He turns and walks to the bar, tossing his jacket on the sofa.

"I'll take that." I walk into the room and grab the jacket.

It smells like bourbon, and...Connor. Earth and leather. Like a predator in the wild.

While Connor pours a drink, I stand there hugging the black Armani jacket. He turns and walks to me, stalking like a jaguar, then hands me one of the filled crystal cut glasses.

"Put it down, Mia," he orders, and my body almost obeys.

"I should be getting back," I say weakly.

Connor tosses back the gold liquid and puts both glasses down on the table beside us. Then he undoes his bow tie and begins to undo his shirt.

Oh God.

I may have seen him shirtless already tonight, but in the dim mood lights of his spacious penthouse, the view of Manhattan in the background, a fire flickering along the wall nearby, I suddenly feel completely out of my depth.

I mean, how strong does a girl have to be to say no to this man?

Strong.

Really damn strong.

Connor drops his shirt and tie onto the sofa, taking his jacket from me and tossing it on top of them.

Fuck.

My core throbs harder, and I think Sienna might be right about ovaries exploding around this man.

He takes a step closer.

"Say no and you can walk out the door right now," Connor says, and I know I should, but instead I stay right there, staring at his beautiful face. "If you are still here in thirty seconds, I'm going to touch you. I'm going to fuck you. I'm going to own your orgasms and your screams."

Oh, shit.

My mouth goes dry.

"Do you understand?"

I nod, and my body begins to tremble.

"Twenty seconds."

Leave.

Go.

Walk away.

But I'm still standing here, and all the reasons why I shouldn't have vanished into thin air. My only focus is his luscious brown eyes and the way they're already fucking me.

Mentally.

Like he owns me.

"Ten seconds," his voice a soft growl.

I open my mouth.

"Do you want me to fuck you, Mia?" Connor asks.

His hand lifts, and a finger nudges some loose hair from my face.

Yes.

Moisture pools in my panties, and I'm so ready to do this. A primal need draws me to him. Our mouths are so close we're sharing oxygen.

"Say yes," he says.

I can't breathe, so I begin to nod, but there's no need. He can see my answer.

"One second."

I swallow.

Then Connor slams his mouth down on mine, and I almost cry out in relief. Instead, he yanks me up against his enormous body, and I'm surrounded by power and his masculine essence.

I grip his enormous biceps as our tongues tangle greedily, desperate to take as much as we can of one another, and pray this is the most amazing night of my life.

It has to be worth it.

Then in a growl, Connor lifts me, my legs wrap around him, and he carries me up a set of stairs. He keeps kissing me, running his hand over my hair, and then pulls it out of the hair tie.

"Fuck, I've wanted to do that since the moment I saw you,"

Connor says, placing me on the floor of what I assume is his bedroom.

The quick glimpse I get is of a room filled with black furniture, an enormous bed, and black silk linens. One wall is floor-to-ceiling glass with a view of the Manhattan skyline.

It suits him.

He removes my top. Goddamn, I wish I'd put on my nice lingerie, but event management is not for the fainthearted. Comfort is a priority. How could I foresee that instead of working, I'd be going home with one of the richest and most gorgeous men in America?

It most definitely wasn't on my task list.

So, nude T-shirt bra and bikini bottoms it is as Connor unzips my skirt and fanny pack, which I'd put back on when we exited the car.

Both go flying across the room.

He pulls me back against him, lapping at my mouth and gripping my hair, tugging it back. It hurts a little, but I like it.

He groans.

"I'll give you all the pleasure you could dream of, but you need to do as I say." Connor's fingers slide along the line of my panties.

I'm not surprised he's dominant in the bedroom, so I don't argue. Honestly, he can do as he pleases. I'm ready for all the pleasure he wants to deliver.

Bring it on.

Especially since we will only have this one night.

I'm going to savor every damn second.

"Much as I want to taste you and thrust my cock inside you right now, we need to talk business," Connor says.

I'm sorry, what?

I still, panic slamming into me.

Does Connor know who I am?

It's one thing worrying my father will find out I'm here, having sex with the billionaire, but the real danger always lurking in my world is far greater. As the daughter of one of the most powerful mobsters in the world, I'm valuable.

Hence my identity being kept as suppressed as it has been for most of my life.

I'm an asset. A very valuable asset.

Who knows what my father would pay if someone were to kidnap me? This fear has been drummed into me since my birth, and it comes flooding to the surface in a rush, nearly paralyzing me.

I draw in a long breath and shove at Connor's chest. Then take a few steps away. "What?" I ask again, my heart pounding.

He stares at me like I've lost my marbles.

"Woah, relax, Mia," Connor says, running a hand over his jaw. "I just need you to sign a document. A contract. It asks you to keep what happens here confidential. I know you couldn't understand the complexities of my—"

"What?" I repeat, shaking my head again.

Contract?

He wants me to sign a contract?

Connor walks to the cabinet by the door and lifts the printed sheets of paper.

So, he's not kidnapping me?

My brain cells start firing again, my shoulders relaxing, but my heart is taking a lot longer to get the message that I'm safe.

"You can't talk to the media. You cannot discuss anything you see or do here with anyone." Connor waves the paper in the air. "And you cannot make any claim against me financially. Blah, blah."

Thank God.

Suddenly, I feel lightheaded, and I remember I didn't eat lunch—or dinner—and I thought I was going to get kidnapped...

My legs start to give way under me, and Connor destroys the space between us. He catches me.

I feel like an idiot, but when you grow up in a mob family and are told every day people want to capture, torture, or kill you, different situations are triggering.

In hindsight, Connor is the most unlikely person in the world to do that, and yet, as my brain went straight into fight or flight mode, I wasn't able to rationalize.

For those few seconds, fear raced through my body, like molten steel.

His chocolate eyes stare down at me in concern, but I also sense his judgement.

Great. It's not like I can explain any of that.

I just killed the most seductive and sexy night of my life.

6

CONNOR

I carry her to the bed and settle on it. "Mia."

Jesus, no one has ever reacted so dramatically before. The agency normally deals with the paperwork, but from time to time, I do meet women I want to sleep with, so I have a contract on file, which I or Mack will print and prepare.

I never picked Mia for the fainting type.

Not that I know her, but I know terror, and something triggered it. She's not going to tell me, so all I can do is make sure she is okay before I send her home.

My cock is as flat as a pancake. Watching a woman nearly faint is not exactly arousing. Nor are the vanilla bra and panties she's wearing, but they weren't a problem five minutes ago.

She pats my pec. "I'm fine, sorry. Just my blood sugar must be low. I haven't eaten today."

To say I'm disappointed is a complete under-exaggeration. The delicious tension that had been building between us now drifting away, like an extinguished flame.

All while Mia continues her *it's fine* mantra.

Her eyes lift to mine, and I become aware I'm just sitting here against my headboard, holding her. When the hell have I ever done that before with a woman?

Then I ask, "*Are* you okay?"

"Yes," she says. "Hungry."

I accept the night isn't going to end how I want it to, and while I suspect she's not telling me the truth, I decide its better if I just go along with it.

She'll be gone in ten minutes.

We need to talk business.

What, in any of those words, could cause someone to have a near panic attack? Because that's what it was. The marine in me recognizes her symptoms and knows how fear feels.

Mia blinks those icy eyes at me, and her cheeks blush.

"You don't need to be embarrassed."

"So stupid," she says, shaking her head.

With my arms wrapped around her, I feel a sense of protection, even though I've only just met her.

I don't want her to go or run, I realize. I want to feed her and see if we can revive the sizzling chemistry that just died a quick death.

"How about some eggs?" I say, running my hand over her forehead, brushing her hair back.

"You're going to make me eggs?" she asks incredulously.

I let out a quick laugh.

"Yes, but full disclosure. It's completely selfish. I want to fuck you tonight, and I'm not a man who gives up easily," I confess.

My eyes drift over her gorgeous features. With her hair down, cascading over her shoulders, she looks older than the twenty-four years she told me in the car. It frames her stunning crystal eyes and those lashes I have no doubt attract the envy of many women.

She blinks when she notices me staring.

My lips curve. "You are very beautiful, Mia."

"So are you," she replies, and when my lip twitches, she adds, "Well, you *are*."

I can't help myself; I laugh.

"Come on," Mia says. "As if you don't get told that every day."

Yes, I know.

My body is strong, virile, and muscular. I've created every ripple. Not to attract women, although I'm not unhappy about that additional benefit. My physique sends a message to those around me and has kept me alive.

It could still keep me alive if the day comes I need the physical power.

It's for survival.

"People don't walk around, telling me I'm beautiful," I reply, moving us off the bed.

She surprises me by blushing when she glances down at herself, still in just her bra and panties.

"Clearly, I wasn't expecting the night to end like this," Mia groans. "I have much nicer lingerie."

"I have no doubt." I find myself wanting to see it, but I don't want her putting on her uniform again, so I lead her into my wardrobe, pull the first shirt off the rack, and hold it up so she can put her arms through it.

"Thanks." She smiles, doing up a few buttons.

It's huge on her, and something inside of me tugs at the vision of her in my shirt.

A stupid business shirt.

Jesus. I need to feed her, fuck her, and get rid of her.

Instead, I find myself sitting on the sofa, listening to her chatter while she sips the hot chocolate I made for her.

Who am I?

"I'M JUST SAYING, if you added some color, this entire place would feel *so* different." Mia is curled up next to me, drinking the last of her second mug of hot chocolate.

I'm drinking whiskey. My arm lies along the back of the sofa, while Mia has her legs tucked up under her. The tail of my shirt exposes her thighs, and while I've seen nearly all of her, the desire to see more is growing again.

Yet I'm strangely enjoying just listening to her talk. Mia is smart, animated, and totally unaware of just how sexy she is.

She yawns, and I'm sizing up that mouth of hers.

I haven't forgotten why she's here.

Fuck her and send her home.

"I like it just as it is," I say, then hear myself ask, "What color?"

She turns and grins. "A couple of plants would be a good start. Some throw cushions. Warm colors. Cream, gold, and perhaps a pink throw."

I nearly spray my Macallan over her.

"I think you've got me confused with Russell from accounting." I wonder if she'll get my joke.

Jokes on me, apparently.

Jesus, the Dark Kings would be grinning their asses off right now. In the past hour, I've dressed this woman, boiled the jug and put marshmallows in her goddamn hot chocolate, and now I'm sitting here, listening to her house décor tips—pink fucking décor —instead of fucking her senseless.

Listening to her chat has been amusing, however. In the past twenty minutes, Mia has asked me a lot of questions—all of which I've avoided answering—and she's told me nothing about herself.

It's been the most non-sexual, real intimate moment I've spent with another human in a very long time.

Which is why she needs to leave.

I have no space in my life for any kind of relationship. Nothing that doesn't contribute to my purpose.

Revenge.

Mia leans forward, her foot dropping to the floor, and puts her mug on the coffee table. Then she turns to me and places a hand on my thigh. I ignore how much I like her touch and resist telling her to move up higher. Only because her brows are bunched, and it looks like she's about to say something serious.

"I'm sorry about earlier. I wish I could explain what happened, but I can't. It's too—"

I shake my head.

"Mia, I'm not a sensitive man. You don't need to explain." Although, I am curious, and something is nagging at me about it. "But I do want to fuck you. If you don't, I can take you home."

She tugs on her bottom, and my cock jumps to attention.

I'm strongly sensing a yes here.

My shirt drapes across her silky olive shoulder, exposing the curve of her breast. I run a finger across it, nudging the material and then taking her nipple between my fingers.

She leans into it, and her lids lower.

"Sign the document and submit to me, Mia. Then let me lick your cunt and listen to you scream."

She gasps, and those crystal eyes sparkle as I pull her closer and take her mouth in mine.

7

MIA

Damn, he tastes amazing. It could be the five-thousand-dollar bottle of whiskey he's drinking, but I doubt it.

Connor Barrett just tastes incredible.

He disappears and returns with the paperwork.

Can I sign it? Sure. But not with my real name. I don't use an alias—Mancini is common enough in New York–but Connor only knows me as Mia. Putting my real name, Maria Luna Mancini, is not an option. My name is powerful, and not a day goes by that I am not reminded of it.

"You can read it if you want, or just sign it," he says, handing it to me, eager to get on with the sexy stuff.

I am too. Especially after those dirty words.

Holy hell.

"I swear, all it demands of you is your silence. Nothing more."

"Where's the pen?" Two seconds later, it's in my hand, and I'm scribbling "Mia Bottini" on the line.

Connor tosses it across the room, tugs me to my feet, and rips his shirt off me.

I gasp and reach out to run my fingers over that sexy ink on his chest. The power I feel under my touch causes my body to shudder.

He's one hundred percent male.

"Now, I taste you," he growls, tugging the cup of my bra down. When his mouth clamps over my nipple, I let out a cry.

"Oh God, yes."

Connor rips his mouth from my breast and somehow removes my bra with skill and speed, leaving me bare to him. He takes my other nipple as he cups my first breast, pinching it.

"Spin around." Connor guides me to the side of the sofa and slides my panties off. "Hands there and ass in the air. God, yes, let me see you."

I feel completely wanton, with him nudging my feet apart and his breath hitting my thighs.

Lick.

My legs tremble.

His fingers slide through my pussy, and he licks some more. "Jesus, you are so wet, Mia, and sweet as fuck."

Connor didn't need my signature on his contract. No matter what happens, after I leave his penthouse, I can never tell anyone.

For both our sakes.

But I want this.

I want this completely delicious moment with Connor Barrett. A man desired by millions of women, who, for some reason, wants *me* tonight.

Lucky me.

In two weeks, they may pull me out of my happy life and force me to fulfill my duty as the mafia princess I was born to be. God, I hope there's no arranged marriage in my future.

Then again, exactly how do I expect to meet anyone I could love in the circles my family socializes in? They're all gangsters and criminals.

Ugh.

So, I'm taking every single second of tonight and enjoying it.

"Here are the rules," Connor says, lapping at me like an ice cream. "When I give you an instruction, you obey. If you want to stop, you say 'Ketchup.'"

Really? *Ketchup?*

"Okay."

"Yes, *sir*," he says.

What? When I don't reply, he slaps my ass.

"Ouch!" I cry, bolting up.

Connor's hand is firm on my back, lowering me back down. "Words, Mia."

Woah, this wasn't what I was expecting, but my body is tingling with delight and wanting more.

"Ketchup. Got it."

More, please.

Now.

"Sir," he repeats, standing, and the loss of his mouth on my core makes me moan loudly. "You call me sir until you leave."

His mouth is on my neck, and he licks up the side of my face. Every single sensation is sending bolts of pleasure through my body.

Holy hell.

"Yes, sir. Please touch me more, sir." God, I need his touch between my legs before I die.

Because I will.

If Connor doesn't start touching me in a more serious and committed way, I am going to explode.

"Good girl. Now, stand up."

He guides my body up and ties my hands behind my back with something. My breasts, small though they are, push out, and I feel so wanton and wild.

I've never used the word wanton in my life.

Then again, I've never had a lover like this.

Connor guides me back to his bedroom and positions me against the glass window, tweaking my nipples as he lowers to my clit.

I let out a guttural sound that both excites and embarrasses me.

"When was the last time you came?" he suddenly asks, his dark eyes rising to meet mine.

A blush hits my cheeks, and I stammer, "Um, what? Why? Sir."

Why does he want to know that?

"Tell me you're not a virgin."

Oh.

Though I might be ten years younger than Connor, I'm hardly underage or inexperienced. But I don't bother arguing the point. I just want his mouth on me.

With a shake of my head, I say, "I'm not. Sir."

Touch me, dammit.

"I'm going to do a lot of things to your body tonight, so remember your word."

"Yes, sir," I reply. My body is burning, and the cool of the glass behind me is a strange, stark contrast sending all kinds of confusing messages to my brain. I'm shuddering with need, and he's enjoying every second.

Then again, so am I.

Connor's tongue reaches out as he spreads my flesh with his fingers, and his eyes meet mine once more. "Then surrender to me, Mia. While NYC watches you."

Oh God.

Why does that turn me on so much?

His mouth surrounds my entire pussy. Connor licks and sucks with the skill of an experienced and passionate lover. He holds me pressed against the glass and consumes me.

"This sweet cunt is mine. All night long," Connor says, lapping at me furiously.

Lord, I nearly come instantly. Instead, he seems to know when to stop. Knows when to lick, suck, and rub to make sure I don't.

I hate it.

I love it.

I need it.

Strong hands keep me wide open, his fingers pressing into my flesh with such domination I feel owned. Those chocolate eyes drifting up my body, moment to moment, sending fire through my veins.

He reaches, takes one of my breasts, and pinches the nipple as I cry out. I feel like I'm in the hands of a maestro. Being played with such expertise, my pleasure is guaranteed.

And Lord, it is.

Circling my clit, nipping it with his teeth, Connor then inserts two fingers, and I close my eyes, savoring the small taste of what it will be like when he replaces them with his cock.

"Good girl," he slowly drawls in that rich baritone voice. "Clench more. I want to feel how tight you'll be when I'm inside you."

No disrespect to those who came—pun intended—before, but Connor feels like the first real man I've been with.

He's so masculine.

So powerful.

So much more.

He speeds up the stimulation on my clit with his thumb, his eyes on mine. "Fuck my fingers, Mia. Fuck them."

Oh hell.

Desire floods my body. His voice. His touch. The feel of him playing my pussy like an instrument.

"You may come now," he adds, and holy shit, my orgasm strikes and I cry out, arching into him, my arms pulling against the silk ties at my wrists.

"Fuckkkkk."

"More. Let me have your juices, Mia," he demands.

This man. His dirty mouth, he's killing me.

Connor wrings every morsel of my orgasm from my throbbing body. Then, as the convulsions begin to subside, he's standing and pushing me to my knees.

"Take my cock," he says as I stumble, my pussy wet between my legs.

I open wide, blinking, pleasure continuing to ghost through

me, and watch Connor fists his cock and direct the head into my mouth.

He's bigger than other men. Smooth and swollen with need.

For me.

When I glance up, I see the wild arousal. His jaw is taut, as if forcing control of his body. He presses in further, and then I'm full of him.

I have never felt so fucking dirty, horny, and sexual in my entire life. I want his cock all the way down my throat. I want him to feel the same pleasure he just gave me.

Without the use of my hands, still tied behind my back, I'm next to useless. Connor grabs the sides of my head and begins to fuck my mouth. He's in control. He's been in control from the start. As I suck and relax my throat, he goes deeper and deeper, until I begin to choke.

Our eyes meet, and that dangerous wild animal within is there, on the surface. He's beautiful, thrilling, and terrifying.

Before I panic, he pulls out, cursing.

"Jesus, Mia. Your mouth," Connor growls, ripping the ties from my arms and lifting me onto the bed. "On your knees."

Powerful men aren't new to me, but Connor handles me like I'm a doll. A sex doll. Those big hands grip my hips and tug me against his groin. Then he moves us back up the bed, close to the headboard. I hear the rip of foil and snap of rubber, then he slaps my ass.

"Ow," I cry out. "Sir."

As in *ow*, that feels amazing, and I shouldn't like it, but I do.

"Good girl. So fucking hot and wet. Are you ready for my cock?"

"Yes, sir. God, yes, please."

I feel pathetic but don't care, desperate for him to fill me. I'm never going to forget this night for as long as I live.

Holy shit. Connor Barrett is about to fuck me.

"You came so big, Mia. I'm going to slip right in this pretty cunt of yours," Connor says. "Ass in the air."

He slaps me again, and I'm throbbing. I may have come, but I need to feel this man inside me, like it's the last thing on earth I must do before I die.

"I'm going hard." Connor slips the head in. "Deep," he says, pressing in further. "Filling you," and further, "and I'm going to fuck you until you can't remember your name."

His groans join mine, his body slapping against my ass as he begins to thrust. Then he slams in harder and faster.

Then again.

Then again.

"Fuck, God," I cry, the feel of his cock against the walls of my pussy the most intensively erotic sensation of my life. I grip the sheets in my hands, my head slightly tilted, and pant out my curses.

Connor lifts my body and directs my hands up. "Palms on the wall. That's it. Such a good girl. My cock loves being in your pussy."

Why do I love hearing that so much?

He repositions us and resumes his thrusting, his fingers finding my clit once more. God, I want him to keep doing that forever.

I'm not shy about pleasuring myself, and I've come with all my lovers, but Connor Barrett takes my body to a whole other level.

I'm dizzy with arousal.

Though I'm not even sure I *can* come again, at the same time, I'm unsure if my orgasm ever stopped. It's the most stimulated my body has ever been.

Then, his thighs bump my legs an inch further apart, and he swivels to thrust deeper. His other hand reaches and pinches my nipple so hard I cry out.

There's so much sensation, my brain is about to go blank.

His mouth sucks my neck, and I arch back into him, wanting him everywhere.

He *is* everywhere.

His cock slamming into me. My clit thrumming, nipple trapped in such painful pleasure, and my head arched as his mouth moves over my neck and then captures my lips.

"Such a good fucking girl," he growls into my mouth. "So sweet and hot."

"Connor. Sir," I moan.

"You take my cock so good. I'm going to keep fucking you all night," he says, lapping at my tongue and slamming into me harder. "I'm going to fuck every part of your body until I'm sated. Until I've had all of you."

I'm gone.

I can't focus on anything except the feeling of him, his taste, the sounds of his growls and his voice in my ear, telling me all the things he plans to do.

As he speeds up, my body gives over control.

"Fuck, fuck!" he cries. "Come on my cock, Mia. Yes, tighten around me. Fuck."

His hands move to my hips as he plows into my body, and then when my hands fall from the wall, he collapses in a controlled heap, taking me with him down to the bed.

Panting, we're both coming, moaning, and stroking one another as we lie there.

I'm somewhere above planet Earth, in a type of heaven, my body throbbing in waves of pleasure.

When our breaths begin to even out, Connor's gruff voice says in my ear, "I'm not done with you, Mia. Not even close."

"Good," I say between gasps. Because I need to make this worth it.

I know I've been followed.

My father wouldn't let me just drive away with a man and not have his security tail me.

I have until lunchtime tomorrow to come up with the best story of my life.

8

CONNOR

Bang.

"Oh, shit," a voice says.

My eyes fly open. Jesus, I can't believe I fell asleep with Mia in my bed. In my penthouse.

No one sleeps at my home. Ever.

I'm clear with the women I entertain—pleasure—they need to leave after we're finished. I don't want to mislead any of them, and I certainly don't want them here with the nightmares I'm prone to from time to time. Showing weakness and vulnerability is not smart and just leads to questions.

Except there were no nightmares, and there was no dreaming. We just collapsed and fell asleep. Not surprising, given how hard I fucked her.

Mia has the single most delicious pussy I've ever slid my cock inside. Plus, those damn icy blue eyes of hers kept making me harder as they pleaded for more.

I've never wanted to kidnap a woman so much in my life, fly her to an island, and spend a week just fucking her.

I do with Mia.

I won't, but it would be a fucking incredible week.

Lifting my head, I see she's already half dressed, sitting on the edge of the bed, doing up that god-awful fanny pack.

It's not dawn yet, but it's close.

Mia turns her head when the sheets rustle.

"Sorry, everything fell out." She slides her phone back inside and zips it up. "Oh, crap." She disappears onto the floor and stands up with a lip gloss in her hand, holding it up and adding it inside as she smiles.

It's nearly comical.

She's way too alert for me. I'm still groggy. I rub my hand over my hair and then my face, fighting the desire to pull her back in bed.

What the hell is wrong with me?

She has a magic pussy, that's what.

I climb out and pull on some boxer briefs, then grab my phone and begin to message Benson. Though I hate doing this to him at this ungodly hour, I want to make sure Mia gets home safely.

Wherever home is.

Mia spots what I'm doing. "No need. Uber is on the way."

I lift my eyes. "Don't even think about it. My driver will take you home."

She lets out a little laugh, and I arch a brow.

I step closer to her. I need to know she got home safe. She's spent the evening here with me—this is my responsibility.

"Cancel the Uber," I say, and she pats me on the pec.

What the fuck?

I'm a big man. Over six foot three, four in shoes. My body is solid muscle. Not as much as when I was an active marine, but pretty goddamn close. I intimidate men, and women either melt or stutter around me.

Mia is unfazed.

"Thank you for last night, Connor. I've got it from here." Then she tiptoes up and plants her lips on mine.

I've got it from here. Is this girl for real?

Without looking, I toss my phone on the bed and pull her body against mine. I deepen the kiss because I need one last taste of her.

But if she thinks I'm letting her walk out the door to fend for herself in Manhattan at four in the morning, she's mistaken.

I release her as her heels drop back on the floor.

"Either let my driver take you, or I'm getting in the Uber with you." I won't. I'll pay the guy the tip of his life, and he can fuck off.

Mia lets out a little sigh.

"Connor, I've lived in New York all my life. Trust me when I say I'm safe."

I feel like I'm missing something.

Also, no.

I walk to my wardrobe and pull on a pair of gray sweats and a Harvard University sweatshirt. Then slip into a pair of Nikes.

When I return, Mia is gone, but she won't go far. The elevator in this penthouse works on a metric system. Without my eyeball, she isn't leaving. When she comes marching back into the bedroom with her arms crossed, I hide my smirk.

She's figured it out.

"Okay, well, this is kidnapping," she snaps.

I laugh.

"I'm trying to get you home safely, not keep you. That's the opposite of kidnapping." I walk to her and cup her face. She keeps her arms down by her side, and I nearly laugh again.

Mia is very sexy when she's angry.

"Look, let me be a gentleman and make sure you get home. I don't want Donna mad at me."

Couldn't give a fuck about Donna.

Mia's eyes fly wide.

"Shit. Your dry cleaning," she cries, beginning to pull away.

Jesus fucking Christ.

I shake my head and growl. "Leave the damn dry cleaning. It was you I wanted."

Her phone beeps.

Mia bites her bottom lip. "Please open the elevator. I don't want my Uber rating to drop."

After staring at her for a long moment, I throw back my head and laugh. I've laughed more times in the last twelve hours than I have in a month.

Then I scoop her up and walk through the penthouse, with her wriggling in my arms.

"Mia, you need to behave, or I will slap that ass of yours so hard you will come."

When she goes still and silent, my cock hardens. Suddenly, I don't want her to leave, yet she can't stay. Regret fills me, and honestly, it's confusing.

We take the elevator to the garage, where I put her back on her feet, and we both ignore the heat simmering between us once more. Silently, she walks beside me to the parked black Maserati. I rarely use it, but I figure Benson deserves some sleep, and I don't trust her not to manipulate him.

Ten minutes later, I pull up outside her building and let the car idle. I turn to Mia. She's been fidgeting her hands and muttering *this isn't good* the entire drive.

When she faces me, she looks worried.

"Is it the dry cleaning?" I ask, frowning. "I can have my PA email Donna if you're concerned."

Maybe she regrets what we did, which I'm not going near with a barge pole. She can book a therapy session.

My cock is happy as Larry.

I'd like to have more of her, but that's not how I work.

"No. But thank you," Mia says, her eyes casting outside the car.

What is she looking for?

I glance around, my wrist resting on the steering wheel. I'm trained to spot danger, but there's nothing outside she needs to be concerned with.

This woman is giving me whiplash.

Is she concerned about her safety or not? One minute, she's

trying to run out my door. Now, she looks worried there might be someone lurking in the shadows.

Fuck sakes.

I get out, circle the car, and find her already on the fucking sidewalk. *Jesus.*

"Come on." I put my hand in the small of her back and walk her to the entrance. It's then I notice she lives in a fancy building. One that would cost far more than an events coordinator would earn.

A light goes off.

Mia still lives with her parents. Who clearly have money. Of course, she's worried about what they will say when she arrives home in the early hours. I rub my mouth to cover my grin, then lean down, tug her against me for the last time, and press my lips to hers.

"You were fucking perfect, Mia."

Big crystal eyes gaze back at me, blinking. "You too."

She runs her fingers through my hair, then steps out of my arms and walks through the glass doors.

And out of my life.

Or so I thought.

9

MIA

I slide my feet into a pair of heels and take one last look in the mirror. My knee-length black dress and matching jacket of the same length are very mafia princess, I suppose.

The dark glasses look a little Jackie O, but then again, I've had less than four hours of sleep, and if I can get away with wearing them, I'm going to try.

I run a rich pink over my lips and spritz fragrance over my head. Then take the elevator downstairs, where my father's driver waits for me.

"Morning, Ms. Mancini," Tony says as I slide into the back of the Bentley. Modified, of course. This vehicle is bulletproof and fitted with weapons, like something out of a *James Bond* movie.

Or *The Godfather*, if they'd had the technology back then.

I only know this because my brother loves to go on about it. God help us when he takes over. He's power hungry, and I doubt many of my father's men are looking forward to the day he becomes the Don.

Perhaps when he matures. At twenty-six, all Cade talks about is killing this person and fucking that woman.

A memory from last night hits me, and I'm filled with heat.

Tony closes the door after I smile in greeting, and I wriggle on the leather seat, feeling the ache in my body. Connor well and truly followed through on his promise. I was well fucked for hours.

Then fell asleep.

I'll find out soon if my father knows about it. It's too late to worry anyway. I made my decision, and *sweet mother of mercy*, it was worth it.

I walk through the luxurious entrance of one of my father's homes in Tribeca. Armed men in black suits line every corner of the place. They're like décor to me but not invisible.

I remove my jacket and hand it to Susanna, who has worked for my family for decades.

"Buongiorno, Maria," she says in greeting.

Maria is my real name. Mia for short. Maria Luna Mancini.

"Ahh, the princess arrives at last," my brother, Cade, says, walking down the winding staircase.

Great.

"Ah, the heir to the throne." I accept his kiss on both cheeks. There is not a lot of love lost between us. Cade would kill for me, but only because of my value. We were closer when we were younger, but now, I just can't relate to him.

But as the future Don, I know I have to respect him.

Cade is much taller than me. Six foot two, at least, and broader. Like my entire family, he has dark hair and light eyes. His are bluer than mine.

Today he's wearing a black suit with a white shirt, but the tattoos on his neck still give him an edge, along with the permanent scowl he has and the single diamond earring.

"Come on. Father is waiting." He tugs on his shirt, hiding his Rolex, and then wraps a smothering arm around my shoulders.

"Ah, *mia figlia*," Joe Mancini says, lifting his head as we walk into the spacious living area. My uncle, who is in an armchair beside him, stands and walks to me.

"Princepessa," Antonio says, kissing both cheeks.

I wish they'd stop calling me a fucking princess, but the one thing that's really aggravating me today is the fact they're all touching me.

It might sound strange, but I just want to feel the memories of Connor's touch on me.

Not theirs.

The way they manhandle me, it's like I'm a belonging. I know it's the Italian way, but today, I hate it.

I step away and drop my Chanel handbag on the table, not greeting my father. I'm playing with fire, and when I turn and see the look in his eye, coupled with the slightly raised brow, I cross the room.

"Papa," I say, dropping a kiss on his cheek.

Just one.

I'm tired and grumpy.

Cade watches me, and I narrow my eyes at him, a chill running down the length of my spine. Something is up.

Is it to do with my two-year deadline approaching?

Does Cade know something?

"Shall we eat?" Antonio says, breaking the tension. "My stomach is growling at the delicious smells wafting through this house."

Despite my mood, I *am* hungry, and lunch does smell delicious.

"Maria, Maria," my Aunt Rosa cries, as if she hasn't seen me for a decade instead of seven days. My father has two sisters, and as Rosa releases me from her hug, my other aunt, Silvia, mumbles in Italian and yanks me into her arms.

They are big women, both widowed. Rosa more recently.

Uncle Antonio's wife, Ariana, walks in with my cousin Riccardo beside her. They have a daughter, Sophie, who is seven and staying with friends tonight. Likely sent away because no one knew how tonight was going to unfold. Riccardo, though, he's just turned eighteen and looks like a gangster poster boy, with his black jacket collar turned up.

He and Cade do the man hug as my father's second-in-command, Gabrielle, enters the room.

"Mia," he says, a firm grip on my arms as he presses harsh kisses to my cheeks. A reminder of who I am.

The mafia princess.

"Gabe," I say, only because I know he hates the nickname.

"Let's eat." My father stands from his chair in a lazy fashion, and everyone moves into action. No one dares defy him. He walks to me, his arm wrapping around me possessively, and guides me into the dining room.

Something is wrong. I can sense it.

Call it survival.

It's as if they all know something I don't, and they're playing with their food.

That, or I'm tired and paranoid.

I calculate the days left of my two-year agreement, and I'm *sure* there are still two weeks remaining. I'm *sure*. So, it must be the lack of sleep, the way I can't stop thinking about Connor Barrett and the night we spent together.

It's like his scent is still on me.

My head is fuzzy, and I'm still floating after the seven or more orgasms. I'm sure the blood hasn't returned to all the correct places in my body yet.

If I close my eyes, I can still see Connor and I lying on our sides, exhausted, my leg over his hip as he slowly thrusts in and out of me, not wanting to stop.

There was little left in either of us, our bodies coated in glossy sweat, and yet his hand clutched my hair, and those deep brown eyes clung to mine as he grunted and groaned out the same desperate pleasure I did.

We fucked until we couldn't keep our eyes open. Falling asleep tangled in a pile of limbs, sticky and almost sated.

I don't think I could ever be completely sated by a man like Connor Barrett. I'd always want more.

He'd always take more.

So, I can't just act as if last night never happened.

The meal is long and laborious, and the more my father watches me, the more certain I am that he knows.

Which irritates me.

I'm twenty-four—this controlling behavior has to end. I don't care if we *are* a mafia family. I'm a grown woman. I'm not the same Mia who left this house two years ago. He knows, surely, I'm not a virgin. There's never been an expectation that I would remain one.

Only that I may be required to marry someone from the world we exist in.

Another gangster.

But nothing of the sort has been raised since my mother was alive and reminding me it was a possibility.

"Go, have fun, but be careful, Mia. There will come a day when you will be expected to play your part in this family. I can't protect you from that. Your father is who he is, and I love him," she would say.

Still, it may be that I'm tired.

Two hours later, there are half-empty plates of pasta, salads, breads, and meats everywhere. Cutlery is scraping, and glasses are being refilled once again.

Everything is normal.

"How is the job, Mia?" Aunt Rosa asks, using my preferred name, and I'm grateful.

"Good." I lift the red wine to my lips. "I love it."

Never miss an opportunity, I say. I'm forever hoping Father will see how happy I am and will let me continue living my life my way.

I know he loves me, so surely, he must see this is what I want. Not a career in crime, murder, and other illegal activities that are too abhorrent to consider.

I've never said it to him directly, but he's seen the look in my eyes, heard my cries, and even watched me run to the bathroom, vomiting, when I was younger and overheard things. Or worse, witnessed them.

Cade would laugh.

Papa would just tell my mother she needed to harden me up. That this was the world we lived in.

"Donna does the most incredible events," Aunt Silvia says. "She did the gala for the Rochford's. You should've seen it. Spectacular is the only word to use."

I *did* see it.

I helped run the event. In fact, the internally lit ice fountain was my idea, and it was all over the NYC media for days.

We helped raise nearly two million dollars to stop the use of animals for entertainment. I was so proud. I hate seeing all those social feeds with photos of people on vacation, where they're smiling and holding a koala, crocodile, tiger, or other wild animal. Don't they know the poor animal has either had food withheld to make them so complaint—a.k.a. starving—or they're drugged?

They are.

So heartbreaking.

My father lifts his fork to his mouth, the enormous gold ring on his finger indicating his role as head of the family. Head of the mob in NYC.

As if its required.

He was born powerful.

His dark hair is now gray, a seventies-style mustache thick on his upper lip and his face lined with knowledge and experience.

And death.

I've watched him flick his fingers, move his eyes, and had men kill for him. A nod and a trigger pulled.

As hard as my mother tried, she could not shelter me from the death and corruption. He wouldn't let her.

This is her future, he would say. *She must learn and respect the family.*

Not a day goes by that I don't hate that my apartment is paid for by blood. My clothes, my phone, my jewelry. At least I can say my groceries come from the work I do each day at Bloom Events.

"Boss," Jimmy "Fingers" says as he walks into the room. Jimmy is Father's head enforcer.

Gabrielle turns his head and watches him like a hawk. He's in on everything going on with the business, and soon, Cade will take his place.

Then one day, step into my father's shoes.

I sip my drink and watch them all, realizing I'm being watched back. Papa is *staring* at me. *Fuck.* I hate that I still can't read him twenty-four years on.

He doesn't move an inch to acknowledge Jimmy, but the man leans down to his ear and says something.

Papa nods once.

"Take him downstairs, and I will be down when I have finished lunch," Joe says.

"Got it, boss." Jimmy leaves, but not before he lifts his arm to indicate one of the guards should follow.

They both walk out.

Papa shoots Gabrielle a glance, and he pushes his chair out. "Excuse me," and leaves.

It's nearly over, and while I mostly hate these Sunday lunches, I do enjoy seeing my family. Just not with the dark cloud of my future hanging over my head.

Despite what they do, I love these mobsters.

Cade watches the interaction with Jimmy and my father— ever the eager apprentice. They share a look as my father wipes his mouth with his napkin and throws it on his plate.

Seriously, this is just another day in the Mancini family.

Hashtag MobLife.

Father takes a healthy drink of his wine, then drops it down, and his eyes land on me.

Directly.

Oh, shit.

"Mia, I have given notice on your apartment. Two weeks, you are coming home," Joe says, and my eyes fly open.

My stomach lurches, nearly bringing up my entire lunch, and it feels like all the blood leaches from my body.

I go cold.

I stay calm, though. It's what you do with powerful, dangerous men. You never show fear.

"I thought we might negotiate," I say slowly, as if this is no big deal.

Cade snorts and lifts his glass to his mouth.

Asshole.

"Two years. That was the agreement," Joe replies.

I nod, lift my drink, take a sip, and drop the crystal glass back on the table. Cool, calm, and holding back a scream.

"Yes. Now, I'd like to discuss an extension to that agreement and the reasons why." Then add, without taking my eyes off Papa, "In private."

The room has gone quiet.

My aunts are staring at me with their mouths open, and Riccardo's eyes are darting between us.

I should've waited.

I should've agreed, then spoken to him when we were alone, but I'm tired, and the words just fell out because the truth is, I'm desperate to keep my freedom.

I'll do nearly anything.

I know I've failed when my father stretches his arms out and places his hands on the corners of the table, palms down, that big ring on display.

I'm not prepared for this conversation. I thought I had a few more weeks.

"No. It's time to come back to the family as we agreed. You must do your part in the business and prepare for when your brother takes over." Papa's voice is strong as he stares me down. Then he waves one of his hands around. "You think all of this comes for free?"

I know it doesn't. I also know the price we all pay with our souls to live like this. The price people have paid with their lives.

But I don't dare say it.

Know your audience, and all that.

"No," I snap. There will be consequences for my attitude. I glance at Cade, and he's staring at me with a smile that sends a cold shiver through me.

I narrow my eyes.

"What part?" I demand, wondering what it is they have planned for me. "What is it you see me doing?"

The darkness that flickers in my father's eyes would terrify most people. It does me, but I'm the least likely person on earth he will kill.

Probably.

I've always pushed the limits, and I suspected it was the reason he let me go off on my two-year adventure, as he calls it. That and losing my mother was a shock to us all, and I know he was aware how much I grieved.

Still grieve.

I played that card hard.

Mom was my best friend. The person who protected me from all of this. And yet, she also tried to coach me for the mafia life.

A life I don't want.

Now I have Sienna and a group of friends, a job and a life I love. I'm not giving up without a fight.

Which, apparently, I'm getting. Papa's hand lifts and slams down on the table. China and silver clang. A glass tips and spills red wine.

I flinch but don't jump.

"You do not demand anything, Maria Luna Mancini," he growls. "Two weeks. Then Tony will collect you to bring you home."

I press my lips together, glaring at him with all the hatred I can muster. In one conversation, he has taken my freedom, taken away all my choices, and taken my happiness.

My life now belongs to the mafia.

As it always has.

I've just been in denial, believing I had a choice when I never did.

Joe settles into his chair and tosses back the last of the red wine in his glass, then pins me with a stare. "And you will end things with Connor Barrett."

My breathing halts. *You what now?*

My father knows about Connor?

Of course, he does.

Wait. End things?

Why on earth does he think it's an ongoing relationship? It was one night.

I glance at my brother, and he's rubbing his jaw, looking guilty as hell. Uncle Johnny is nodding at me, as if this is the right thing for me. I nearly scowl at him.

"We will find you a husband," my father says. "I have a few in mind once you get settled. The last thing we need is all the media attention, with you dating that man."

"What?" I gasp, unable to take it all in.

I'm. Tired.

And my life and independence have just been ripped from me. I rub my eyes and stare at everyone around the table. My family just sitting there, doing nothing, as my soul dies in front of them.

No way.

I can't do this.

I won't do this.

"I can't marry them," I cry.

Think, Mia.

"You will," my father says firmly, in a tone indicating it is already done.

"I can't," I repeat.

Then, a sort of insanity overtakes me. That's the only excuse I have for what I say next.

"Because Connor asked me to marry him. And I said yes."

Moments later, the entire room erupts into chaos.

I'M FINALLY FREE to go. After my father screamed, paced the room, sent everyone away, and punched a wall while letting out a whole bunch of *you will tell him you won't marry him's,* I told him I had to go.

I told him I would not cancel the engagement.

My fake engagement.

The one Connor knows nothing about.

Holy shit, what was I thinking?

I head up to my old bedroom to grab a pair of shoes I've been missing. My entire wardrobe was far too big to take with me two years ago, and most of it designer. Not exactly event-planning wear.

As I exit, I hear my brother from his room, talking in loud hushed tones, so I figure I should say goodbye. Fine, I'm being nosy. When I get closer, a few words I make out cause me to freeze.

"It doesn't matter," Cade snaps. "By the time it's done, she *will* be married to Salvo."

I take another step and lean forward. He's on the phone, pacing.

"It *has* to happen. This engagement will secure the partnership," Cade growls. "We'll deal with Connor Barrett."

Salvo?

That's who my father wants me to marry?

Salvo "Sly" Vitale?

My stomach lurches for the tenth time today. Salvo is fifteen years my senior. Balding, enormous belly, hair growing from his ears—that might not be true, but in my head, he has—and he does this slurping thing when he eats.

Revolting.

More to the point, I do not love him.

No fucking way.

I race across the hall and down the stairs, grabbing my coat from out of Susanna's hands, then out to the car.

Tony glances up as I leap in.

"Ms. Mancini," he says, startled. He hates that he didn't get to open the door.

"Go, please. I'm…I'm in a hurry. Late for a meeting."

At approximately the speed of a snail, he turns the engine on, and we cruise slowly away from my family home.

Angry tears slide down my face.

10

CONNOR

My eyes flick open for the second time this morning. Mia is gone, but I can still scent her on my sheets, my body.

God, what a night.

I lie thinking about her, about the way she looked as she came multiple times, then lay sated in my arms.

There was something different with her, and I'm not sure why. She's not an escort, obviously, but I've slept with other women not sent to me by the agency and never reacted to them like I did her.

Mia has a sparkle in her eyes that, as ridiculous as this sounds, made me feel alive. She made me laugh. Sitting talking to her was refreshing and...fun.

When was the last time I had fun?

I don't know anything about her, except what she does for a job—obviously has wealthy parents—but I sense she has a story she's not sharing with people.

Has she lived abroad?

Lost a parent?

There's a depth to her most people don't have.

And for some reason, I didn't intimidate her. At least, not when I didn't have her tied up and screaming my name.

I push back the desire to have more of her.

No seconds. I don't do seconds.

Not even with Mia...Mia? Whatever her name is. It'll be on the contract.

I toss back the sheets to get on with my day and life.

Sunday mornings, I usually wake up early, go for a run around Central Park, and spend an hour in my gym. Grab a coffee and breakfast and scroll through emails for a few hours.

Then my focus is solely on Dark King's work.

Not that it's not front of mind every other day of the week, but after nearly twenty years, I've learned to control my anger and obsession.

After leaving the marines, I created The Dark Kings, a covert organization made up of myself and two former marines, Nathan and Decker, who I served with.

Men I would die for.

Men who every day put their lives at risk to help me find the mafia asshole who destroyed my entire family while I watched. The same mob who would kill me if they knew who I was.

Who think I'm dead.

All I have is one name and a face etched into my childhood memory.

Carlos.

One day, I will find him and he will stand—or rather, kneel—before me, pleading for his life. Once he's screaming and barely alive, I will slit his throat and watch his blood seep from his body and stain the floor.

Just as my mother's did.

As my father's did.

As my sister's blood did.

For my family, I will seek revenge, and only then will I welcome in the light, which will heal my soul and release my heart from the devil.

Until then, darkness remains my solace.

Until then, I have nothing to offer emotionally. I cannot love when I hate so thoroughly.

My empire is my cover, funding the real work.

I have an entire secure room in my penthouse, which looks like something out of an episode of *CSI* or some crime documentary. I covered the walls with images of mafia families from the United States and other parts of the world.

Which mafia is the question I ask myself every day.

I was nine when the men turned up at our house, storming it with machine guns.

My father was helping me with the setup of my train set when we heard the cars. His face paled, and he screamed for my mother. She came running into the room.

"Get Rebecca," he yelled, referring to my sister, who was three.

Then he grabbed me and tore open the door under the stairs, held my face, and said, "Stay silent, no matter what you see. Do you understand?"

I nodded, my heart pounding.

"Don't cry. Don't let them find you. And never tell anyone who you are, son. Run! Run when it's safe and find Detective Scott. Give him this, and he will work out the rest."

Then he ripped a chain off his neck. On it hung a key. He put it over my head, tucked it under my sweater, and said, "I love you, Connor."

Seconds before the door burst open, he shut me inside.

Then my world collapsed.

Through an air vent, I heard and saw them grab my father, pull my mother and sister from downstairs, Rebecca crying, and then smash them with the butts of their guns.

My mother fell to the floor, blood pouring from her head. My sister, tumbling from her arms. My father, screaming.

It took everything I had in me to follow my father's instructions. Tears fell down my cheeks, and my fists clenched, anger and terror filling every cell in my body.

I knew then I could be next.

I *would* be next if they heard me, or if I had stepped out of that room. All I had left was the key, cold on my chest, reminding me of my father's orders.

"Carlos. I have them," a man with an accent said. He waved a brown folder. "Let's go."

Carlos nodded at the other man, who I couldn't see, only hear, and lifted his gun. "You traitor, Beaufort. You piece of fucking shit."

"You cannot kill me, Carlos," my father said from his knees. "Leave. You shouldn't be here. You know that."

"Fuck you," he had said, then swiveled the gun and shot my mother in the head.

Rebecca screamed. My father roared, drowning out my gut-wrenching muffled cry as my hand slapped over my mouth. I had nearly vomited.

"You will die for this, Carlos," my father said, reaching for my mother. But he never got to her.

Carlos turned the gun at him and sprayed dozens of bullets at his body.

By then, I was numb from shock.

Rebecca, three years old, sat on her bottom, crying, terrorized and alone. My hand was on the door handle, ready to fly out and save her.

"Leave the girl," a man nearby said. "She's innocent."

I watched Carlos look around, grunting something out, then slowly, he spotted something.

"Where's the boy?" Carlos asked, picking up the framed photo on the cabinet in the hallway and poking the glass. "He could be in the house. Find him. He's old enough to talk."

Rebecca continued screaming as the men took off to search for me. I pressed myself far into the corner of the cupboard, shaking and in terror as another shot suddenly sounded out.

Then there was only silence.

Carlos had killed my little sister.

An innocent child.

I slunk to my knees, my hand over my mouth, my scream frozen, awaiting the moment I could release it.

I'm not sure I ever have.

He had killed my entire family in minutes. When the others returned, saying I wasn't there, Carlos ordered them to hunt me down and kill me too.

I don't know how long it took me to finally move and leave the space under the stairs, but it was the longest and most terrifying time of my life.

The bodies of my mother, father, and sister, drained of blood, greeted me once I did. I vomited multiple times, collapsing and crying in convulsions, until I eventually crawled to the phone and rang the police, asking for Detective Scott.

When I gave him my name and told him what happened, he took over. The house swarmed with police, and I was whisked away with a new name and put into a boarding school in Switzerland.

Well, a new surname.

I didn't realize it then, but it was protective custody.

For the next four years, I grieved for my family and acted out. I fought and tried to run away multiple times. If it hadn't been for a strict headmaster and one compassionate nun, I don't know what I would've become.

Sister Maxine told me to seek peace in my heart for what ailed me. But I couldn't tell anyone, Detective Scott said, or they would find me and kill me. And so, I did as she said—I chose a purpose for my life.

Revenge.

I would grow powerful and find this Carlos, no matter how long it took. Then destroy him.

You see, I knew when I turned eighteen, I would inherit one hundred million dollars. Detective Scott had visited me only once after getting me settled in the school, giving me enough information to act on when I was old enough.

The life insurances, cash, and assets of my family were mine.

And the key, which I had never given to the Detective.

I'd forgotten and then was too scared.

It sits in a box, along with files the now FBI agent had given me.

You traitor, Beaufort.

What had my father done?

I didn't want the answers to that question—just wanted revenge. I didn't want to know if my father, who I had loved and looked up to, could be responsible for what I'd witnessed that day.

So, I didn't.

Instead, I focused on avenging my mother and sister. And my father. I started putting together a plan. Joined the marines, built a strong body, invested the money, and began to learn about buying businesses. Fast forwarding a lot of years, by the time I left the marines, I was a billionaire.

It was in the marines I met my two best friends, Nathan and Decker.

One night, in the dark deserts of the Middle East, I finally told them my story. We'd returned from a two-hour shootout with the enemy and had barely left with our lives. I wasn't sure I would return to U.S, soil with my life at the end of this tour and needed to know someone else would hunt down Carlos if I was gone.

Nathan and Decker, as it turned out, shared a hatred for the mafias as well. They each have their own stories and a desire for vengeance similar to mine.

It was like the stars aligned.

Mafias caused a whole raft of pain and suffering around the world, with the drugs they pedaled, people and sex trafficking, and more. While taking on that motherfucking huge job was a recipe for failure—mostly because there was corrupt law enforce-ment, which allowed it to go on—it didn't mean we were going to sit back and do nothing.

We were vigilantes in the making.

But we weren't fucking saints.

We could find one man and avenge those who had destroyed our lives.

The three of us sat up all night talking that evening, about what we wanted to do and what we *could* do about it. By the early hours of the morning, we had formed the Dark Kings.

Best decision of my life.

I step into the gym and turn the treadmill to mid-speed. I'm a little jaded after my Mia-workout all night. As I begin to jog, my mind goes back to the Dark Kings, to the moment we realized just what we were undertaking.

"Fuck yeah, I'm in," Decker said, reaching out his hand, and we shook, slapping shoulders.

"You only have a name and a memory of what this Carlos looks like?" Nathan asked, rubbing his shorn head.

"That's right," I answered.

"Shit, man. This could take years," Nathan replied.

I didn't care. I'd search for a decade, if that's what it took. My family deserved to be avenged.

"It will take as long as it takes. I have the funds, and I will keep hunting the fucker until the day I die."

Which defied logic, since Carlos was much older than me. Someone gave him the order. Or he was working alone.

I doubted the latter.

After hearing Nathan's story, I knew he was on board. His brother had been fucked up by the mob, somehow getting involved with heroine. Every day, I saw anger and ghosts in his eyes. He needed an outlet for that rage. Just like I did.

"If you join me, we'll bring these mobsters to their knees. This is a partnership. Even if we find Carlos, my funds are yours to avenge your loved ones. It's not one or the other. This will be *our* life," I reiterated.

"Then I'm in," Nathan said.

"So, the mafia think you're dead?" Decker asked.

"Yes."

Detective Scott had heard from people on the inside that there was no talk of looking for a kid with my name, and now, so many years had passed, we both agreed it was unlikely they were looking for me.

"They probably thought you were a cousin in the photo. Whatever, there's no noise about it. You're a kid. Hardly a threat to them," the detective had said when I asked him again before leaving for the marines.

"Do you have anything else to go on?" Nathan asked next.

"Not yet," I replied.

I had the key—to what, I didn't know.

And while the FBI had taken all our belongings, Detective Scott said he had put some personal things in storage for me when I left the boarding school. All of it was now in my possession, along with a new alias: Connor Barrett.

Connor Beaufort no longer existed. Nor did I feel like that person anymore.

I increase the speed on the treadmill.

We left the marines and spent six months setting up a strategy, looking at what we knew. My father had something of theirs and called him a traitor.

But which mob? That was the other fucking question.

I had narrowed down their accents to either the Mexican cartel or the Italian mob. Yeah, I know they're fucking different, but when you are nine years old and men are screaming and shooting your family, accents are fucking accents.

I hadn't given a shit.

What I had eliminated were Irish, Russian, and Chinese.

Which left Italian or Spanish.

So, then we decided to focus our efforts there and worked our way into the Mexican cartel—Decker—and Italian mafia —Nathan.

That was six years ago.

And despite multiple leads over the years, we still haven't found Carlos.

Among the images on the wall in my office are facial recognition artists' and software drawings of what I remembered Carlos looking like.

Every day, I stare at it and let my rage flow.

There are also images of all the mafia, their families, connections, and other gangsters he could've been working for or with. We put together profiles on all of them. It is like a fucking episode of *CSI* in there.

I knew this was going to take time, but my patience is running out.

Six damn years.

One of the biggest issues is getting close to the inner circle of the mob bosses.

They don't trust easily, and both Nathan and Decker are Americans. Neither Italian nor Mexican.

We are at a disadvantage.

Frankly, I am getting concerned they have been in there too long. Both of them have done things they've despised to prove themselves and fit it.

Things that destroy a man's soul.

There is only so much I can do to counter it on the outside without compromising them. I feel useless some days, wanting in on the action, but my face is too well known by most Americans, so it is impossible.

Instead, I keep the Dark Kings safe. I pull strings when needed with law enforcement and get them out of tricky situations.

Detective Scott is now working in the FBI, nearing retirement, and the one man aside from the Dark Kings—which includes Mack—who knows what I am doing. He doesn't completely agree, but I don't give a fuck. Let's just say, he is going to retire a wealthy man, and not because of his pension. So, he helps when I ask.

Tonight, I am meeting with Nathan.

It is always risky to connect, but we keep most meets tight and fast. When Decker was on U.S. soil, we met at our Dark King's headquarters in Lower Manhattan.

My phone beeps with a message from Mack.

A new location has been set.

AN HOUR LATER, my workout is done, and I step into the shower. Mia enters my mind again.

Damn, she was sweet. All that cinnamon and honey, like Christmas time, only hotter.

I press the button on the wall, direct the seven shower heads to different angles, and power them up. Fuck, yeah. The muscles in my body begin to relax.

I should've fucked her in the shower.

A missed opportunity.

Another button and the water stops. Reaching for a thick black towel, I dry off and then walk back into the bedroom naked, rubbing the towel across the back of my head.

I reach for my cock, wishing that woman was lying on my sheets, when something catches my eye. It's white and sticking out from under the bed, near where Mia dressed this morning.

Did she leave something? I recall her dropping her bag but didn't pick her as the type of woman to plant something so she had an excuse to return.

I'm also thinking I probably wouldn't mind another taste. Crouching, I reach for the object and end up with a business card in my hand.

As I stand, flipping it over, I see the name, and my blood freezes. Mia Mancini—Event Coordinator.

Mancini.

I stare blankly at the carpet.

You have got to be fucking kidding me?

I storm down to my office, buck naked, punch the code into the security panel, and push through the door.

No goddamn way.

I find the Mancini mafia and stare at the notorious boss, Joe Mancini. My eyes trail down. Like a family tree, I have all the names and faces of the Mancini family—and others—showing their roles and any other information I deem important.

Motherfucking fucker.

My chest tightens when I find her photo and name right there on my goddamn wall—Maria Luna Mancini.

Jesus.

She's younger in the photo. The data was collected when she would've been eighteen, at most. She wasn't anyone we paid much attention to because she was a child.

The little Nathan ever said about Mia was that she spent most of the time with her mother, until the woman died. It was Cade, her brother and heir to the mafia throne, we needed to keep an eye on.

Recently, he's been causing trouble. He throws his power and influence around town, being mostly a nuisance but making enemies. I'd love to know what Joe thinks about it, but that will never happen. We aren't close enough to him to have a clue.

We do know Cade isn't much liked but is respected because of his position in the family. I call it respect, but it's not really.

I stare back at Mia's photo and curse. It's her. Maria—*Mia*—fucking Mancini. The mafia princess. The woman I fucked for several hours last night.

"Wait a damn minute," I say as something occurs to me.

I storm down to the living room and lift the contract off the ground when I find it. Flicking the pages, I find her signature.

The little minx. She signed a false name.

I slam it down.

Well, well, well. The voice in my head tried to tell me something, and I didn't hear it. I'm nearly impressed with how she fooled me. Not that she has any idea who I am and why I know all about her and her family. About every mafia on this planet.

What is she doing working for Donna?

I know for a fact her residence isn't a Mancini-owned property. Did she get to me to drop her off somewhere other than where she lives? For a moment, I'm worried if she got home.

"Fucking hell, Connor. She's Joe Mancini's daughter. Who cares?" I growl out loud.

Then my brows shoot up when an idea occurs to me.

I kind of hate myself, but there's no way I can ignore it.

A door which has been shut to the Dark Kings for years has just cracked open, and its name is Mia Mancini. Is there a way to leverage a relationship with her? Could she be a way into the upper echelon of the Mancini family?

That's a big fat fucking yes.

Am I going to walk away and let this opportunity slip through my fingers?

No. Hell no.

I grin.

"Mia Mancini, you are about to be the first woman asked out on a date by Connor Barrett. And while I'm at it, I'm going to fuck your sweet pussy a few more times," I say out loud.

Two birds and all that.

Mia fucking Mancini.

"You might be fooling everyone else, but I know who you are, princess."

And she just became my pawn.

SEVERAL HOURS LATER, I'm sitting in a random bar downtown when Nathan slides into a barstool next to me.

We don't look at each other.

He orders a beer.

Nathan has a new tattoo on his neck since the last time I saw him. Nearly seven weeks. I hate that it might not have been his choice. But then again, being inside the Italian mafia *is* his choice. We all have our reasons for doing this, and Nathan does too.

I lift my cheap, shit-tasting whiskey to my lips. There is no Macallan in this bar. I didn't bother asking or looking.

Though I might be recognizable in NYC, with my baseball cap, bomber jacket, and jeans, I look just like any other American guy.

The no-brand clothing helps. And I left my thirty-five-thousand-dollar watch at home.

"'Sup," Nathan says when the bartender slides the beer across to him.

"Nice ink," I reply.

He just nods, leaning his thick forearms on the wooden bar. We're both watching baseball on the screen in front of us, just drinking our beverages. We wait for the commentators to go nuts about something and then make it look like we're discussing it.

"Cade Mancini is preparing to take over," Nathan announces, and my brows rise on their own—like right the fuck to the top of my hairline.

There is no way The Rock—Joseph Mancini—is stepping down. His son isn't ready, nor is he someone anyone on either side of the law wants in the top seat.

Fuck me.

Joe Mancini is a dangerous man, but Cade Mancini is a narcissistic psychopath. Twice as dangerous and ten times more unstable.

He's also Mia's brother.

"How much support does he have?" I ask Nathan, knowing without asking this is a coup.

They happen in the mafia. Most are shut down before they get much momentum because someone gets scared and talks. When it's a family member, the chances of success do increase.

Yeah, I analyze this shit. Know your enemy, and you'll always be one step ahead.

Nathan lifts his beer and takes a long swill, then points it at the screen. "Some key influencers on the team. Reasonable concern."

I signal the bartender. "Another one."

The shit is burning my throat, but this is all for show. I'm tempted to ask him to add fucking lemonade, but I'm not a pussy.

"Names?"

"Giordano, Botticelli, The Icepick, and..." Nathan glances at me, then spins on his seat to survey the bar behind him. It looks like he's just chilling, but he's carefully making sure there is no one listening or watching. "Salvo Vitale. New partnership."

My breathing halts, and I wait to hear more. It's like I'm having a psychic moment or some shit. Or maybe I just know too much about how these families work.

And Mia is of age.

"Promising expanded distribution of the white stuff in the state but a smaller cut. Oh, and Vitale gets the sister," Nathan says.

Jesus.

Mia.

Not only does this mess with my plan, but I also fucking hate that she's going to be traded as property. Which she isn't, but to them, she is. It's how these things work.

Am I any better? I planned to use her.

Now, unless we intervene, I'll have to let this play out.

"When?" I ask, fiddling with the Bud coaster.

"Soon," Nathan says, pulling out a twenty and dropping it on the bar.

I don't know much about Salvo Vitale. Nathan is my source for accurate information. Vitale has always been small fry. A new kid on the block and not on our radar for the purpose of finding Carlos.

Nathan makes to leave.

I need to know about the gangster, so I do something I shouldn't. Turning as Nathan stands, I meet his eye. It surprises him. I see the flicker. Otherwise, he doesn't respond. The guy has so much control, he even impresses me.

"Salvo Vitale?"

"What's the question?" Nathan asks after a long moment.

"Is he dangerous? For her?" I ask, knowing he'll connect the dots. Mia is the only woman we mentioned.

Nathan stares at me, then nods. "Yes. He's brutal."

Fuck.

11

MIA

ngaged? To Connor Barrett?

What was I thinking? I *hadn't* been thinking—that was the problem. I can't even explain where the idea came from. The words just fell out of my mouth.

Let's call it survival.

Now, though, I am in an even bigger pickle. My family thinks I am engaged to one of the wealthiest men in the U.S. Connor thinks I am a girl he enjoyed—hopefully—great sex with last night. Someone he will never see again.

If he finds out, I will look like an idiot.

I have to fix this.

But my situation is far worse than I thought. Salvo Vitale? Surely, my father can't force me to marry someone I don't want.

Right?

I mean, I know how these things work in the family, but it's not the last millennia anymore. Right?

And it's kind of illegal. *Right?*

I nearly snort at my legal argument. As if that stops mobsters from doing anything.

My father demanded I end the engagement while asking a whole lot of questions.

When are Mr. Barrett's people announcing our engagement?

Is he ever planning to ask for my hand?

Does he have a death wish?

When is the wedding planned for?

Am I pregnant?

All of which, of course, I have no answers for.

Except there is no baby, and we aren't actually getting married —least of all because Connor knows nothing about it.

I have to tell him, and fast.

There's every chance, despite me agreeing to bring Connor over to the house—I know, I'm insane!—that my father could go over my head and contact the sexy billionaire directly.

I don't trust my father.

It's better Connor hears it from me.

Herein lies my next problem. I have no way of getting in touch with him. We didn't swap phone numbers, and aside from hovering outside his building like a crazed ex-lover, I'm not sure what else to do.

I could go to his office tomorrow. Or ask Donna for his number. Which would need an explanation, and I don't have any spare brain cells left to conjure something clever.

I could break into our company database and pull his details? I doubt he has his personal phone number listed, and sending an email will be intercepted by his PA.

Can you imagine it?

Dear Connor, so turns out I forgot to mention I'm the Mancini mafia princess. Also, I told Joe Mancini—mob boss and also my father —that we are engaged. Don't worry, I'll get us out of this, but for now, can I move in and live with you?

Yours sincerely

Mia Mancini

Jesus, I'm in deep here. Which is why I'm currently chewing my thumbnail while my friends keep giving me weird looks as I sit opposite them at Toast Bar.

I should've stayed home instead of joining them at the bar,

but there's no way I could relax and sleep, although I'm physically exhausted.

"Mia, are you okay?" Sienna asks, scooping nachos loaded with sour cream into her mouth.

"Hmm, yip. Fine. I'm cool." I nod.

Duncan snorts. "Cool as a forest fire."

"Huh?" I ask, then laugh awkwardly. He's a NYPD firefighter, and if he can fit a fire analogy into a joke, you bet your life he will.

Fortunately for him, he's hot and women like men in uniforms. Just not his jokes.

Isabelle lets out a groan, proving my point. She's immune to his muscles and pretty blue eyes.

"No, I just had a late night," I say, leaning my elbow on the table and resting my head on my hand.

Sienna squints. "Did you go out after the Gala? Jeez, I was exhausted."

Everyone stares at me while I try to come up with an answer. I obviously can't share my situation with them because a) they don't know who I really am, and b) I might've signed a false name on Connor's contract, but I won't break his confidence.

I understand why he wants his privacy. Plus, I don't want to find myself in the *NY Times*. Connor is featured every week for one reason or another. Mostly business or appearances, but also gossip about his relationship status.

I trust my friends, but I agreed, and my lips are sealed.

So, I lie.

What I learned about lying from my father was, you should keep it as close to the truth as possible. Then people are more likely to believe it and shrug off any doubts.

Yeah, like I said, I'm no princess.

My dream is to have my own business, but I have no idea what I want to do. I'm endlessly working on a business strategy for an idea that's not fully formed—and changes by the day, if not the hour.

"I was working on my business plan. Couldn't sleep. It

happens after a big event sometimes," I say. "My feet and body might have been tired, but my brain wouldn't shut up."

They all know how passionate I am about my business ideas. Most of which I run past them and end up hitting a brick wall, but you have to start somewhere.

"Yeah, that happens. Sometimes you get overtired," Sienna says, nodding. "I wish my apartment had a tub to soak in. Although, I'd most likely drown."

I snort.

"Magnesium," Isabelle says. She's studying natural therapies so is always giving us advice on some supplement or another. Magnesium is the answer to many things, I've learned in the past two years. "Relaxes your muscles and calms your nervous system."

I nod. "Thanks. I'll try that."

I won't.

Magnesium isn't going to fix this. It won't stop my gangster father from forcing me to marry some old disgusting mobster or breaking up my fake engagement with an unsuspecting billionaire.

Lord, what a mess.

"Well, here's to another successful event," Sienna says, lifting her glass of wine, and we do the same, then drink.

"And Mia's business ideas." Isabelle winks. She's been a freelance designer for six months while studying and is always encouraging me to follow my dreams.

I'm so proud of her. And envious.

"Thanks, Iz," I say, taking a long sip of my wine.

Perhaps a few glasses of Dutch courage will help, while I work myself up to do the inevitable. I can't hide my head in the sand over this. I have to tell Connor.

Tonight.

Then, if I can buy myself some time, I will find a way out of this situation. To live independently of my family. To get out of the arranged marriage to Vitale.

The truth is, no one leaves the mafia. Certainly not Joe Mancini's daughter.

But I have to try.

Which is why, two hours later, I find myself outside Connor Barrett's apartment building.

A little drunk.

12

CONNOR

hat the hell?

"Mia?" I ask, stepping out of the vehicle and watching her pace in front of my building.

What is she doing here?

I've been going back and forth over the conversation with Nathan and concluded I have to forget about dating her.

You mean, using her?

Now I'm curious as hell to understand why she's here. If I'm honest, I'm not unhappy to see her.

"What's going on?"

"Trust me, this is not what it looks like," she says, and my brows lift in response.

"Okay, perhaps it is. Well, no, it's worse," Mia adds.

Worse?

Okay, now she is really getting my attention. Why has the Mancini mafia princess come back for seconds? An assumption, I realize, but what else could it be?

On second thought, I can't see her being one of those clingy one-night stand types.

Plus, she looks stressed.

"Explain," I say, taking in her sexy-as-hell tight jeans, which hug her ass perfectly, and a silk green top which drapes in a cowl neck, hinting at those perky little tits I had in my mouth many times this morning.

She looks completely different from her Bloom Events uniform. Tonight, her long dark hair is flowing in silky waves down her back.

I don't want to be this attracted to her, but Mia is gorgeous. And complicated. At least, she's a complication to me.

If I'm going to use her to get to the notorious Italian mafia's inner circle, I need to remember she would just be an asset.

Nothing more.

Fine, she's a great fuck as well.

It can be both.

Temporarily.

"I think...I don't know. It doesn't matter. Well, it does. I think. Shit. I'm here because I didn't have your number," Mia says.

Obviously.

Not many people do.

"There's a reason for that," I say, walking past her toward my building. She follows, and I open the door and glance at her. Mia figures out it's an invitation to enter, while Mack stands back, watching me.

"Head home. I'll see you in the morning," I instruct him.

"Yes, sir," Mack says, walking back to the car. He and Benson will wrap up for the night, my other men in the foyer starting their evening shift.

I turn to Mia, waving her in, and we walk to the elevator to my penthouse. When the doors open, I go straight to the kitchen and pull out two bottles of water.

She paces the floor, biting her nails.

Curiosity is nearly killing me, if I'm honest.

I open one of the bottles and put it on the kitchen bench between us. She looks at it, then at me as if snapping out of her thought pattern, but she continues her pacing.

Christ, this is going to take forever.

"I know who you are," I say, hoping that might speed things up.

Mia stops walking and freezes. She's staring at me, and I guess I can appreciate that she's waiting to see what I will say. I know what it's like to protect your true identity.

"Mia...or should I say, Maria Luna Mancini," I add, to be clear we are on the same page.

Her body slumps. "I'm sorry."

Interesting.

I lift the bottle and take a long drink, watching the defeat in her body language. Where's her sass gone? Something has happened, and a thread of anger weaves through me.

I push it aside.

She's my enemy. Or at least, her family is.

Pawn. Remember that.

I put the cap on my bottle.

"Is that why you're here, Mia? Guilt for not telling me your real identity?" But I don't care. I simply want to keep her talking because it's clear there is more than this going on. "Or because you signed a false signature on our agreement?"

If I'm going to play this, I must be smart. I can't let her know I care about what her family does. Or that I have a vested interest. Theoretically, if I was simply a businessman wanting to ensure his privacy wasn't at risk after a night with a woman, I would be concerned about that contract.

That's all.

"No!" she says. "No. I'll honor that. I just can't sign my real name. I couldn't. Surely, you can understand that now. Or maybe you can't. There's...My life isn't normal. I can't explain."

I do. I understand more than she realizes.

"Good to know," I reply and lean a hip against the counter. "So, why are you here, Mia Mancini, mafia princess?"

She cringes, and I watch her curiously.

I wait.

"So...God...My father knows I was here last night," Mia says, and I raise a brow.

"And?" I ask coldly.

Despite the fact he's Joe Mancini, do I care? I'm Connor fucking Barrett. He's hardly going to come knocking down my door for fucking his daughter.

Well, he might.

"Unless Wikipedia has it wrong, I'm pretty sure you're over eighteen," I add.

"You googled me?" she asks, giving away a hint of pleasure, and I suppress the smile I want to give her.

Instead, I push away from the counter and throw back the rest of the water.

"When you learn the daughter of the Italian mafia was in your bed, it's always good to check she is of legal age, don't you think?"

"I'm twenty-four," Mia confirms for me again.

I didn't Google her. I have all the information about her on my office wall. She'd be creeped the fuck out if she saw it.

I toss my water bottle in the trash, and I can see she's wondering why I'm not quivering in fear.

She won't get that from me.

"So, your father's going to send someone to shoot out my kneecaps, is that it? Is that why you're here?" I smirk.

Joe Mancini can try, but his goons won't get close enough. Everyone who works in my personal or protective roles has military training and is far more skilled than they need to be.

Or perhaps, do *need* to be.

One day.

Mobsters might be ruthless killers, but they aren't trained. They'd be dead before they lifted their weapons.

Mia crosses her arms. "Don't joke about that."

I laugh dryly.

"Don't worry about me, princess. I can take care of myself. Your father doesn't scare me," I say firmly. It's important Mia knows, if I'm to work my way into her life, I am powerful enough to face her family. I want her to feel confident introducing me to them quickly.

This is a turning point for me and the Dark Kings.

"Good, because he wants to meet you?" she says, a blush hitting her cheeks.

What?

I stare at her, taken by surprise.

Jesus.

It's like life is being handed to me on a silver platter. The Mancini family and the sweetest pussy I've ever had. Except I'm not a fucking idiot. There's something she's not telling me. I walk around the kitchen island and stop a few feet away from her as she lifts her face.

Mia's holding her breath, and my heart is thumping away in my chest.

"What have you done?" I growl, crossing my arms.

She mirrors me, but it's a protective stance, and for a moment, I don't like the vulnerability I see in her eyes.

Pawn.

"Mia, talk."

"Before I say any more, I want you to know I didn't plan this. It just fell out. There is no way I could've known I would, you know, end up here last night, and so...I got scared,"

"Of me?" I ask angrily. I do not want her to be afraid of me. That is unacceptable.

"No," she replies quickly, and I nod.

"Keep going."

"So, I've been living this double life, and my time is up, and then my father says I have to move back home. He's canceled my lease, and I have to quit my job. Then I overheard my brother saying they've lined up Salvo Vitale to be my husband. God, he slurps his food."

My brain is trying to take in the data, but all I hear are Nathans words: *He's brutal.*

Staring at her and imagining that asshole with his hands on her...Well, I don't like it at all.

She's worried he slurps his food? Fuck, that's the least of her fucking worries.

Double fuck.

"And he's older, you know. Like, fifteen or more years older. I know you're older. But like, good old."

My brows lift and then drop in a frown. I may not know Mia well, but I do know when someone won't stop talking, it's because there's something they do not want to say.

Usually, it's followed by bad news.

What the hell has she done?

"Mia," I say roughly.

She looks up at me, and her eyes are filled with tears. I take a step closer, my arms dropping.

"What. Did. You. Do?"

Ice creeps into my bones as Mia bites her lip and looks pleadingly at me. My eyes hold hers, pressing for the answer.

"Well, I said I can't marry anyone," Mia replies. "Because...Oh god." Her head drops into her hands. "I told my father...I said I was engaged to you."

I draw in a sharp, audible breath, then curse.

Jesus fucking Christ.

The head of the mafia thinks I am engaged to his daughter.

Me.

The man who wants to destroy him.

"I'M SORRY," MIA cries as I spin away and run a hand through my hair.

Jesus.

I don't know whether to strangle her or kiss her. This could be an incredible opportunity. Or an enormous risk.

Marry the mafia princess?

Am I insane for even contemplating the idea?

Whatever I decide in the next few minutes, what I need to do is ensure Mia thinks I'm shocked—which I am—and need convincing.

I shoot her a glance, then start to pace, my hands roaming over my head and across my face. Multiple times, I turn to face Mia, who stands there with her arms wrapped around her middle.

She's worried.

"What do you think is going to happen here?" I finally ask. I need to know what her expectations are. What she's thinking.

If I'm to proceed with my idea.

"Not that you will marry me," she says firmly. "Honestly, not that. I just need to buy some time until I can get my own place. I have to move out of my apartment in two weeks. Papa is taking away everything."

Papa, like Joe Mancini is some guy who used to take her to Saturday ballet, instead of leading one of the country's most dangerous gangs.

If he has taken away her apartment, it's likely he will cut her off financially as well. It's how you control trust-fund babies. I see it all the time.

"And?"

"I just need a few months to get a deposit together and furniture." She waves her hand around, like she could afford anything in my penthouse. Most people couldn't. "Then I'll convince my father I don't love you, or something. Once I have everything set up, I'll be independent enough to tell him I'm not coming back."

My eyes widen, and I nearly laugh.

Is she insane?

This is her grand plan to escape the mafia? Her family, her destiny, and the role she was born into as a mafia princess.

If I didn't know the security in my penthouse was the best in the world, I'd suspect I was on a hidden camera show.

It's like she's in complete denial.

Or desperate.

"Mia, I don't know much about mafia families," I lie, "but I'm sure it's not that easy. Why don't you sit down with your father and discuss how you feel."

I know it won't work, but again, I'm playing a role here. If I say yes and go along with her plan, she'll be suspicious.

She flings out her hands and lets out a groan.

"I'm not marrying Salvo Vitale. Do you know...No, you don't. They don't treat women well in my family. We are...Anyway, forget it. I can't say anything to Papa. I just hate what they do...We do. Ugh. I know this is crazy. I shouldn't have come. I've had too much to drink, and...I don't know...I thought maybe you might..." Her eyes lift to mine, and for a moment, I'm pulled into those crystal blue eyes and feel a genuine desire to help her. "I get it. There's nothing in it for you. Well, there is. I get my trust fund if we *did* marry, but it's not like you need the money."

Now, that's something I can work with.

I watch Mia unravel as I reformulate my plan. Little does she know, there is *a lot* in it for me. The thing I want most in life. Revenge. And she could be the key to unlocking the door Carlos is hiding behind.

I must do this. No matter the cost.

Of course, I don't need her money, but I keep that to myself. It's essential Mia believes I have selfish reasons for agreeing to what she's asking.

Being a businessman, money is something I would be interested in, so I ask, "How much?"

"What?" Mia's eyes go wide.

"How much is your trust fund?"

"Two million," Mia says, and I force back my reaction.

Her father has an estimated wealth of one hundred times that, and he's giving her two measly million?

It's becoming clear Mancini has set up quite the invisible prison for his daughter, and it surprises me he has let her have a job. Something I plan to ask more about another day.

I polish off my mental plan. Mia flops down onto the stool, defeated. I sit beside her, my body dwarfing hers.

Taking a moment to run my eyes over her, I feel a familiar desire run through me. She's utterly gorgeous, and I'm strangely excited about having her in my life for a bit longer as I proceed with this insanity.

"I know it's not much. You can say no, and I will understand." She locks her eyes to mine. "You think I'm crazy, don't you?"

Yes.

"No, Mia, I don't," I reply, drawing in a long slow breath and then exhaling.

She watches me.

"I think you're fucking gorgeous. I think I enjoyed last night with you very much, and I thought about you several times today."

She blinks in surprise.

"I think I want to fuck you again, Mia Mancini. Something I don't usually do with other women. I am a powerful man. With your background, I'm sure you understand why a relationship is impossible for me."

She nods.

I had no doubt she would understand that concept.

"So, this may suit me. Temporarily, of course."

Mia nods faster.

"The agreement will need to benefit us both," I add, my voice darkening and my hand stretching past her along the marble bench. "So, I will have my own stipulations."

She nods slower, more wary, and glances at my hand now lying beside her.

"What would you want?" she asks, swallowing nervously.

"I want all of you," I reply.

"All of me?" she asks and begins to hop off the stool.

I stop her with the palm of my hand on her hip.

"If you want to be my fake wife, I'll have all of you while you live here. Along with one point five million dollars once we are married. That is my offer."

I watch as reality sinks in.

Mia chews her lips, glancing at me like it's not a bad deal. She enjoyed last night, and we can both feel the chemistry still simmering beneath the surface.

If she does agree to go ahead, I'll need to be very clear I know the price. Mia will be my pawn. Nothing more, nothing less.

Afterward, she will hate me.

13

MIA

"Okay, I accept."

"Are you sure?" Connor asks.

I'm pretty sure by *all of me* he means sex, but I need to clarify it further. Even if he does, I *am* sure about accepting his offer. At first, I was shocked, but would sleeping with Connor Barrett a few more times truly be a hardship?

The answer is no.

Especially given I'm asking him to be my pretend husband and to face my father, a mobster. I'm sure he is a busy man, and it wouldn't be all the time.

Plus, the money.

No money is worth giving up my freedom, so I will happily hand it over.

"Yes, I agree to your terms. If this gains me my independence, then I'll happily do it." For a second, I glance over his shoulder into the darkness outside and wonder what I'm getting myself into.

I've completely lost my mind, I'm sure of it.

But what other options do I have?

Run away?

They'd find me in a hot minute.

"Okay, then you'll move in immediately," Connor says as I nod. "You will wear my ring, and we'll announce the engagement early this week," he adds. "Then you'll introduce me to your father, and we'll tell him we plan to marry in six months."

Holy shit.

I can't believe he's agreed to this.

He leans an elbow on the bench. "You *will* marry me, pay me the money, then we can divorce whenever you are ready."

"And we sleep together," I say, but he knows it's a question and that I'm looking for clarity.

"You will live here as my fiancé, and you will fuck me. When and where I want." Connor moves his hand from my hip to the space between my thighs, inching them apart. "I will be reasonable in my demands, but expect it to be frequent."

My breathing falters. "You can't be serious. I have rights. You can't just demand sex from me."

Can he?

If I've agreed to it, then of course he can. The question is, will I agree to this or walk away?

"On the contrary." Connor presses his thumb against the denim covering my clit. "You want something from me? I want something in return."

I hate how quickly he can affect my body. I'm wet and aroused. My sharp nipples are visible through my top.

"That's...I'm not a whore." I try to back off the stool, but his hand holds me firm. I need space.

This man is intoxicating and dangerous, and he wants me to be his sex slave.

"Is it prostitution, though, when *you're* paying me?" Connor smiles darkly, and it sends a shiver through me.

I'm trying to think, while my body is craving his touch, his cock, and the release I know he can give me.

These are his terms. I either agree or walk away.

I'm not a whore, but that's not what this is. I'm attracted to Connor, more than any other man I've met. I could think of this as a short-term relationship I know isn't going to lead to anything permanent.

I won't expect him to love me, and I'll ensure I keep up a strong boundary so I don't get attached to him.

He's simply a means to an end while I create a new life for myself, independent of my family.

"No more than five times a week," I negotiate.

Dark eyes graze my face for a long moment, then he nods. "Agreed."

"What else?"

"No one can know about this. The risk is too great for my organizational reputation. I expect complete secrecy," he adds, then his eyes meet mine. "And for your safety."

My lips press into a smile. I like that he seems to care, or at least consider me. It's nice.

"After we marry, you have thirty days to deposit the money into my account," Connor says.

I chew my lip and glance away.

This will be worth it one day. Six months at most, then I'll have my independence.

One day, I will fall in love and get married. Have a family. I won't be bound by the mob, and I'll have a thriving business of my own.

It *will* be worth it.

There is one question I'm curious about, though.

"Why do you want the money?" I ask. "You have a net worth of sixty-five billion dollars." His wealth is widely known and spoken about everywhere. Monitored, analyzed, and judged.

Connor shrugs. "Compensation. Some of it will cover the ring, media management, your living expenses, and the wedding. The rest is profit. Or we could call it 'services rendered.'" He smirks in a tease, then climbs off the stool.

What a smartass.

"I'll drive you home so you can take the night to say goodbye to your old life, then tomorrow, you'll move in. I will arrange credit cards and a ring for you," Connor says, as if it is a done deal.

We both know it is.

We stare at each other, and he reaches out his hand to help me off the stool. Then he pulls me closer. My body presses into his, and he cups my cheek. It feels nice. Like all day, this is where I have been wanting to land.

"So, I guess I should pop the question," Connor says, his dark chocolate eyes roaming my face. "Mia Mancini, will you fake marry me?"

Holy smokes, we are doing this.

"Yes," I reply, dread filling my tummy.

Connor's mouth descends on mine, and I can't help but feel like I've sold my soul to the devil.

14

CADE

Fucking Mia!

Engaged? None of my soldiers have reported seeing her with Connor fucking Barrett. On Saturday night, yes. But not any other time.

I don't believe it for a second.

Has someone leaked my plans to her? If there is a traitor in my team, they will find themselves in a pool of blood.

Barrett is a powerful man and very influential, but I need him out of the way. Easier said than done. Getting to him through his tight security and without cameras will be difficult, so I need to think this one through.

Otherwise, he's going to wreck everything.

I am the next in line to take over the Mancini family. We are the most powerful mafia in New York. In the United States. My father isn't getting any younger, but I'm getting older.

I'm twenty-six years old and sick of playing second fiddle to the old man. It's time to take my place on the throne. Wear that ring on *my* finger.

For the past nine months, I've been building relationships and a loyal team to back me when I do.

Yeah, a fucking coup.

I light a cigarette and click my Zippo lighter shut, then pocket it, blowing out a large cloud of smoke. Shoving my other hand in the pocket of my black jacket, I watch as two of my loyal guys kick the shit out of a junkie.

The guy is two months behind in payments, and he came to us wanting more smack.

Is he joking? I know the game now. There is no way this cunt is going to be coming up with the money.

Teeth go flying.

"Enough," I yell.

I walk over, reach down, and grab a handful of his hair so his bloody eyes are looking at me.

"Five days and I want the money. You got it?" I say, then spit in his face. "No more smack until you have it. Oh, and I see that pretty little wife of yours has a new job on 57th Street."

His eyes fly open, and he starts to moan and kick. "No, please don't touch her—"

"Get me the money, and nothing happens to her. *Capise*?" I drop his head to the ground, and it bounces.

Piece of shit druggies.

No idea why they fucking touch the stuff. I don't.

I jut my chin at Sonny, and he rounds up the men, leaving the guy behind. Someone opens my door, and we climb into the black SUV and pull away.

A few minutes later, my phone rings.

"Cade, how's my wedding planning going?" Salvo Vitale asks.

I shake my head and give Nathan a glance. He's sitting up front with the driver. Nathan's new to my team and built like a fucking marine. Which he was.

He turns and smirks at me.

Vitale is an asshole.

But he's a key player in my plan.

Finding someone disloyal to my father wasn't as easy as I thought it might be. Vitale, though? He's a greedy cunt and keen to expand his distribution of snow, diamonds, and girls through New York's boundaries. For that he needs Mancini permission.

My father denied him.

When I found out, I went to talk with him.

Months of negotiations have landed us here. Vitale gets his shit through our gates. I get a healthy cut. He provides the manpower while I take down my father.

And for that last bit, he gets Mia.

For life.

"Small glitch, but I'll sort it," I reply.

"What kind of glitch? I want the girl, Mancini," Vitale growls through the phone.

I must tell him. Joe said the announcement was going to be made this week, so it's better Vitale hears it from me first.

"She's engaged to Connor Barrett, the entrepreneur."

I pull the phone away from my ear as he curses.

"Let's head home," I say to my driver, then put the phone back to my ear, hoping the noise is done. "You done?"

"How the fuck are you going to sort that out? Barrett isn't some guy. He's...him," Vitale says.

I know.

I fucking know.

Of all the men for her to choose. Of all the goddamn timing.

"I'm not going after him," I reply. "You just do your part. I will bring Mia to you, and you will have your fucking wedding."

Then I hang up.

Salvo Vitale needs to remember I'll be the Don very soon and keep his tone in check.

"Nathan, call those girls we had over the other night. I need a blowy."

He pulls out his phone and starts texting. "You got it."

15

CONNOR

I'm fucking engaged.

How the hell did that happen?

I know *how* it happened—I proposed to her. Once Mia said yes, I dropped her at home. It took some willpower not to fuck her beforehand. But I said I'd give her one night to say goodbye to her old life, and I have.

Do I think she'll change her mind?

No.

Tonight, after she finishes work, movers will arrive, pack her things, and move her to my penthouse. Mia will then live with me as my fiancé for the next six months. Or however long it takes for me to learn if Carlos was part of the Italian mafia...and a lead.

She's the key to getting to the top echelon of the Mancini family, which has evaded Nathan these past six years.

I'm confident Mia bought into my motivation in agreeing to the fake engagement. Sex and money. I'm a man with needs, and after our explosive evening together and the chemistry clearly still alive between us, it made sense that's what I would want from her.

And while there's a small part of me that feels like an asshole, I do want to fuck her.

So that's not a lie.

Knowing Mia has given me access to her pretty wet pussy whenever I want it is a fucking turn on. Tonight, she's all mine, and that's one part of our deal I won't have trouble faking.

Being a fiancé and husband? That might be a little more outside my comfort zone. I've never been in a relationship before, and while it doesn't look like brain surgery, we'll both need to be alert and make sure we look like we're in love.

As for Mia achieving her goal, I don't have high hopes for her.

She seems almost too innocent to have come from a mafia family. Then again, Nathan said her mother protected Mia most of her life, and she has been off at college. Now, working for Donna. It's about as far removed as any mafia family member could get. Now they want her back, and she wants her independence.

And she's clearly willing to do quite a bit to achieve it. Such as marry me, hand over her trust fund, and fuck me for six months.

Thing is, once she divorces me, her father will bring her back into the fold and marry her off to whoever he wants.

Which is not my problem.

I focus back on the sweet smell of revenge and formulating a plan. Today, I'm getting everything lined up for our fake engagement announcement and buying Mia a ring.

"That everything, Mr. Barrett?" my secretary, Lilly, asks.

She's been with me for over five years, and while she doesn't know my secrets, Lilly is reliable and trustworthy.

My public relations manager, Tim, leans his hip against the sofa, arms crossed with one hand rubbing his jaw.

He knows something isn't right.

Too fucking bad. He's not getting any information.

I canceled all my meetings this morning and pulled them both in for a briefing. Mack stands near the door—his usual spot, if he's not taking a break.

"Yes."

"Okay, so I've got on my list here to make sure the flowers are sent to Ms. Mancini at Bloom Events by ten. And the movers need to meet her at her apartment at five this evening. I'll have Harry Winston present rings to you at midday today." Lilly glances at Tim. "The media team will ensure nothing leaks until we're ready to send out the press release tomorrow morning."

I nod.

Aside from my team needing time to prepare, I need to get word to Nathan. Hearing I'm engaged to the mafia princess out of the blue, when we'd met just last night, would take him by surprise.

We work on a no-surprises basis where possible.

Given I'll be stepping into his world, into the Mancini residence, and meeting my fake father-in-law, well, Nathan needs a heads-up on that.

"We'll do a press meeting," Tim says. "This afternoon, we'll send out invites, but they won't know what we're announcing until they arrive. We'll have media packs for them."

I glance at Tim, then back at Lilly.

"That's all. And another coffee." I glance into my empty cup.

"Yes, sir." Lilly makes her way out of the office.

I stand, stretching my body. I missed my daily workout this morning to get a head start on things, and I'm feeling it. After being a marine, sitting behind a desk has taken some getting used to.

"Connor," Tim says, and I glance his way. "Is there anything you're not telling me? I need to be prepared for all possibilities and questions the media could throw at us, so with respect, I'd appreciate if you could share everything now."

I hired Tim because he's astute, so I'm not surprised he smells a rat. Today, though, he needs to just do his damn job.

"Mia being the daughter of Joseph Mancini is a challenge, I understand," I reply, not answering his direct questions because he doesn't demand things from me. "However, I trust you'll navigate it. Focus on the fact we are in love and all that."

The look he gives me says *bullshit.*

He's right, but that's not his job.

"It's important we're clear Barrett Industries has absolutely no involvement with mafia business. And we never have. We continue to be a law-abiding organization that contributes to the community. You can quote me on that."

Tim nods. "For the media packs, do you and Ms. Mancini have any photos we could use to show your dating history?"

He knows there aren't any.

The fucker is digging for information.

I trust him but not enough to sell the scoop of his life and make a clean ten mill.

"Draw up the media release and have it to me by lunchtime," I say, ignoring him again, then walk to my chair and sit down. I wiggle my mouse to wake up my laptop. "Speak to Lilly if you need anything else. Otherwise, Mia and I will be here in the morning by eight."

I wonder what kind of ring Mia would like. Lilly has already emailed me a gallery of images from Harry Winston to start looking through.

"Yes, sir," Tim says. "I wouldn't be doing my job if I didn't warn you the media are going to be skeptical about this…"

I glance up at him.

"And wonder why you're engaged to a woman related to the most dangerous mob in America."

He's trying my patience. "So do your fucking job. If you need a reminder of why you're standing in this office, Tim, go check your last pay slip."

He presses his lips together.

Tim earns nearly more than any of the executives on my team because public relations is damn important and he's one of the best. Which is why he's challenging me.

Tim is right. He's doing his job.

But this isn't a rebrand or business merger, for goddamn sakes. This is my personal life.

"I'm not giving you any more details. I am marrying Mia

Mancini, and we are in love. That's it. Make sure the media believe it, and don't question the organization has any links with the mafia," I say, then more darkly add, "because we don't." I'm out of patience. Or maybe I'm stressed when I say, "If you can't do your job, then I will find someone who will."

Tim runs a hand through his hair and quickly retreats with a *got it.*

Mack catches my eye as Tim passes, and we share a knowing look. This was never going to be easy, but I hope its fucking worth it.

JUST BEFORE FIVE in the evening, I climb into the back of a rundown heap of shit. Mack organized it, and there's a chance I now either own a Toyota Corolla, circa last century, or it's stolen.

Nathan slides in, pulling his cap low and collar up.

"I've got five minutes."

"Then I'll get straight to the point. I'm engaged to Mia Mancini. Media will be told in the morning."

As expected, he jerks his head around, shocked.

"Jesus, Connor. I thought Mia was lying to her family. This is real?" Nathan says. "Explain."

He knows I never joke about women or the mafia.

"We met a few nights ago, and she told her father we were engaged. The opportunity just fell in my lap."

"Why the fuck would she do that?" Nathan asks. "I take it the engagement is not legit?"

My brows raise. "Oh, I *will* marry her. Unless we get the information I want sooner. I doubt it will happen that fast. Whatever it takes."

"Whatever it takes," Nathan replies, repeating the Dark King's motto.

It was the last thing we said that night in the desert, as we all shook hands and agreed on a future we had no clue we were about to create six years ago.

"Mia wants out of the family, and we need to get closer to Joe." I rub my face. "I need you to know I'll be visiting with her. She's moving in tonight. To look legit."

Nathan watches me, then shakes his head. "Jesus, Connor. Do you like this girl?"

I look away and stare into the front of the dirty Toyota. What I want to say is, she's a sweet-tasting pussy for the duration of the job. But the words won't come.

I'm not going to disrespect Mia like that.

It's true, but I don't want Nathan or anyone to think I'm using her sexually. I am. But I'm not. We both agreed to the terms, and it's important Mia continues to believe this is what I wanted from her.

I do.

If I were a better man, I might not touch her. But I'm not and I will.

And I can't fucking wait.

"She's an asset," I reply.

"Fuck, Connor. This is dangerous. I've been getting closer. Cade is starting to trust me. What's our move if we find ourselves in the same place at the same time? They could link us."

Yeah, fuck. I thought about this overnight. Still, I believe the potential benefits outweigh the risk.

I hope.

Nathan joined the Italian mafia using his real name and identity. His story was he was angry with the U.S. government after being stationed overseas and wanted to stick it to the man and make some real money.

So, they knew he was a former marine. The fact no marine worth his weight would ever dream of joining a mafia seemed to elude them.

As for me, it's public knowledge I'm a former marine. Every

bio and article written about me mentions it. Connor Barrett, entrepreneur and U.S. Marine...blah, blah, blah.

We just needed to make sure they never have cause to link us in any way. Or for any reason.

"For now, let's not do anything to get them to connect the dots. Keep your focus on Cade. I'm not coming in hot, so there's no reason for them to think you and I have a connection. Its Mia they'll be worried about," I say.

Losing their princess is a big deal.

Especially if they had a marriage with another mobster lined up.

"Yeah," Nathan says, adjusting his cap. "Still a fucking risk."

I get it. He's nervous. I'm not going to pretend to know how he feels. He's been living a double life with these assholes for so long now. I know he's over it.

There is no vacation when you are undercover.

"Sorry, man." I sigh. "Hopefully, this is the break we've been waiting for. Meantime, stay vigilant."

"Always fucking am," Nathan says, and we sit there for a moment, making the most of being able to just be who we truly are.

Marines.

Men with revenge always on our mind.

"Joe Mancini will try to manipulate you." Nathan turns to look at me once more. "I doubt he's going to let you marry her."

I know. At least, he thinks he'll be able to stop me, but he won't.

"Cade is going to be a problem. He needs this marriage to Vitale to go ahead."

I know that too.

"Fuck, Connor. This is messed up." Nathan blows out a breath, adjusts his cap once more, then puts his hand on the door handle. "Stay alive."

"You too."

The next moment, he slips out of the car and is gone. I let out my own sigh and run a hand over my face. This could be the best or worst decision of my life. This morning, I was sure this was the right thing to do. Now doubt is creeping in, and I'm beginning to wonder.

I trust myself and I trust my team.

What I don't trust is my ability to be completely neutral when it comes to Mia. Already, I'm trying to find a way to ensure she has her freedom so no asshole can get their hands on her when I divorce her.

The idea of Vitale near her makes my fists clench.

You don't want anyone touching her. Be fucking honest.

Mia is not my concern.

Except I've decided she is.

16

MIA

The roses arrive to the minute I am expecting them. Connor texted to say he was sending them and I was to tell my colleagues they were from him.

He completely took the lead after I agreed to his fake proposal.

I lay awake most of the night, questioning what I was doing, but in the end, I just told myself to stay focused on the prize at the end. My freedom.

Tomorrow, we are announcing our engagement, so Connor thought the flowers were a way to break the ice and let my work colleagues know I'm dating him.

So far, everyone has swooned over the enormous bouquet. Donna raised her brows at me and went back into her office.

I'm not sure what that means.

"Holy shit, there are at least thirty roses in here. So beautiful!" Sienna says, pressing her nose to them. "But Mia, when the hell were you going to tell me you were dating Connor Barrett?"

I hear the hurt in her voice. We tell each other everything.

Well, except the bit about my family.

"I can't believe I said those things on Saturday night, and you're banging him," Sienna continues, and I choke on my saliva.

"It's not completely new. He asked me to keep it quiet. We met, um, earlier and just hit it off."

God, I am crap at this.

I have this entire story prepared and can't remember one single bit of it.

"Hit it off, my ass. There are *thirty-six* red roses here. Long-stemmed, with individual little water tubes on every stem." Sienna is still running her fingers through the bouquet. "That's serious."

Which is what Connor wants you to think.

I shrug and put them on the table in our office. It takes up half the round space. "Well, he's rich, so—"

"A multi-billionaire isn't rich. That's *filthy* rich." Sienna flops into one of the chairs. "And hot."

I bite my lip.

Connor is most definitely hot. Smoking hot. And I get to sleep with him for the next six months. I keep flopping between being creeped out by it and horny as hell.

"Yeah, he really is. And he's also caring and cuddly," I say, lying through my teeth. I doubt he is either of those things, but I am going to be marrying the man, so I have to appear to be head over heels.

I have to lie to everyone. My friends, my family. Donna.

Everyone.

Tomorrow, the world will learn about our engagement and my real identity. Not that I've used a false name. I've just never told them who I *truly* am.

I'm not sure how they will react, and honestly, I am more nervous about this than the fake relationship. My father's reputation is well known and bad. There is no way it won't reflect on me.

"Wow, you really like him, huh," Sienna says with a sigh.

"Yes." I cross the room and close the door to the office we share.

Sienna's eyes follow me, her brows dipping. "What's going on?"

"I have something to tell you. Please hear me out before you freak out," I say quickly.

"Oh shit. Are you pregnant?" She gasps, sitting up straight. "To Connor Barrett. Oh God. Sorry, freaking out."

I laugh.

"No, I'm not pregnant." I make a mental note to make sure we use double condoms and to religiously take my birth control. "I'm moving in with him."

I hold my breath, waiting for her response.

"Oh." Her eyes widen, and she sinks back into her chair. "That seems...fast."

And in three, two, one...

"He asked me to marry him last night," I add, "and I said yes."

Sienna's mouth falls open, then she jumps to her feet. "Shut the front door!" she cries, staring at me. "Is this what you want? Do you love him?

I nod, smiling.

She crosses the space between us and throws her arms around me. "Congratulations, honey. My God."

I close my eyes for a second, welcoming her warm loving embrace, and hope she can forgive me for all the lies I am about to share next.

And soon, when this is all over.

"Sienna, there's something else." I pull back out of her arms. My smile fades, and regret rushes through me.

Sienna leans her hip against the desk and frowns. "Okay, I'm all out of ideas. No baby...You're getting married. So, go. Tell me."

I walk to my chair and sit down, then sigh.

"My name is Mia Mancini, but I haven't told you who I *truly* am." I wince at her reaction. "My father is Joseph Mancini."

I let that hang, while Sienna stares blankly at me. Then I see the moment she figures it out. She straightens away from the desk, and her mouth drops open.

"Mancini," she says, staring at me, like I'm a freak.

I nod.

"The mobster."

I nod again.

"Daughter."

I press my lips together.

"My God. Are you...I don't even know what to ask."

I reach for my bottle of water and take a long sip. After two sleepless nights, I'm exhausted and emotional. This lying business is not for the fainthearted.

"I couldn't tell you. No, that's not true. I want to tell you the truth." I wince, knowing that's only half true. Goddamn. "I didn't *want* to tell you. I wanted a life independent of the mafia, and I have. For two amazing years. Your friendship is so important to me, and I was hoping you would never need to know. I'm sorry."

"Why tell me now?" she asks. "God, all this time, Mia."

"Tomorrow, we're announcing our engagement to the press. They know who I am. I'm boring, so never in the news, and I don't think they'd even recognize me. Now I'm marrying Connor. It will be all over the news," I say. "You can't say anything. Please. Not until it's released."

"Yeah, of course. No one wants to cross the mob." She lets out a dry, awkward laugh.

I hate it.

I hate that this is out and between us now. She'll never look at me the same. I want to say it's not like that, but it is.

Sienna glances around the room, then back at me. "I guess you can't tell me anything."

"No." I shake my head. "Trust me, you don't want to know."

"Is it horrible?" she asks, and I can see my friend once more.

"Yes."

"Is this why you are marrying Connor?" she asks perceptively but not as accurately as she might think.

Now the lies begin again.

When will I be free of them?

"No. I love him," I reply firmly. It's going to be imperative people believe me, so if I can get Sienna on board, then surely, I can sell the lie to others. "Apparently, love at first sight is a thing."

She sits there, shaking her head in disbelief. Not at my lie, as she should, but at the truths I've told her.

"Wow. You're going to be the wife of a billionaire. And you're a mobster," Sienna says, and I hear the unsaid words.

You're not one of us anymore.

You are not who I thought you were.

I remind myself this is temporary, and at the end of everything, I'll be free and can once again just be Mia.

Which is just one more damn lie.

17

CONNOR

The last of the boxes are taken upstairs, and I leave Mack to see the movers out. Since leaving the marines, I haven't shared a living space, so it will take some adjusting having Mia in my home.

The novelty of having her sexy body to fuck whenever I want will soon wear out. Not that it's why I've agreed to marry Mia Mancini, I remind myself.

I'm playing two fake roles here.

The first as her fiancé, as far as the world and her family are concerned. The second as a billionaire who wants a woman to fuck while benefiting from the trust she'll get paid once we marry.

Jesus, she must think I'm an asshole.

I walk upstairs and find Mia in the guest room, going through a box. She's in a pair of light sweatpants and a tight sleeveless sports top.

"You can store things you don't need in here, but you will sleep in my bedroom," I say, sticking with the role I've adopted.

I'm mildly concerned about the nightmares, but she'll hear them if she's in my bedroom or the guest room, so I'll deal with it when it happens.

Mia turns her head.

"I know," she replies with a sigh. "Do you really want me sleeping in your bed? Why don't I sleep in here, and we can...you know...then go our separate ways."

I almost smile.

Instead, I crouch and make her look at me. "And when your family visits and sees your bedroom? What then?"

She lets out a groan.

"I'm not fucking with the mafia and doing this halfheartedly. If I'm going to lie to Joe Mancini, we do it my way, or not at all."

She turns back to her box and mutters something about *I could say you snore.*

"Mia..."

She climbs to her feet in a rush as I stand. We collide. I grab her arms and fight the urge to slam my mouth down on hers.

"What?" she asks breathlessly, just as affected by our closeness.

Which is not the plan.

I'll fuck her and enjoy it, but I don't want to desire her this much. This powerfully. Not like this. Not like I need her lips on mine in the next sixty seconds.

Then, I remember. I'm not a gentleman, and I've told her I will take what I want from her, so I pull her tightly against my chest and lean down so our eyes meet, our mouths inches apart.

"Kiss me," I demand.

Her pupils turn dark, the mist of that blue ice sparkling as she fights her desire. Then her lips part, and as I start to close the gap, Mia's meeting me with the same passion we had the first night.

Our lips crush.

I sweep my tongue inside and reach around to press her against every inch of me. My other hand threads through her long dark hair and grips it as our kiss deepens.

God, I wasn't imagining it. She still tastes so damn sweet. Cinnamon and honey.

I take from her, wanting to throw her over my shoulder and

fuck her on every surface in this damn penthouse. Then I remember I have something important to do. When I force myself away from her moist, hot mouth, she lets out a sexy moan. I hold her eyes, then lick my lips.

Mia slides down my body slowly and looks at me in question. Waiting.

I take a step away, my hand on her hip, and slip my hand into my pocket, pulling out a small box. I glance quickly around the guest bedroom filled with boxes and hate this is how she's being proposed to.

Nathan is right. This is fucked up.

A flash of anger spears through me. No one gave my family a second thought when Carlos was shooting bullets into their bodies. When he shot Rebecca dead at only three years of age.

Mia Mancini is a means to an end. My doorway to the revenge I deserve.

Get on with it, Connor. This is fake.

I release her hip and open the box. Her eyes drop, then she gasps.

I hate how happy that makes me.

I understand why, though. The eight-carat square solitaire diamond set in platinum is simply stunning.

Her eyes dart to mine in awe, then she breathes out my name. "Connor."

Goddamn her.

"It has to be believable," I growl, ignoring the wistful look in her eyes, and take her hand. It's warm in mine, and I fight the urge to squeeze it and make her smile.

This is so fucking wrong.

I slide the two-million-dollar ring on her finger. When our eyes connect, I see her vulnerability and hate myself.

"One day, Mia Mancini, a man who deserves you will do this a whole lot better that I just have. Someone who loves you." I then drop her hand and walk away.

I ignore the noise she makes as I keep walking.

Because I can't do this if I care.

My family deserves to be avenged.

I will protect Mia as much as I can, but the fact remains, she will hate me at the end when she learns the truth.

I WAKE WITH Mia lying across my chest.

She was already asleep when I went to bed. I wanted to give her space—or perhaps it was me who needed it, after putting that fucking ring on her finger—so I undressed, slid under the covers, and pulled her body up against mine.

Our limbs were not strangers after our first night together, but it surprised me when she wriggled in her sleep and then settled.

My cock hardened, and as my fingers drifted over her hips and down between her thighs, her body reacted. Her legs slid apart to give me access.

"Good girl," I growled into her hair, pressing inside her.

When she arched and let out a little sleepy moan, I began pumping. Slowly at first, then harder. The need to fuck her, the woman now wearing my ring, overcame me in a way I did not expect.

I thumbed her clit, and it didn't take long before she was panting and pleading as her orgasm struck. As if she had needed my touch all day. I then flipped her onto her back and positioned myself, lifting her legs over my shoulders.

Icy blue eyes connected with mine in the moonlight, and fuck me, they had the power to reach under my skin.

"Condom," she said, and I cursed.

Fuck. How could I have forgotten?

Once sheathed, I slid the head of my cock inside her and lifted my eyes to hers again. When she blinked, I stilled.

"Tell me you want this," I growled, realizing there was no way I could do this without her permission.

"I want my freedom, so yes," Mia replied, after a really fucking long second.

Fury stormed through me. I leaned down and gripped her jaw. "Then tell me you want me to stop."

She winced, her body tugging my cock inside her, and I smirked.

"Didn't think so," I replied and thrust deeper inside her.

Mia arched, gripping my arms, and her nails dug into me with all the passion and desire she was trying to hide. One arm on the sheets beside her, the other on her hips, I slammed in deep, pulling back and then again. Anger and desire weaved its way between us as we fucked each other for our own reasons.

She wanted freedom.

I wanted revenge.

I realized then there was no way this was going to end well.

Afterward, Mia closed the door in the master bathroom, and when she came out, I did the same. I tossed the used condom in the trash, cleaned up, and then leaned my palms on the marble and stared at myself in the mirror.

I am a hard man; I know that.

Seeing your parents murdered in cold blood would do that to a man. But Mia's touch, those eyes, the softness of her skin, is doing something to me.

Perhaps it is a natural need to protect someone innocent, but the thought of her being handed to a gangster who will fuck her rough and abuse her makes me want to kill.

Nobody touches Mia. She is mine.

The hell? She doesn't belong to you.

Stay on task.

When I returned to bed, Mia was rolled in a ball, unlikely to be asleep but clearly wanting space. I lasted about twenty minutes, lying prone and staring at the ceiling, until I pulled her into my arms, and within minutes, I was asleep.

I stayed asleep.

No nightmares. I don't have them every night, but I'm pleased she won't wake and question me about it so soon.

It will come, I have no doubt.

Now she's breathing softly, her hair tickling my chin and hand tucked around my bicep, which is flexed because my arm is propping my pillow up. She's like a damn jigsaw piece fitting against me at every angle.

I watch the sun rise behind the buildings, creating an orange haze in my bedroom, and as I glance around, I wonder what Mia sees.

It's huge, with a giant bed covered in black silk sheets. There's also black cabinets and a chaste lounge in the corner of the room. Black, of course. But there is a cream cushion.

She probably likes that.

And the matching soft cream rug, which lies in the middle of the room over the polished wooden floors.

Everything is hard and masculine. Like me.

Even the artwork hanging on the far wall.

She must hate it. I will let her redecorate, but no fucking pink.

"What's wrong?" Mia asks, startling me.

My eyes drop to hers, and I brush the hair from her forehead.

"Morning." I shift and tug her against me. Playing the part.

After all, she's here for my sexual enjoyment—that's the deal we agreed to and what she expects from me.

"You look unhappy," Mia says, blushing. "Sorry, I didn't mean to use you as a life-size pillow."

Yeah, I'm miserable. Waking up with a gorgeous woman draped over me is hell. Utter hell.

"I think I can defend myself." I smirk.

"So, you're just not a morning person?" Mia's eyes graze over my face. She's trying to analyze me. It's what people do when they've lived with controlling parents. The goal is to be one step ahead of the issue to survive.

I don't like that she doesn't trust me, but she shouldn't.

"I could show you how much of a morning person I am, but I suspect you might be sore," I say, letting that sink in.

She presses her lips together, and I palm her ass, nudging her against my hard cock and suppressing a groan.

"Get in the shower while I go workout. We have press to meet with this morning."

Mia sighs, her eyes moving to my lips as if she wants me to kiss her. Does she?

Then something else occurs to me.

"Think you can pretend to be my fiancé?" I ask. "Appear to be madly in love with me. Kiss me like you can never live another day without me?"

I'm taunting her.

"I've kissed you," she says, sounding almost offended.

"Like you want to fuck me, not marry me," I reply, my brow quirked.

Her eyes move from mine and roam the space behind me. I can't help but wonder what she's thinking. She hasn't asked me the same question in return.

Can I convince the press I'm in love?

I don't know.

It's not like they'll expect I've turned into Ryan Gosling overnight because I met a woman I loved. I'm not the type of man into public displays of affection.

I'm stoic.

Yet we need to be convincing.

"I don't know how I'd kiss a man I love," she finally says, surprising me. "I've never been in love before. Have you?"

"No," I answer without hesitation.

We need the world to believe us, so we better get it right. Convincing her father will be a whole other challenge. While I've not met Joe Mancini, I know powerful men. They're clever and astute.

He also knows his daughter, and I bet he'll spot a fake relationship a mile away. We have two days until we go to dinner to perfect our act.

Either she's an excellent actress, or I need to make it look like we're madly in love. I decide a little manipulation is in order.

"Well then, you'll probably be as unconvincing as me," she says, pressing at my chest.

I rise over her, and my nostrils flare when she draws in a little gasp. "Sweetheart, I'll make the world believe you're the love of my damn life. I'll kiss you so damn passionately, even you'll be wondering."

Then I lower my mouth, and as those big blinking eyes watch in anticipation, I move to the side, kiss her neck, then climb out of bed.

"You'll have to wait for the cameras." I walk out of the bedroom and head to my gym.

Naked.

I know she's watching my ass.

18

MIA

Connor has his hand on the small of my back, directing me through the Barrett Enterprise offices. There are dozens of eyes watching us.

Watching me.

Mack congratulates us, glancing at the rock on my finger. I don't know if he's aware of the truth or not. I will have to ask Connor when we have a private moment alone.

I suspect he does.

Connor pushes open the door to his office, greeting his secretary. "Morning, Lilly. This is Mia."

A mid-thirties woman in a tailored navy dress stands and greets me. She's very pretty, with shoulder-length blonde hair and perfectly painted nails.

Very corporate.

"It's a pleasure to meet you, Mia. And congratulations." She sounds genuine and glances at the Rock of Gibraltar, as I've named my enormous ring.

It's impossible to miss and likely worth more than some people's condos. The sparkle in the bathroom light is the most stunning thing in the world. Connor caught me playing with it this morning and made a strange growling noise.

I feel guilty making him do this, but he is committed, and today, we're going public, so there's no turning back.

My phone is full of upset messages from Cade, my aunties, and one from my father. They've asked me to come home and hold off on making the announcement, but I told them it had to happen because of Connor's profile. Keeping our relationship a secret would be impossible and create rumors that would simply be a distraction from the important work he is doing at Barrett Enterprises.

A line Connor fed me and I'm passing on.

"Thank you," I reply to Lilly, giving her a smile.

Connor leads me inside his office. "Send Tim in when he arrives," he calls out to Lilly, then removes his jacket.

I try to keep my eyes off him, which is the opposite of what I should be doing, given he's my fiancé, but Lord, it's difficult. The man is sex on two legs.

When he walked downstairs earlier this morning while I was eating my bowl of cereal on the kitchen bench, I nearly choked. Connor Barrett, freshly showered and in a fitted Tom Ford gray suit, is a piece of art.

It didn't help I was still processing that near kiss. He left me hanging, and while I know this is fake, it still filled my stomach with stupid lusting butterflies.

I'm a little embarrassed at how much I desire Connor, when it's clear this is just a sexual contract to him. Yet when he demanded my consent last night, I realized he's not the cold, hard asshole he presents to the world.

It's something I'm still processing.

Still, I know he's powerful and holds all the cards here. I'm not stupid.

Introducing him to my family on Thursday is going to be terrifying. So many things could go wrong, and I don't know how they are going to react to him.

Connor, on the other hand, is cool as a cucumber.

I walk to the window and stare out across Manhattan. I am

worried about so many things. My friendship with Sienna, losing my family, how I will achieve independence…I feel like I'm flying on an out-of-control magic carpet which needs a tune-up.

Or top-up in magic.

I feel Connor's body behind mine, his hands on my hips. Without thinking, I lean back into him as his arms wrap around me.

Wait. Are the cameras here?

"Bet you regret spilling that drink on me now." His voice is low, and his breath sends shivers down my neck.

Do I? It is hard to think around this man. I turn my face to his, waiting for him to claim my lips. He smiles and moves away.

What the hell?

He's making me dizzy.

"Tim. Meet Mia," Connor says, his dark eyes sparkling at my response. Then he turns. "My public relations manager."

I park my reaction and smile at Tim.

He's everything you'd expect a corporate media person to be. Expensive suit, curly styled hair, and cool glasses. As he walks toward me, I spot quirky socks under his pants.

"Mia, nice to meet you." Tim extends his hand. We shake, and he walks to the round table a few feet away, places his tablet down, and slides his hands into his pockets.

Then he studies me.

"First question. Are you media trained?"

Connor walks to his desk and begins to tap at his laptop.

"No," I reply.

Tim nods and continues studying me. "That could be a good thing. They're going to ask a lot of questions, mostly for Connor, so let him do the talking. But they'll want something from you."

"I want you to manage that closely," Connor says, and I watch him lean back in his huge black executive chair, looking as powerful as any man can.

Perhaps more.

His tattoo may be covered, but I know it's there, and the edge it gives him is different to the powerhouse he presents himself as here in his billion-dollar empire.

Which in and of itself is sexy as fuck.

"On that. Let's discuss what you *are* willing to discuss." Tim lifts his tablet and taps on the screen. "The obvious questions will be about your relationship, but they'll be curious about your family, Mia."

My eyes dart between the two men. "I can't speak about my family."

The media, government, and police are our enemies. At least, that's what I was told as I was growing up.

"Be generic. Something along the lines of, 'Both Connor and I are looking forward to blending our families.'" Tim lifts a shoulder as if it is no big deal.

It is.

And I have no idea about Connor's family.

We hardly know each other. From what I have read, he is an orphan. Yet, he seems to have thrived anyway and made his place in the world with outstanding success.

"Mr. Barrett, I have your cards." Lilly walks over to his desk and hands him an envelope.

"Thank you," Connor replies, ripping it open. "Let us know when the media arrive." He briefly lifts his eyes to Tim. "I need a private moment with Mia."

Tim nods and glances at his watch as he walks to the door. "Ten minutes."

My stomach lurches. Soon the world will know who I am. Soon they'll believe I am Connor Barrett's fiancé, and our plan will be locked in place.

Holy shit. Am I doing the right thing?

As the door closes and we find ourselves alone once more, I turn.

"Maybe we shouldn't do this," I begin as Connor walks over to me. "I'll figure out another way. I'll..."

I'll do what?

Where would I live? I'd have to go home, and the first thing they'd do is marry me off to that creep, Salvo Vitale.

The thought makes me feel nauseous.

"We are doing this, Mia." Connor hands me two plastic cards. "These are yours."

I glance down at the black credit cards and swallow.

You can do this.

"You'll need to act the part, dress the part, and spend the part," Connor says. "Update your wardrobe and ensure you have outfits to attend events and dates with your fiancé. We'll be photographed together, and the media will want to know who you are wearing and all that bullshit. Make sure you know."

I can do that.

I'm not a stranger to designer clothing. I came from money—dirty money. Most of my more expensive outfits are still in my wardrobe at the Mancini residence because they aren't suitable for my current life as Mia, the events coordinator.

Now I am engaged to a billionaire.

It already feels like my old life is fading away, but I have to make sure it doesn't. I am happy. I love my friends, and Sienna is important to me.

She is not mad at me about being a gangster's daughter—like I had a choice—or rather that I didn't tell her. Sienna was curious and asked questions, but I could sense she felt there were more lies hidden. She is right.

But what upsets me more than anything is the way she now looks at me.

Like she doesn't know me.

It hurts.

She is the one person who knows me more than anyone now my mom has passed.

Will being a mafia princess and marrying one of the most powerful men in America—unexpectedly—make me so unrelatable now?

Fine, it sounds ridiculous to me as well.

Six months and then this will be over. I just need everything to go to plan. Engagement. Marriage. Inheritance.

Then divorce and I'll have my freedom.

I slide the cards into my purse. "How much is on them?"

"Don't worry, you won't run out of money," Connor responds. The corner of his lips twitch. "Give it your best shot, though."

"I could buy an island," I challenge him. Playful Connor is sexy as hell, so I am totally encouraging it. I mean, if I have to spend months with the man, it is worth having fun with him.

Maybe we can be friends as well as lovers.

"Not sure they take American Express at the Buy an Island Shop. But you can try." Connor grabs his jacket back off the hanger and slips it on, his eyes sliding down my body.

I'm wearing a Gucci sleeveless black jumpsuit clinched with a silver belt, my long dark hair straightened and lips a glossy rose pink. My lashes are dark and long after three coats, and I chose my stupidly expensive Chanel pumps for the occasion.

Classy and stylish.

The media will have to dig deep to find anything at fault with this outfit.

"What?" I ask, jutting out a hip when Connor keeps staring.

He closes the distance and pulls me to him. "I never told you how ravishing you look today, my beautiful fiancé."

Huh?

What is he up to?

Those dark chocolate eyes of his lock me in place, and suddenly, I'm wishing this gorgeous man truly wanted me.

Stupid.

But the way he holds me, touches me, watches me...He's intoxicating. I challenge any woman to ignore this man's brazen sexual masculinity.

"Well, then, maybe you should kiss me," I say.

We stare at each other for a long moment, and when I think he's going to finally drop his mouth to mine, he steps away.

"Come," Connor says, leading me out of the room.

Damn this man.

CONNOR

"HOW LONG HAVE you been dating Ms. Mancini?" the reporter from the *New York Times* asks.

Predictable questions so far.

"Long enough to know I want to spend the rest of my life with her. Next question," I reply, my hand resting on Mia's hip. She's tucked up against me, and I can feel the tension in her body.

She's nervous.

Tim's team has set up our huge conference room, and all the top media in the city are here with cameras and their microphones. It's a daunting scene for someone not used to being in the public spotlight.

She has nothing to worry about. I could do this in my sleep.

"Claire," I say, nodding to the dark woman in the front row. I know them all by name, given most of them follow me around or have attended every press conference I have given over the years.

"Will you share your proposal story with us?" She smiles cheekily.

Yawn.

"No," I reply, glancing at the next raised arm. "Roger."

"When's the wedding? Will you have a long engagement or marry fast?" he asks.

Roger wants to know if Mia is pregnant. I glance down at her, smiling. I predicted this, and this is the one response we've planned.

The floor is yours, gorgeous.

Because, fuck, she is absolutely stunning, and her vulnerability only makes me want to protect her more.

In three, two, one...

"We've yet to set a date. Once we speak to our families, we'll decide," Mia answers, smiling back at me, then out to the cameras.

Perfect.

"Teresa." I nod at the woman in the second row.

I give Mia a little squeeze. She'll get my cock later for that incredible performance.

"How will you ensure there's no mafia influence in your business now you're associated with one of the most notorious mob families in America?"

My jaw tenses. Despite expecting this, it still fucks me off.

"This is a marriage, not a business merger. Not Mia, nor any of her family members, will be working with, or for, Barrett Enterprises. Last question. Vicki."

"Has Barrett Enterprises been working with the Italian mafia previously? Is that how you met?" the small-framed older woman asks.

Sneaky bitch.

"I—"

"Our meeting was completely random," Mia says, cutting me off and placing a warm hand on my chest.

My hand lands on hers as she lifts her face to mine.

What is she doing?

"I poured a drink down the front of him, and he was furious," Mia continues, and oh my fucking God, she's terrific. "And now I'm marrying the most amazing man in the world."

Jesus.

Why does that make my chest swell?

The world around us disappears, and the need to kiss her overtakes every nerve in my body. I lose complete control of my mind and turn to her. Mia stretches up onto her toes as I cup her jaw.

I'm aware the cameras are clicking like mad, but I don't give a fuck. All I care about is claiming those glossy lips.

Keep it family friendly, Barrett.

My mouth lowers to hers, and as a white-hot need spreads

through me, I kiss her hard, taking all the sweetness she'll give me.

Holy hell.

I release her mouth, my eyes never leaving hers, and I see the same surprise I know she sees in mine. That was more than lust. And we need to keep it bottled up.

There is no room for emotions in this arrangement.

None.

19

MIA

"Is he going to follow us everywhere?" Sienna asks, and I nod.

Connor insisted I have a security team, and after much debate, I agreed to one man. Although, George is the size of two men. Much like Connor but with short brown hair, and I'm not sure he knows how to smile.

Then again, that's not his job.

I'm used to having protection, but for Sienna, this is new. Along with the paparazzi trailing us. They're keeping their distance, and I suspect it's because they think George is a mobster—something I'm not going to correct.

"Yes," I reply, pushing open the door to Toast Bar. "It's better than having cameras right up in our face, trust me."

"They weren't *not* in our face." Sienna shoots me a look as we spot Duncan and Isabelle and wave. "They literally swarmed you when we walked out of the building."

It could've been a lot worse, but I don't argue. None of this is fun or normal for her. Or for me. I've been in the shadows of the Mancini mafia world, protected and of little interest to the U.S. media.

Now that's all changed because I'm marrying Connor. The fact my father is Joe Mancini is just an added bonus. The response from the public has been a mix, and Tim said that's to be expected.

Mostly, it's positive, aside from the broken hearts of women around America. To quote Fox News.

On my end, my phone has been going crazy with my relatives and friends from my other world. They're shocked and wondering what my father thinks.

The answer is, he's not happy. I haven't heard from him since the news broke, but he's expecting us for dinner, and I know he'll have a lot to say.

Or he'll threaten Connor and tell him to break it off.

I'm not sure. This is unchartered waters for me.

For tonight, I organized drinks with my friends so they understand this engagement doesn't change anything. After this is all over, I will pick my life back up, and I want these three to be a part of it.

I won't be a mafia princess—technically—and I won't be a billionaire's wife.

I'll just be Mia.

Isabelle leaps off her stool and grabs my hand.

The Rock of Gibraltar is totally the star of the show. One of the morning shows did a whole segment on it. Even I learned a few things watching it on my phone in Connor's office. When I glanced at him in surprise after hearing the diamond is graded a D on the DIA scale—the highest and most rare rating you could buy—he just shrugged.

"I could hardly get you a ring from Diamonds Are Us."

"That's not even a real place." I laughed, but I knew what he meant. A billionaire would buy the woman he loved an important ring of value.

Isabelle squeezes my fingers and gasps. "I can't believe you're marrying Connor Barrett. You kept that a big secret. Oh my God, look at this thing."

"It's insane," Sienna says, ordering us two glasses of the house wine.

Our usual.

The plastic cards in my purse seem to be screaming at me. Along with Connor's *to make this look legit, you need to look like a blushing, happy bride-to-be and spend my money.*

"Let me, Sen." I grab the bartender's attention. "Two bottles of your best champagne." I wave the black plastic at him, and his eyes widen as he nods.

Sienna frowns at me.

"The chardonnay would've been fine," she mutters, then slips onto a stool.

I'm stuck in the middle of trying to be *just Mia* and also keeping up with this billionaire's wife charade. It's impossible.

I want to tell her, but I can't. It's too risky, and I promised Connor. I trust Sienna, but she doesn't know the stakes here, and if for some reason she said something, it would impact a lot of people.

And Connor's organization.

And my future.

"I can't believe you're the mafia princess," Duncan says, shaking his head. "Mancini. I remember seeing your photo in the paper when I was much younger. You had this black dress on... Was it a funeral?"

My mother's. But I keep that to myself. I want this to be a happy night.

"Can't believe I didn't piece it together," he continues.

Isabelle wriggles in her seat excitedly as the flutes are placed in front of us and the champagne corks popped.

Dom Perignon.

Not my favorite, but it looks fancy enough.

"I think it's exciting. What's it like being in the mafia? Some of those guys are *so* hot. Dangerous, I know, but it's kind of thrilling," Isabelle says, and I glance down to hide my cringe.

She's just the type of blonde they'd love to play with and toss away. Not hot.

"Trust me, it's not as romantic as the movies make it out to be," I reply. "Also, I'm not *in* the mafia. I was born into it. I love my family, but I'd do anything to live a normal life."

"By marrying a billionaire?" Sienna lifts her glass full of golden bubbles, studying them.

Ouch.

I push back the hurt, even though I see the immediate regret on her face.

"Sen!" Isabelle cries. "You can't choose who you fall in love with. I bet he's nice."

I nearly snort. Nice isn't a word to describe Connor.

Serious, sexual, mysterious, demanding...Those are words, for starters. Nice? Hell no.

"I'm sorry. I'm still trying to understand how you dated a man, fell in love, and are now engaged, and I didn't know a thing. We talk and see each other nearly every day," Sienna says.

Because it's not true.

Guilt laces through me, and I reach across and squeeze her hand, my eyes pleading for her patience. Sienna gives me a small smile.

"Well, congratulations, Mia. I hope you and Connor are very happy together and that you don't forget us," Duncan adds.

"Congratulations," Isabelle and Sienna say simultaneously, and we all clink glasses and sip away.

"I'm not going to forget any of you." I place my flute in front of me. "I'm getting married, not dying. I just live at a different address and will have a husband."

A fake husband

Temporarily.

I feel almost desperate for them to believe me. Once I get away from the bonds of my family and divorce Connor, things will be back to normal. I'll be single, independent, and a business owner. Whatever that business might be.

Note to self: *create a profitable business in six months.* I have some ideas, but with limited experience and only my business degree under my belt, I know it could take years of learning, failing, and one day succeeding, but I'm asking for a miracle.

I need to financially provide for myself, and when I divorce Connor, I'll only have the remainder of my trust fund to support me.

It's more than most people ever have, but it won't last forever.

"So, what's he like?" Isabelle asks, leaning her chin on her hands, like I'm about to tell a romantic story.

The strange thing is, I blush.

George leans against the bar nearby and accepts a glass of water from the barman. I really hope he's not listening.

"He's..." How do I explain Connor? "Intense. Romantic," I add on the end and quickly gulp my champagne.

There's not a romantic bone in Connor's body.

"Well, he did send her about seven million red roses yesterday." Sienna takes a long swig of her champagne.

"Thirty-six," I correct because we both counted them.

She sends me a grin.

"Did he get down on one knee?" Isabelle drawls, and Duncan rolls his eyes. I've often wondered if there is anything between the two of them. Either way, it's clear Duncan likes Iz as far more than just a friend.

Whether she's aware or not is another story.

Isabelle is still waiting to hear the details of the proposal. The one where Connor said he had *better ask me to marry him*. The one where he slid the ring on my finger, told me another man should do this, then left me standing alone.

Alone.

Engaged.

Wondering what the hell I am doing.

I blink and focus back on my friends, then give them the story Connor and I agreed on.

"It was romantic. We were out on his yacht, cruising along the

Hudson, the sun setting. We were in the back of the craft with a blanket over us, drinking champagne and listening to the sounds of the water," I say, getting far more poetic than Connor had. "Then he just suddenly sat up, kissed me, and slid to his knees. It surprised me, of course. We had only been dating a brief time."

Isabelle has little hearts in her eyes as she sighs.

Sienna narrows her eyes. "And you said yes that night? Wait, when did you go out on the boat?"

Shit.

She basically knows everything I do every day.

"Oh, well, it was the other weekend," I lie.

"Didn't you say he asked you last weekend?" she asks, looking increasingly disbelieving.

Crap.

"Maria, my sister," a masculine voice says from behind me, and I spin around.

Cade?

Any distraction would've been good. But not this one. Not after hearing him discuss a marriage between me and Salvo. I hate that he hadn't warned me. Or been on my side.

I guess I'm just upset with him, and I certainly don't trust him.

I turn and force a smile, wondering what he's doing here? Did he follow me?

"Cade?" I say, trying to get down off my stool, but he's crowding me. I glance at George, who pushes away from the bar and makes his way over to me with haste.

"Step away from Ms. Mancini, please, sir."

"Oh my God." Isabelle gasps dramatically. "Are you mobsters?"

Jesus, Isabelle, no.

"Yes, ma'am. Big dangerous baddies." Cade smirks, shooting his men standing behind him a grin, then shifts his eyes back to me, completely ignoring George. "Mia, you need to stop this nonsense and come home."

Despite George's presence, I wish Connor was here. I know

the marriage is a sham, but I don't like that Cade's calling it nonsense. I have no doubt my fake fiancé would have something to say to Cade, if he ever had the nerve to say it to Connor's face.

Does Cade really expect me to grab my purse and say, *You're right, I'm an idiot. Let's go.*

He's an idiot.

"Is this your brother?" Sienna asks as George says, "Sir, I need you to please take a step back."

My eyes dart around, aware this is about to escalate. I am furious my friends are going to witness all of this because my brother can't keep his nose out of my business. I hate that they're nervous...Well, except Isabelle, who is thrilled by it all.

"Cade—" I start.

"Get the fuck away, man. This is my sister," Cade demands, and two gangsters step up behind him in support.

"My God." Isabelle gasps dramatically.

"Izzy, shut it," Sienna growls.

"Cade, please don't make a scene. I'm with my friends, having a drink, and I'm not going anywhere." I lean closer to George and glance at the two goons behind my brother.

I'm suddenly grateful Connor insisted on the big guy, even if I don't believe my brother would hurt me. Or force me. Although, I'm starting to wonder, as I watch anger fill his eyes.

"Did Papa put you up to this?" I snap.

George pulls out his phone and lifts it to his ear.

Cade ignores me, and his eyes drift over the scene. My friends, the champagne, my outfit I wore at the press conference. "This engagement is bullshit. You need to come home right now. You have responsibilities, Mia."

George steps in between us and holds up his palm.

"Ms. Mancini is leaving."

I am?

"Do you know who the fuck I am?" Cade asks, shoving at George's shoulder.

So much happens in the next ten seconds.

George spins and grips my brother's neck, growling at him to move away. Cade's men pull out their guns and cock them, pointing at George's forehead. Isabelle squeals. Stools screech along the floor.

"Fuck," Sienna curses under her breath.

"Jesus Christ," Duncan says, sliding off his chair and tugging Isabelle with him.

"Cade, stop it!" I cry, as two new men in black suits descend upon us with guns raised, pointing at the two gangsters.

Connor's security.

"Drop your weapons," one of the men says with complete and deadly calm and no question that he will act if they don't obey.

I know. I've seen men in action all my life.

Cade glares at me.

George's hand is still locked around his neck.

"Bad move, sister of mine. Tell them to step aside and come with me."

Fuck.

"Ms. Mancini, please come with me," one of the security men says, reaching out his hand.

Fuck, fuck, fuck.

This is bad.

When my father hears Connor's men have pulled weapons on his people, including my brother, he'll be furious.

But the more I think about it, I just can't see my father sending Cade to retrieve me like this. He knows we are coming to dinner in a few days.

"I'm not going anywhere with you, Cade. Tell them to drop the weapons before the police turn up," I say angrily, then lean in and whisper so only those closest to us can hear. "I'm engaged. I'm not yours to boss around or sell to the highest bidder anymore. Leave before this gets messy. There are dozens of reporters outside. Joe won't like that, and you know it."

Cade's eyes flare, but he holds mine for several moments, then finally nods. George releases him, and Cade says, "Let's go."

His two goonies lower their guns, and Connor's men take a step back. It's like a well-orchestrated dance, each man taking a step back and to the side, until Cade and his guys finally turn and leave the bar.

Isabelle lets out an audible breath and clasps her hands to her chest. "Holy smokes, I cannot believe that just happened."

George is crowding me, but I glance at Sienna, who's shaking her head. "You okay?"

"So that's your life, huh?" she says.

"No. It's not. That's my brother being upset about the news. That's all," I reply.

It's way more than that.

Cade retreating confirms something to me. Joe, my father, didn't send him. I'm starting to wonder exactly why my brother is concerning himself with a marriage contract involving me.

Whatever it is, he needs to back the truck up. I'm marrying Connor.

Honestly, I don't know if there is anyone in my family I can trust since my mother died. I want to trust my father, but we want different things for our lives. My uncle Jimmy will take his side. I hope my aunts will act as advocates now my mother has passed, but if I'm being honest with myself, I'm on my own.

Even Connor will only protect me for the timeframe of our agreement.

Six months. That's all I have.

"Yeah, well, my brother would probably just send me a shitty text, not pull a gun, you know," Sienna replies.

"You don't have a brother." I try not to grin, but when she stares at the huge security guys around me and her eyes return to me all *Jesus, they are hot,* we both laugh.

Because they are.

"I'm so sorry, you guys," I say, my smile fading. "I promise this is not what life with me is going to be like."

I had put them at risk.

"Ms. Mancini. Care to tell us what just happened?" a guy in a bad suit asks.

Great.

The media.

Connor is going to kick my ass.

I groan.

"No comment," I mutter as George nods at me that it's time to leave. Grabbing my purse, I give my friends a smile and slide off the stool. "I'm so sorry. Stay, enjoy the champagne, and I'll see you tomorrow, Sen."

"Text me when you get home so I know you're safe," she says, darting the three huge security guys behind me a look. Then blushes. "Which I'm sure you will be."

As they whisk me out of the bar, past the media, and into a waiting car outside, my phone rings.

"Mia Mancini," I answer.

I know who it is. I can see the name on my screen.

Connor's dark voice says, "Your ass better be in the car and on the way home."

I let out a sigh.

MACK HOLDS THE elevator door open as I step out. Connor is standing with his back to me, his arms crossed. He turns and, ignoring me, stares at Mack over my shoulder. They do some silent exchange of information, then Connor nods, and I hear the elevator door slide closed behind me.

Connor's eyes finally meet mine.

I knew he would be pissed, mostly because of the media, but this seems a little extreme.

"Are you okay?" he asks, first in a growl, his voice incredibly dark.

"Yes," I reply, then lower my brows. "Why are you so mad?"

I'm getting a little over all these grumpy men around me. All I wanted was a few hours with my friends. Now I want a bath, to read a book and just zone out of this insane world I have somehow created.

"Your brother tried to take you from me." Connor stalks toward me, and I swallow, heat flushing through me.

Despite my body reacting, I didn't miss his terminology. *Take me?* What is it with these men seeing me as a goddamn possession.

"I'm not a painting, Connor. No one can take me from anyone. I belong to myself." I plant my hands on my hips after dropping my purse to the floor.

He's right, though.

I saw it in Cade's eyes. Given the chance, Cade would've pulled me out of Toast Bar and taken me back to the Mancini residence.

Or worse. Vitale.

An icy shiver runs through me.

What would my life be like right at this moment if it weren't for this powerful man standing furiously in front of me, protecting me?

"From now on, you'll have three of my men with you when you walk out the door," Connor says, ignoring my comment.

My mouth drops open.

"Why don't you just tie me up and keep me here?" I say, shaking my head.

"Sweetheart, I'd gladly do that if it wasn't against the law," Connor replies, and my mouth suddenly slams shut.

I'm not sure if I'm highly aroused or terrified.

Both.

And...now my panties are soaked.

Connor takes the last few steps and grips the back of my neck with one hand and the small of my back with his other, tugging me up against his large, solid body. "Right now, I need to claim back what's mine."

Oh God.

Yes, please.

But also, I'm still irked at his claim of me. Perhaps this just isn't the time to argue. Wet panties and all that.

I'm bent backward as Connor's mouth descends, and he begins ravaging my mouth. Sucking, lapping at my lips, my tongue, my chin, my jaw.

"*My* fucking fiancé," he growls, and I'm breathless as he scoops me up and plants me on the hall table, shoving up my dress.

I tremble in need, shaken and aroused by his unapologetic claim.

"Fuck," I whimper as he tosses my panties, spreads my legs, and then drops to his knees while palming my thighs on either side of my pussy.

"Connor," I say, gasping.

"Louder," he demands, his tongue sweeping through my folds, flicking with the right amount of force.

Jesus.

Pleasure fills my core, and I'm worried I'm going to come immediately. I don't want it to end. I never want it to end with this man. I press into his mouth, my body arching as I grip the edge of the table.

"Oh God, oh God, oh my God," I groan.

"Sweet fucking pussy," Connor says, his fingers teasing my hole. "No one is taking this from me."

Oh shit.

He keeps teasing, his mouth clamping onto my clit, and then I scream his name. As my orgasm hits hard, waves of it continuing in bursts, Connor rips off his shirt, and I run my hands over his rippling muscles. His pants drop to the floor.

"Mia," he cries, slamming into me, one palm on the wall above my head.

With those deep eyes locked with mine, I gaze into them like he's all I could ever hope for. I don't want anyone to take me from him either.

But I don't belong to him. I'm my own woman. I will never sell my soul.

Even though it feels like Connor Barrett already owns it.

20

CONNOR

I hold Mia's hand as our car speeds toward her father's house on Long Island. No one is around to witness this display of affection—if you can call it that. After hearing Cade Mancini tried to coerce Mia back to the family, I'm feeling a little protective.

Mia is mine.

For now.

I'm lying to myself that it's because she is the key to me getting close to her father, but I know it's a little more. I like Mia—that's all. I like having her in my life and in my bed. That's probably normal.

If you ignore the fact that we're faking an engagement and I'm using her to avenge my slaughtered family.

After I fucked her in the hall, she kept apologizing about the media. I didn't care about them. Well, I do, but *that* I can deal with. Losing Mia, not so much.

George was stressed as fuck once we got to talk with Mia out of earshot. Putting the heir to the Mancini throne in a neck lock wasn't a good move, but I told him he'd done the right thing.

She belongs to me.

Cade is not to be trusted. His little stunt adds a level of tension to tonight's family dinner. My skin crawls at the thought of the Mancini's being my in-laws.

But needs must and all that shit.

I considered arriving via helicopter, but for security reasons, landing blind in the gangster's property isn't smart.

I'm not sure what to expect, and Mia has been less than helpful. She keeps shrugging and saying it will be fine.

Fucking hell.

In the vehicles behind us, I have eight of my men. All former military. It is unlikely I'll need that many, but it is a clear message to Joe and Cade Mancini—and the entire Italian mafia—that I am a man of power.

And Mia is now under my protection.

She is.

Mia gave me a look when I took her hand, which I ignored. I fucked her so hard last night, I'm surprised she can sit upright. She didn't argue either. It was like she needed it as much as I did.

"It's going to be fine," Mia says suddenly, glancing up at me.

I turn to her. "What?"

"Tonight. It will be fine. You don't need to worry."

I hold back a laugh.

With my head slightly tilted, my lips soften for the first time in nearly twenty-four hours. "You think I'm nervous?"

Her fingers tighten around mine, and I glance down. This time, I laugh and release her hand, pulling her into my arms.

"Mia, I am not afraid of your father or your family. I'm fucked off they challenged me."

Her icy blue eyes narrow.

"Cade didn't challenge you. He ambushed *me*," she snaps, attempting to pull away. "This is not about your ego."

I lower my head. "No, it's about taking what's mine. You belong to me. Whether its fake or not."

She wriggles like a kitten in my arms, so I release her.

"I don't belong to you. And I don't belong to them!" she snaps again, moving a few inches away along the leather seat.

I let her go, focusing on the landscape flashing past us while I contemplate the evening ahead. I have a clear strategy, but it will take my total focus, and I need Mia on board if we are to succeed.

So, I give her space to defuse, and then, as we grow closer, I turn back to her and tug her body up against me. Her questioning gaze meets mine, and she lowers the mobile phone she's been scrolling on.

"In a few months, you'll be my wife, Mia. Whether this marriage is legitimate or not, it will be legal. You are under my protection and belong to me. That is what we agreed."

She fish-mouths for a moment, looking stupidly gorgeous, but before I let her say anything, I have more to add.

"It's in your best interest to let me dominate and claim you in front of your family. If you want your freedom, then this is what's required."

She glances away, but I know she understands this more than most any other woman. Her family is all about power. This is the language they speak.

If she'd chosen a weaker man, they would chew him up and spit him out.

"Fine. In front of others. In front of my family. But you do *not* own me, Connor Barrett. No one does." She won't meet my eye.

I grab her chin, and she slaps my hand away, but not before I see the moisture in them. *Fuck.*

This time, I force her to look at me. My words jumble inside my head. I was going to growl and tell her she *is* fucking mine, but she isn't.

Mia's just a pawn in my game of revenge.

But the need for it to be real right in this goddamn moment, knowing she could've been taken or decided to walk away, consumes me. Not for the reasons it should.

I'm fury and heat. Impatience and dominance. I want to scream and marry her now so it can't be undone.

Instead, I smash my mouth down on hers and take what she isn't offering.

I'm a thief when it comes to Mia Mancini.

Revenge has always been my first thought when I drift off at night and when I wake. Until now.

Now, I wake and reach for her.

Now, I think of all the ways I want to pleasure her, enjoy her, protect her. I look forward to taking her to places I've felt alone, showing her my life and having her on my arm.

Yet she has no idea about any of this, and it needs to remain that way.

As I ravish her mouth, I'm filled with both desire and anger. She's a dangerous distraction. The need to fill her with my come every fucking day is becoming more than just sexual greed—she's like a drug.

Maybe having her in my bed is a poor decision. Remaining focused on the darkness inside me which fuels my revenge has to be my priority, or I'll fuck up this opportunity.

I release Mia roughly.

"Connor," she gasps, blinking.

"We're nearly there," I snap. "Remember your role. You're my fiancé. Or the deal is off."

I shut down any emotions and focus on my game plan.

First, Joe Mancini will see me as the enemy—we already are, but he doesn't know that—as the man stealing his daughter. Then he will grow to trust me. I'm not sure how yet, but I will find a way. I didn't build a billion-dollar empire without shrewd tactics.

Once I learn whether Carlos was, or is, part of Mancini's gang and who gave the kill order, I will give Mia her desired freedom. It might mean destroying those she loves.

Until then, she is mine to use as I choose.

OUR VEHICLES ARE waved through the gates. We cruise along the circular driveway and pull up outside the Mancini Mansion.

The mob's soldiers are everywhere, armed with machine

guns, dressed in what appear to be black pants, zipped-up jackets, boots, and sunglasses.

The same outfit Nathan wears when we meet.

As my team positions around the vehicle—a stark contrast in their tailored black suits—Mack opens the door and gives me a nod.

I climb out, look around, then reach for Mia. She takes my hand and glances up, letting me drop a kiss on her lips.

"Good girl," I whisper.

Her obedience is going to give me a fucking hard on. But then I spot the subtle anger still sizzling beneath that blue ice. I better get used to it. She's going to hate me more by the time this is all over.

"Maria, *mia figlia*," Joe Mancini says, stepping out of the house with his arms wide and greeting his daughter in Italian, completely ignoring me and the eight armed men I have around me.

The Don is dressed in a navy suit and red tie over a crisp white shirt, which stretches over his large belly.

Like me, Joe knows my security won't harm him. The consequences are too great for men like us. We'd need a very good reason to give them a kill order.

Mia stays by my side until I release her, and then she moves into his arms. I don't miss his twitch as he acknowledges her choices.

Sorry, your girl is mine now.

I'm not sorry at all. This man could be responsible for the slaughter of my family. He could know who and where Carlos is.

If he does, I will find out.

"Daddy, this is Connor," Mia says, after he kisses her cheek three times. "Connor Barrett."

His warm demeanor hardens when he faces me. I don't approach him, staying a few steps away, as he decides how he wants to play this. Joe runs his eyes over my body and then at the men around me—as if he hadn't already done so from the window when we pulled up—and nods.

"Mr. Barrett," he says coldly.

"Please, call me Connor," I reply with little emotion.

His eyes lower back to Mia's. "Bring your man inside. We will eat and then talk."

Man?

Fuck that. I'm not going to be dismissed by this asshole. He thinks I'm Mia's fiancé, and he knows my position of influence in this country.

Joe Mancini is testing me.

If he thinks he can fuck with me, he's sorely mistaken.

I am Connor fucking Barrett.

"Mr. Mancini, I am not Mia's pet. I am the man she is marrying. If you cannot speak to me directly, then I will take my fiancé and return to Manhattan."

Mia's mouth falls open. Her mobster father halts his progress inside and slowly turns.

"Conno—" Mia starts, but her father interrupts.

"Perhaps if you'd asked for my daughter's hand in marriage, we may have begun our relationship on a better footing, Mr. Barrett," the man says darkly. "It is you who did not talk to me directly."

He slides his hands into his pockets and stares at me in challenge.

I nearly grin.

Game on, gangster.

Instead, I shrug. Just to piss him off.

"You would've said no, and I wasn't willing to lose the moment with such a beautiful woman who has stolen my heart." I know this is what he wants to hear. "My loyalty is to her and her alone. However"—I shrug all *whatever*—"Mia wishes us to be a family."

In other words, I don't want to be here, but I'm doing it for her.

Untrue, of course.

I'm here for me. For my family. For my sister who never got to see her fourth birthday. Possibly because this asshole ordered her dead.

Joe glances at his daughter. This time, I see affection and realize I've hit the bullseye. Family is important to the mafia—I already know that—so I took a chance that he's not a complete psychopath and loves his daughter. I was right.

I don't take my eyes off him, but whatever he sees in Mia's face shifts something within him.

The Don glances back at me, then nods.

"Family is everything. Come. Let's eat," he growls, and I watch as he takes in all the security around us. Joe points to one of his black-clad soldiers. "Let three of his men enter. The rest remain out here."

Three.

That is acceptable.

If shit goes down, I make four.

21

MIA

I feel Connor's hand in the small of my back as I follow my father. Talk about tense. Two powerful men meeting for the first time, with me standing between them.

Not something I want to do again.

But we still have more family members to introduce my new fiancé to, and I know both of them won't make it easy.

I can't work out why Connor has become so protective and possessive. I appreciate he's a man used to being in charge and getting what he wants, but does he really care that much about one point five million dollars and sleeping with me for six months?

He's taking this very seriously.

I suppose coming up against the head of the mafia is no small thing, and I should be grateful. He's saving me from a life of pure hell with men like Salvo.

But it's not just that.

No one was there when Connor fucked me into submission last night. No one was sitting opposite us during the long drive to my family home tonight, while he held my hand so tightly my fingers almost lost feeling.

As if I would run away if he let go.

Or someone would steal me.

It is just confusing. I haven't had that many lovers, but there is an intensity about sex with Connor that feels emotionless, like the damns are about to smash open and let it all out.

There are moments when it almost scares me.

But he notices every nuance and will soften a little and bring me back to him. His fingers will slide through mine, or he'll cup my face with an *I've got you.*

I'm not sure it was meant to be like this. It is more intimate than either of us acknowledges.

Even now, despite my furious rejection of being owned, I feel like I *am* Connor's. Forget labels of fiancé, girlfriend, or wife. I belong beside this man.

I just don't know how to work that out logically.

"Sit," my father says, waving a hand around the enormous living room.

This is the house where I spent most of my life growing up. We would go to Manhattan for periods of time, but this is my home.

Technically, it's a mansion with three levels, thirty bedrooms, as many more bathrooms, five living areas, an enormous yard with a lap pool, bar, hot pool, and entertainment area. The kitchen is a chef's dream, which is handy as there are three on staff.

The huge glass doors to the outdoor area are wide open, letting in a cool breeze after a warm June day. Mack and the other two men position themselves nearby as we sit on one of the sofas.

Father sits in his usual large armchair and waves at me. "Mia, go find your brother. I told him to be down here at seven."

I go to stand, but Connor puts his hand on my arm. I sit back down, not unhappy after Cade's actions last night, but I shoot Connor a look, wondering if he is going to defy my father at every point.

Joe Mancini isn't a patient man. Sooner or later, he'll snap. I don't want anyone getting hurt over my desire for freedom. That isn't a price I am willing to pay.

My father stays silent as a tray of drinks is handed out. They offer the men whiskey, while I accept a vodka dry.

"Now you are pushing my patience, Mr. Barrett," Papa says, nursing the crystal glass in his hand.

And there it is.

"Your son accosted Mia while she was out having drinks with her friends last night," Connor says without flinching. "I initially thought it was at your instruction, but something tells me he was acting alone."

My father stares at Connor for a long moment and then glances at me. "Is this true, Mia?"

I nod, then let out a sigh.

I suddenly want to know the truth. Was it him, or was it Cade who decided to come and interrupt my night.

"Yes. It was horrible, Papa. Guns were drawn, my friends were scared, and I know you don't care about the life I've created, but they *are* my friends, and I never wanted them to see any of this," I admit, feeling my shoulders sag.

He glances back at Connor. "Who drew first?"

"Mancini men," Connor replies. "However, Mia's personal security detail did need to intervene as your son went to grab her by pushing him aside."

My father's brows lift, and then he's back looking at me.

I feel like this entire thing is my fault. If I hadn't said I was engaged to Connor, I could be...Well, I'd be packing my bags, knowing I'd be moving home.

I'd be told I was being married off to Salvo Vitale.

Ugh.

I wish my mom was here. It all catches up with me now that I'm sitting in front of my father. I blink away the emotion, and he notices.

"I don't *not* care about your life, Mia. But you belong in the family. It is just how these things are. In saying that, I did not order anyone to bring you home. Least of all your brother."

I'm relieved.

So relieved. My father has the power to force me home if he really wants. Connor thinks he can stop him, but I'm not convinced he can.

"Okay," I reply, pulling my lip gloss out of my purse and sliding it over my lips. "Can you tell him to back off before someone gets hurt? That was not cool."

"No one is getting hurt," Connor growls, laying a protective hand on my thigh.

Possessively.

"Your brother won't harm you." My father watches every move Connor makes. "I will speak to him."

It is just as I thought.

Cade won't harm a hair on my body. He'd be punished if he did. My father might want to curtail my life and freedom, but he would never let anyone harm me.

Including my brother.

I glance around at the empty room. I was expecting the entire family to be here, interrogating us.

"The others will join us shortly," Papa says, reading my mind. "For now, I want to get to know the man who thinks he is marrying you."

I roll my eyes, but Connor ignores the jab and says, "Whatever you want to know, just ask."

Papa lifts his glass to his lips. "Good. Tell me about yourself, then, Mr. Barrett. Things I cannot find on the internet."

And so, it begins.

CONNOR

I RELAX ON the cushions of the sofa, stretch out a leg, and wrap an arm around Mia. Joe doesn't like it.

Tough shit.

"There's not a lot about my life that's not on paper already," I reply. *There's nothing I'm going to tell you.* "My life is mostly work and very little play. Recently, I met your beautiful daughter, and I fell for those stunning eyes."

Mia glances up at me, and I smile. Then I fucking hate myself when I see those blue globes sparkle. She deserves to be genuinely loved by someone, not being used for the cold revenge I'm after.

Yet here we are, and I'm not walking away.

I'm also not leaving her unprotected, now I'm sure I know what Cade is up to. It's clear Joe Mancini loves his daughter, but if the right partnership opportunity arises, he would marry her off.

It's sick to think Cade would even consider handing Mia over to Vitale. *He's brutal.* Nathan's description of Vitale a constant reminder. Has her brother given a single fucking thought to her safety or happiness?

Fury runs through my veins.

I press her closer against me, and I see the question in her eyes, but I can't give her any answers. I never will be able to. Which sends my thoughts in a spiral. Right now, Mia is in my arms, but until I know she's safe, I'm not walking away from her.

Which may impact my plans, and that's a fucking issue I'll deal with tomorrow.

Right now, Joe Mancini is sitting in front of me, and I need to make him think I love his daughter.

"And what do you have in common?" he asks, glancing between us both. "Marriage is about partnership, loyalty, family. How do you see this working?"

Jesus. I was expecting him to threaten my life, not marriage council us.

"One day at a time," I reply. "Together. Dealing with life's challenges."

Mia leans into me, grinning, Goddamn her. So far, she's been an excellent little actress, but the attraction between us is real.

Really fucking real.

When she's in my arms and around my cock, there's just her and pleasure and my need to chain her to my life.

"What he said." She smiles at me and then at her father.

God, I'm a cunt.

"Basically, Connor will do whatever it takes to make me happy," she adds, and when her eyes meet mine again, my brows lift..

Then she smirks at me.

Little minx.

Joe barks out a laugh and goes on to ask several more questions about how I achieved my success and the causes I give to. I don't ask about his. We all know how he makes his money.

When he prods about my inheritance, things get a little close for comfort.

"So, you lost your family when you were young."

Yeah, and you may have been the asshole who gave the order to have them assassinated. But I will withhold judgement until I'm sure.

Actually no, that's bullshit. I hate you more than you could know. The drugs you pedal, the children you traffic, the women you sell, it's disgusting.

"I barely remember them," I reply, instead of saying any of that. It's a story that's out in the world, so I stay on script. "They died in an accident, and I inherited their insurance payout when I was twenty-one. Still in the marines at that point. I invested and got lucky, I guess."

Luck has never factored in my life. Unless I consider Mia walking into it and handing me access to her father. I call it an opportunity.

"My condolences. What did your father do?" he asks.

I force my heart rate to stay calm.

That fucking question haunts me. The truth is, I don't know.

The boxes of files I have from the FBI and that key need to be looked into.

But what if I find my worst nightmare?

If I find out my father was involved...if he was the reason...

I steady my breathing.

These are the things that could destroy the very essence of my life's purpose. I'm not going down that rabbit hole as I sit across from my enemy.

"No idea. All I know is, he worked in an office." I lift the glass to my lips. "Things that were boring to a little boy interested in cars and trains."

Joe nods and accepts a top-up of his drink without even looking at the woman. His eyes remain on mine.

He's like a predator seeking his next prey.

But I'm a snake.

"That's difficult, losing your parents so early. Mia, as you know, lost her mother," Joe says, and I nod. "Will you two be having children?"

Christ.

Mia spits out the vodka she's drinking and begins coughing and patting her dress. "Dad. Jeez. We've just got engaged."

She stands, reaching for a cocktail napkin, and dabs at it.

Joe shrugs. "These are questions your mother would've asked, Mia. Things you should discuss before marrying."

I notice she's embarrassed, and my mood improves. She continues muttering *oh my God*, then lifts her face to mine. Her cheeks are rosy, and it's adorable.

"We are definitely having children," I say, enjoying watching her blush deepen.

God, we would have gorgeous babies.

Not that I'm ever expecting to have children, but Mia is a beautiful woman, and I know I'm a good-looking guy. Between us, I could just imagine the offspring we could create.

Jesus, this fake marriage is going to my head.

"I need to get some soda on this, or it will stain," Mia says and runs out of the room.

I shoot Mack a glance, but he's already following her.

When I turn back to Joe, all the warmth is gone. Time for the men to stop playing games and get to the heart of what this meeting is really about.

"I can see Mia is very taken with you," Joe says, his voice low. "You have a very impressive career and have amassed far greater wealth than I have or ever will."

Facts.

"I'm sure you're an influential man, Mr. Barrett," he adds.

"Please, call me, Connor." I force back a smile because it will only antagonize him. I need his trust, not to make an enemy out of him. He has no idea *how* influential I am.

I have information about the Mancini mafia that could devastate his organization in a matter of days, should I choose. People in powerful government positions owe me favors, who would make sure the damage is painful.

And I have his daughter.

I *am* influential.

I'm the biggest threat to his business, life, and family, and he has no idea.

That's not the goal today.

I want answers. I want Carlos, and whoever else is responsible for my family's death. I want to watch them scream as they take their last breaths, just as my baby sister, Rebecca, did.

"However, I see you do not love my daughter, as you claim," Joes says, ignoring my offer.

I don't respond straight away. Not because he's right, but because I'm not going to address it head-on. I'm as cunning as he is, and whether he likes it or not, I *am* marrying Mia.

"Perhaps marriage—partnership, as you called it earlier—is not so much about love as it is a mutual understanding and sharing the same objectives," I reply.

Jesus, I need to be careful.

That's getting a little too close to the truth. Not that the mobster will have any clue who I am or what I am up to. If he did, I'd have a bullet between my eyes right now.

Joe takes another slow drink, watching me over his crystal cut glass.

A chill runs down my spine.

I've seen that look in a man's eyes before, and it's dangerous.

I stretch out my arm along the back of the sofa and cross my legs, not letting him intimidate me. He may be the head of the mafia, but I could snap his neck before he finishes his next sip if I wanted to.

My men are fast and trained. They'd have bullets in the men surrounding the room before they could touch me.

Joe lowers his glass and leans forward, placing it on the table. "You remind me of a man who double-crossed me once, many years ago. Don't make that mistake, Connor Barrett."

The fuck?

Is he referring to my father?

I do a quick calculation. There's no way he could know who I am. My identity is so deeply buried, no one will ever find it. Not even him. If he did and Mancini is the man who gave the kill order, I'd already be dead.

This is simply intimidation.

He doesn't want me to have Mia.

Tough shit.

It is time to let the head of the Italian mafia know exactly who Connor Barrett is. The man I hide from almost everyone, except the Dark Kings.

I lower my arm from the back of the sofa, lean forward, my forearms on my knees, and look him straight in the eye.

"I don't like threats, Mr. Mancini. Don't mistake me for a while-collar guy with a gym membership. I'm a marine, and I protect what's mine. And Mia is mine."

♔

WHEN MIA STEPS back into the room, the air is thick with tension, but we've said what we had to say, and now our boundaries are clear.

Cade Mancini chooses that moment to come into the room. He has two men with him. They stop behind Mia.

Shit.

My heckles rise as I stand and go to her, while doing everything I can to not make eye contact with Nathan.

What the hell is he doing in the Mancini family home in Long Island?

He's head to toe in black, a leather jacket with the collar up, despite the early summer heat. And he has shades on his head.

Mia turns, and when she spots them, I see her reaction. She knows Nathan. Which makes sense. He's been working for her father for six years.

He winks at her and sticks a toothpick in his mouth, chewing.

The fuck?

I pull Mia to my side and glare at him. I trust the guy with my fucking life, yet I want to smash my fist through the side of his head.

Our eyes meet, and he grins at me. *Motherfucker.*

But he's playing the role he should, and I am trying really hard to remember that as Mia leans into me.

Cade laughs and shoots Nathan a shit-kicking grin.

Smile, asshole. One day, I'm going to wipe it off your face with your blood.

"About time, Cade. Go get your aunts and uncles. It's time for dinner," Joes says. "And meet your future brother-in-law."

Now, it's mine turn to smirk and watch his smile fade.

22

CONNOR

etween Mia's aunts telling her they're happy—but *shouldn't you choose someone Italian...and Catholic*—and her uncle Antonio glaring at me across the dinner table, I've had enough of the Mancini family.

But it's Cade who holds most of my attention.

His behavior is odd. Given I know about his coup, I expected to meet a man with a sense of personal power, ready to take over the kingdom, but instead, he seems both childish and rebellious.

A spoiled child with a machine gun.

A dangerous fucker.

I can't get a read on Joe's feelings on his son. He keeps them very close to his chest. Which I respect. He's probably hoping that he'll mature and grow.

I keep going over our conversation. Maybe I should've lied and told him I loved Mia, but he wouldn't have believed me. He's astute, and I probably gained an ounce of respect by not bothering.

Reality has kicked in, and I know if I want to make progress, joining the family sooner rather than later is my best move.

I've demanded his respect. Now it needs to be earned.

"So, when's the wedding?" Cade asks, shoveling the last of his meal into his mouth, dropping his cutlery onto the plate.

"We haven't set a date," Mia says.

"We should. Late July. A summer wedding," I say, laying my arm along the back of her chair possessively.

"This July?" her aunt Rosa screeches.

Mia whips her face to me. "That's less than eight weeks away."

"That's too early. July?" Silvia cries.

I think it's perfect. It will keep everyone busy and lock this agreement in place, destroying Cade's plans. He glares at me from the other end of the table.

I lift my fork to my mouth, meeting his stare.

When I finish my mouthful, I drop my eyes to Mia and add, "We'll have a wedding planner, sweetheart. You just need to choose your dress. We can fly to Italy if we need to. Whatever you want, you can have."

Cue the women around the table, clutching their pearls and swooning in Italian as they discuss what her dress should look like.

Mia glares at me momentarily, but the family is on a roll.

Family will need to fly in. The priest will need to be booked. Flowers must be some damn color.

Who will be her bridesmaids?

"Given I'm paying for it, we should discuss the dates and details privately," Joe says.

"Oh." Mia's eyes go wide.

"You're not paying for a thing," I state firmly, and the room goes silent.

Even Cade raises a brow, taken aback.

Nobody was privy to our earlier conversation.

I've been reasonably quiet, mostly because Mia wants me to fit into her family. Fake or not. Her family is important to her. However, it's time I set those same boundaries with everyone else.

This is a mafia family, and again, if I want their respect, I need to claim it. They're like a pack of fucking dogs. If you don't bark loudly, you'll find yourself at the bottom of the pecking order.

Or the ocean.

"Mia is my fiancé and my responsibility. We will be paying for our wedding. Buy us a nice gift instead." I smile dangerously.

Let me translate: *I'm far richer than you. Your daughter belongs to me now.*

Cade loses his shit and tosses his napkin on his plate. "Are you going to allow this, Father?"

Joe sends a death look down the table at me. "No, I won't. We will go halves."

The fact he even offered a compromise makes me want to laugh. It didn't go unnoticed, as Mia's aunties nearly break their necks staring between me and Joe. Cade continues ranting, but my attention has shifted to Mia, who has gone quiet.

I glance down at her, and she's gritting her teeth.

"Mia?"

"Hello. Bride here. Do I have a say?" Mia asks as her eyes move from mine to the rest of the room.

The entire table says *no!*

Now I'm mad. I take her hand, and she turns angry, upset eyes to mine.

"Would you like to get married here?" I ask, privately. The section is enormous. I could've landed the chopper on the front lawn. There's plenty of room for a marquee and hundreds of guests.

It's perfect.

But as her eyes begin to glisten, I realize the momentous mistake I just made.

Shit.

"Forget it," I say, dropping my napkin.

What was I thinking?

This marriage is fake. The last thing Mia wants to do is fulfill some childhood dream of getting married at her family home.

"Do you, Mia?" her father asks, and I flinch.

Crap, I thought I had spoken quieter.

"I need to think about it," she replies, refusing to look at anyone.

That's it. I'm taking her out of here.

I stand.

"I accept your offer of paying half, Joe," I say, only because I want us to leave. "Now, I'm afraid we must be getting back. I have a late-night conference call."

I don't.

The only thing I'll be doing is fucking this gorgeous woman and making up for what I just did.

And planning my next move.

23

MIA

I throw my purse down on the kitchen bench and grab a glass out of the cupboard. Turning on the tap, I begin to fill it, then feel Connor come up behind me.

He was quiet on the ride home, but then again, so was I. The entire evening was exhausting. In the car, I curled up my legs, and he pulled me into his chest where I snoozed, both of us deep in thought.

"I'm sorry." Connor lays his hands on my hips. "About the house. I didn't think."

But is he sorry about setting a wedding date without speaking to me? No.

I turn. "It's fine."

"No, Mia, it's not. I won't take those things from you," he says, and it almost offends me.

Sometimes, I forget this relationship is fake, which I know is ridiculous because we're not in love, but Connor is so intense and the way we spend our nights...Well, there is nothing fake about those.

Things are getting so fuzzy in my head.

"You just surprised me," I say, then when he tilts my face to

179

his, I sigh. There is no hiding from Connor Barrett, and I know he won't let this go until I share what I'm thinking.

God forbid he ever do the same.

"Tell me."

I sigh again.

"I used to plan my wedding when I was little. My mom would play along, and we'd imagine what my dress would look like, and she'd show me how she'd do my hair."

Connor runs his fingers up my arm, his gaze roaming my face. I wonder why he cares. Or *if* he cares. I continue because I want him to know. Fake or not, he's going to be my husband, and we're sharing our lives under this roof.

For now.

If I married a mobster in an arranged marriage, it could be way worse. There'd be no love. At least I'm attracted to Connor.

Highly attracted.

I know he desires me because ninety percent of the time we're together, he's touching me. Not just sexually. Every night, we have sex, but there's a difference between a man wanting sex and one who wants *you*. It's in the way they look at you, the time they take while touching you.

This man confuses me so much.

This relationship confuses me, and yet, I know I'm safe with him.

Watching him with my father was terrifying but thrilling. I've never seen anyone meet Joe Mancini on the same level before. Now that I can breathe again, I can admit it was one of the sexiest things I've ever seen.

I mean, Connor is gorgeous, but seeing him stand up to my father was goddamn panty-destroying.

Then he went ahead and spoiled it by deciding we are getting married next month. That was annoying, but when he brought up the venue, my heart splintered.

Fake wedding or not, I want my mom.

My whole family knows I want to marry in Long Island. I

spent half my childhood dressed up as a bride, zooming around the house with curtains on my head.

If I don't, it will be very odd, but how can I?

How can I marry this man, who doesn't love me, in the one place where my mother raised me while wishing she was with me?

Does my freedom mean that much to me?

Can I dishonor her?

"I used to dress up and pretend to walk down the aisle with a bunch of flowers," I tell Connor. "I'd steal from the front entrance bouquet. Susanna would get angry and curse in Italian, throwing her arms in the air, until momma would tell her it doesn't matter."

Connor smiles as I laugh, then a little unexpected sob escapes me. He curses and pulls me into his arms.

"Fuck, Mia. I'm an idiot."

"You didn't know," I say into his chest.

"I should've fucking known." He takes my chin and forces me to look at him as a tear slips out. His eyes shut for a moment, and then his thumb wipes the tear away. "You deserve so much goddamn more than all of this. It's not right."

All I can do is blink and stare at him.

His expression is pained, and it surprises me. I can't tell if he regrets this or cares about me.

Perhaps that's it.

Getting involved with my family is a risk to his organization's reputation. Was tonight a reality check?

Why did he agree to all this?

For me? For sex? For a measly one point five million dollars?

I was so desperate on Sunday night when I came to him, topped-up on wine and with a confession. I'm beginning to really question the validity of why he agreed to it.

His reasons.

I can understand a man like him would want a regular sex partner without commitment. Unlike an average man, he can't be seen picking up a woman at a party or taking out every single girl in town, without expecting bad press and getting a reputation.

Sure, there are wealthy men in Manhattan who do, but Connor isn't a playboy. Surely, there are women who would want this job. For want of a better word. A regular arrangement with Connor, which is discreet and, speaking from experience, highly pleasurable.

The risk is high. I see it from his point of view. Women fall in love easily.

How could they not?

The difference here is, I needed his help. With me, it's a partnership, where both of us have agreed to go our separate ways at the end. I get what I want. Connor gets regular sex and the money at the end.

This really is a win-win for him.

And me.

He was willing to take the hit with the media and face my father. He wasn't threatened, and why should he be—he's one of the wealthiest men in the United States *and* a marine.

It's nearly like I've found the perfect man.

What I didn't expect were all these emotions.

Or his.

What does the look in his eyes mean? Does he regret it after meeting my family? I need to know, or I will worry.

We either move forward with our plans, or we don't.

"If you've changed your mind, we can tell everyone I've called it off. Make it my fault. I got you into this, Connor, so it's my responsibility. I'll even face the media," I say. "I can leave right now and stay with Sienna."

It would only be for one night, anyway.

The moment my family hears I'm no longer with Connor, they'll scoop in and take me home, lock the door and throw away the key.

Connor shakes his head slowly.

"Whatever is going on in your head, forget it, Mia. You are not going fucking anywhere," he says in a growl. His mouth covers mine, and I melt into him completely.

Because for reasons I'm not ready to acknowledge, I don't want to leave.

CONNOR

THE ONLY THING I've changed my mind about is which position I'm fucking Mia in tonight. I want her wet, from top to bottom.

I have some making up to do after asking if she wanted to marry at the Mancini Mansion. She's opened up to me, and I'm honored. But deep inside, she's a little girl who lost her mother. I know a thing or two about losing your family.

I lift her off her feet and walk into our bathroom.

Our?

"Dress off, Mia," I say, reaching to turn on the shower.

I unbutton my shirt as her dress falls to the floor, and she stands before me in a peach-colored bra and panties. They have little silver hearts dangling from them.

Her long dark hair falls across her shoulders, and she's so damn perfect, I'm hard immediately.

Tossing my shirt, I reach for my pants, but her hands are on my pecs, sliding down my chest, and she's starts undoing my belt.

"I want control," Mia says.

"No," I reply firmly as my pants fall to the floor.

"Commando." Mia smiles, wrapping her hand around my swelling cock. Then she licks her lips.

"Don't play with me," I warn her. "If you want to suck it, get on your knees."

The smile may have gone from her mouth, but I see it in her eyes. She's testing me, pushing the barriers to see how far I will let her go.

Not far.

Slowly, she crouches and licks the tip of my member, settling on her knees. I twitch in her hand, wanting more of her hot wet tongue. She darts out and swirls around the end.

More teasing.

"Mia," I warn, tempted to grip her head and take what I want. Yet I find this side of her sexy as fuck, and it's turning me on.

With a flicker of those long lashes, she wraps around the entire head and she sucks, releasing it with a pop.

Jesus fucking Christ. It's like I love torture.

I let out a groan while she takes me down deeper. Then again, over and over, until suddenly, I'm deep in her wet hot mouth, and she's working me hard and fast.

I throw back my head and groan, one hand palmed on the shower wall, letting her have all she wants. My thighs are spread, and a beautiful woman is on her knees, sucking my cock. Life is feeling pretty fucking great right now.

Heat zips down my spine as I get close. I drop my head and slide my fingers through her long dark hair, gripping and taking control.

"I'm going to come down your throat, hard," I grind out, and her eyes tell me to do it.

I wasn't asking.

"Good fucking girl." Both hands on her head, I stroke her mouth, and almost immediately, my hot seed spills as I throw my head back. When Mia gags, I release her head and start stroking my cock, covering her lips and breasts.

As if marking her.

I gaze down at her, my semen dripping from her lips, and it fucks with my head. I want to own this woman every way possible for the rest of my...

Stop.

Snapping me out of that insane thinking, Mia stands and removes her bra, then her panties, and steps under the water.

I'm still fucking recovering. And not done yet.

Following her into the shower like a rabid animal, I take her by the hips and lift her onto the built-in shower seat.

"Hey, ohhhhh," she purrs when my fingers go straight to her pussy, finding the creamy moisture I'm after.

I lick my fingers, then claim her mouth.

"Taste yourself," I say, and she moans against my lips.

Rubbing her clit, I kiss her again, as if it's the last time I ever will, until she's rocking against my fingers, wanting more.

"You going to marry me, Mia?" I ask, my mouth moving along her jaw. "You going to let me fuck you however I want and make you mine?"

What am I saying?

"Yes," she cries, arching into me, desperate. "Yes."

"Tell me what you want," I order her.

"I want you."

She doesn't mean that—she means my cock. I'm starkly aware of that fact and know I shouldn't care. Know I should be just fucking this woman, but we both know I'm not. I wish she didn't, but even I know I'm giving her much more than I promised.

My protection.

A piece of my soul.

"You want my cock or my mouth?" I stand to stare down at her startling icy blue eyes, that have the ability to make me do things I never would before.

"Um, I...," Mia starts, and I grin at her indecision.

My fingers press inside her, and she cries out again.

"Choose, Mia." I'm fucking her hard with two fingers now, about to take her choice away. I stroke my cock with my other hand.

My patience is running out.

I need to be inside her. To be connected and pleasure her. To claim what feels like belongs to me.

When she glances down and watches, I know she's chosen.

"Yeah, baby, such a sweet little pussy," I growl, pressing my cock against her entrance. Pressing inside, inch by inch, I go deeper and feel her tighten around me. The sensation is so intense, I have to force myself not to runt her, like the animal I want to be.

That I am.

"Oh God, fuck," she cries. "More, Connor, more."

Hearing my name on her lips makes me even harder. I take her chin and tilt her face up to mine. "Keep being a good girl, and I'll get you your freedom."

Right now, I'd give her fucking anything.

"Yes," she cries.

"Until then, you belong to me," I grunt when I'm balls-deep. "Do you understand?"

She doesn't respond, so I thrust again.

"Mia," I growl.

Her nails dig deep into my arm, her legs wrapped around me. I slam a hand on the wall of the shower above her and demand her submission again.

"Tell me."

I'm a fool. We both know I can't ask it of her, nor honor it if she did. Still, the desire and defiance in her eyes kills me, so I crush my mouth to hers while my cock thrusts along her channel.

When her pussy tightens, it takes me over the edge, and we both cry out together.

Pleasure blasts down my spine as I spill into her.

A few moments later, Mia's legs begin to slide from my body, but I'm not done. Not even close. I grab them, turn the shower off, and carry her to our bed.

Our.

"I haven't washed yet," she says into my neck.

"You are about to get real dirty, sweetheart. I'll wash you after. Now get on your knees."

I know she's not mine to own, but the desire to possess this beautiful woman is all-consuming. Tomorrow, I will think about what the fuck I'm doing. Right now, I need to know I own her in ways she will never understand.

Or agree to.

Tonight, I lie and tell myself it's all part of the plan so I can avenge my family.

None of it's true.

For the first time in my life, I'm not thinking about them.

24

"**B**oss."

Fuck.

"Wait...Just...Fuck, tell him to wait," I say, pressing down on the woman's head as she sucks on my cock. I shove my hips up to speed things along. Then let out a moan. "Yeah, yeah, yeah, fuck."

As the jet of my come releases, she tries to lift off, but I hold her there, pressing down her hot throat.

"Fuckkkkk," I cry, and she gags as I throw my head back and open an eyelid. The roof of the car greets me, reminding me we're down by the docks, awaiting Salvo Vitale.

Who has now arrived.

Who is now waiting for me to finish getting my cock sucked. Because he kept me waiting, so now, I'm doing the same.

"Jesus, Cade," the girl whose name I've briefly forgotten says as I release her.

Fine, I never knew her name.

I rub my come over her lips.

"You are getting better at that. I'll be five minutes. Ten at most. Get that pussy wet, and if you come before I shove my cock into you, like last time, you are off the team."

189

Team. Harem. Whatever.

She glares at me.

I grip her chin and yank her face. "Lose the attitude, or you won't get your hit, bitch."

Her eyes lower.

Much better. Goddamn junkies these days.

I pull my zipper up and tuck in my shirt. Then I climb out of the car.

Freddy, Nathan, and Dean are leaning against the paintwork, shades on, jacket collars flicked up, sleeves tugged, looking gangster as hell. Dean is puffing out a smoke, Nathan chewing on a pick, as he seems to always do.

A couple of yards away, Salvo's SUV is parked, and he has a couple of guys standing around it like mine are. They're more alert, mostly because of my surname.

Mancini.

We own this city and the distribution of basically everything illegal. From guns to drugs to women.

Salvo's door opens, and he steps out. He's over a decade older than me, tall with a paunch, dark brown hair, and today, he's wearing a fur coat.

What in the ever-loving God?

"It's fucking eighty-five degrees, Vitale. You auditioning for the Godfather role?" I ask, laughing.

My guys snigger.

"Fuck you, Mancini," he says, stopping in front of me with a scowl.

Which has zero effect on me.

"No thanks. Got a bitch in the car for that when we've finished here. So, let's get this over with. What did you want to talk to me about?" I reply, shoving my hands into my jacket.

Where I have a gun stashed.

"Sounds like we have a little problem with our agreement. And your payment," Salvo says, pulling out a cigar and lighting it.

Jesus, he's going for the full Pacino look today.

A couple of times, I've cringed at the thought of Mia being manhandled by this guy, but honestly, who wants to think about their sister having sex? It's creepy as hell.

His hair is beginning to thin on top, but he's not decrepit. There are way worse matches going on in Italy in our extended family. She won't be grateful, but she should be. Or rather, when I'm the Don, she won't open her mouth and complain.

I'm sick of Joe having the reins. He needs to stand down and let me run the show. I have far more energy than him and ideas he won't listen to.

The fuck, he even kicked my ass for trying to have a drink with Mia a few nights ago.

Sure, I was hoping she'd come with me so I could drop her at Salvo Vitale's. If she had, we could've fast-forwarded our plans.

And when I say "kicked my ass," my father slapped me around the head and shoved me up against the wall. My neck still has bruises.

Asshole.

"There's no problem. It's simply a delay. You will marry my sister," I say. "Then, when my father is removed, we can expand your distribution and get the money flowing."

"How? Barrett has three men protecting her now," Salvo growls. "Three. And they're goddamn ex-military."

I narrow my eyes.

"You know that how?"

"Because I don't fucking trust you. My men are keeping an eye on her." He shrugs.

I take a step closer. "Touch one hair on my sister's body before I hand her over to you, and you'll lose body parts. And your little soldiers," I say, shooting them a look.

"Soldiers you're going to use to take the fucking throne, Mancini."

I grunt.

That might be true, but it's irrelevant here.

Mia is far too valuable to the family.

"She is the princess. Don't go near her." Despite my plans, Mia belongs to the family first and foremost. We are all responsible for protecting her.

My father had plans to marry her off one day soon. I'm just moving faster than him.

This engagement to Barrett is bullshit. I can see right through it. Men like him don't marry and settle down suddenly. How she's done it, I don't know.

Maybe she gives magic blowjobs. Ugh.

Anyway, if Salvo tries to take her and if Barrett gets a hint there are people trying to kidnap his fiancé, he will lock her down hard. I saw the possession in his eyes.

Love? I doubt it. But he knows her value.

What he plans to do with it is the question.

One my father is currently asking.

"He wants something," Joe said after they had left the dinner. "I don't know what it is yet, but that man does not love our Mia."

"He's clean. Business-wise," Uncle Jimmy had said. "Could just be looking for a good wife."

My father had stood there nodding for a long moment. "Perhaps."

Whatever Barrett is up to, he has the money and power to do it. Including protecting Mia. Which makes my next move harder.

"Get everything set up. I will have her delivered to you when I can."

He blows out a thick plume of white smoke. Fortunately for him, not in my face.

"Good. We are ready to mobilize when you give the word," he says, then grips his balls. "And so are my other soldiers."

With a grin, he turns and leaves.

I stand watching, with my men at my back, until they drive away. Then I turn and roll up my sleeves.

"Give me ten minutes, then let's go."

Dean lights another cigarette as they all nod.

I climb into the car and find Sally...no, Dianne...fuck,

whoever...with her legs spread, skirt up to her waist, and her fingers in her pussy.

Closing the door, I unzip and pull her onto my lap.

Then rip open her shirt so I can play with her tits while she rides me.

Life is good.

And about to get so much better once I'm in control of the city.

25

CONNOR

I lie awake as Mia sleeps beside me. My arm under her neck, her bum pressed up against my hip. She refused to submit to me, and part of me is furious about it. My need to protect her is growing, and it's complicated things.

I shouldn't have reacted to Nathan tonight.

I shouldn't have told Joe Mancini I didn't love his daughter. I'm distracted and can't focus.

I slip out of bed and go down the hall to my office. After I punch in the code, the door opens, and I stand in front of the wall with all the photos and Post-it notes. Seeing her photo now seems odd.

In fact, I fucking hate that it's up there and want to tear it down. *Maria Luna Mancini*. Daughter of Joe Mancini.

She doesn't feel like theirs. She is mine.

Soon, she'll be Mrs. Barrett.

Another lie.

My name is Connor Beaufort. Was. My change of name was legally done and then buried so no one will ever find it.

Still, the idea of her having my name, real or not, sends a strange feeling through me I know doesn't belong in my life.

One which threatens to destabilize me.

How, though? How the hell has she crept inside me without trying?

Mia wants her freedom, but I can't give it to her. Temporarily, while she is with me, yes. After that, no.

If her family gave the kill order on my family, it will be worse than that. I will destroy her family—the people she loves—and she will hate me.

I am her enemy.

I stare at the trail of names, details, and roles of the people on the wall. Do they know who Carlos is or was?

He could be dead. I'm aware of that.

It has been twenty-three years since the deaths of my family. Nathan infiltrated the mafia six years ago. Ditto Decker in Mexico. Neither have heard of a single mention of the man.

My phone on my desk beeps.

Fuck.

That phone number is only accessible by three people: Mack, Nathan, and Decker. The Dark Kings.

Saw the news. What the fuck? Decker.

I knew he would eventually be in touch. It was more important to speak with Nathan first. Any contact is risky, so I waited for Deck to reach out.

Not legit. Door opener. I reply.

On U.S. soil in two Fridays. Decker replies.

I rub my forehead, thinking.

He's in the country infrequently, so we have to take advantage when he is. A Dark Kings meeting is completely overdue, so I make the call.

Friday 7pm. King's base.

Got it.

Then I shoot a message off to Mack to let him know so he can get a message to Nathan. The stakes have never been higher, so with me being inside one of the mafia's, we need to debrief and get clear on our strategy.

Especially between Nathan and me.

I also want Decker briefed on Cade's planned coup. A change in the top job can unsettle the other cartels around the world.

Right now, my plan is to stop him. First, if Joe is responsible for giving the kill order, I want his fucking head. I'm not that arrogant to think we have full control over this, but we're in an excellent position to do so, with both Nathan and I having access.

There's another thing on my mind.

Joe's comment keeps playing over in my head.

You remind me of a man who double-crossed me.

If my father, Ian Beaufort, was somehow responsible for all of this, it will fucking break me. Blaming others has been far more comfortable.

I don't want to learn my father was one of them.

26

MIA

Over the next few weeks, Connor and I fall into a rhythm. We go to work, come home, and have dinner together. Then he either works for a few hours in his private office, which is weirdly always locked, or we watch TV.

Sometimes, we chat.

It's during those quiet conversations I've been learning more about him. Tonight, I ask about his train set, which is laid out on a table in the far corner of the room.

"I started it about eight years ago. When I retired from the marines," Connor says, staring across the room at it. "I've hand-made every single piece."

I'm surprised by that.

"I can't imagine you having the patience to build models."

He smiles slowly at me. "You think you know me, Mia Mancini?"

I shrug. "No, but you can't tell me you're a patient man. I know you're not."

Connor glances away. "I'm not. Which is why I need to do it. You should always push yourself in areas of weakness."

I think about that. About how I can apply it to my life and future business. The one that doesn't exist yet, but will one day.

"Also, it gets me out of my head. While I'm focusing on the details, I don't think about anything else. It's freeing."

Freedom I can relate to, but what does Connor need to be free from? Is this about his past, I wonder?

I decide to ask.

"Is this about your family?"

He's silent for a moment, and then his face hardens. "We should go to bed. It's late."

Then, just like that, he's shut down. I want to demand he tell me something about himself, but what right do I have? Sure, I'm going to be his wife, but it's not real. Yet every day we live and act like a couple. We fuck, we laugh, we get annoyed with one another, and we wake up the next day, entangled in each other's arms.

So, tell me, what part of all that is fake?

Because I see the way he looks at me when he's deep inside me, the way his eyes run over me when I step out of the bedroom in yet another gown to attend one of his business events, the way his hand slides over my hip protectively when another man looks at me.

The way he huffs when he has to get the breakfast bowl down for me each morning because I can't reach his silly tall cupboards —and growls at me for climbing on a stool to get one. The way he won't simply move them to another cupboard because I think he *likes* doing it.

Or maybe I'm imagining it all.

But what he won't do is tell me about his life, his past, his family or friends. What's so secret that he can't share a little bit about his childhood so I feel less a stranger?

"Fine, goodnight," I say, climbing off the sofa and walking upstairs.

Connor never comes to bed with me.

Every night, he'll brush his hand over my cheek or slap my bottom, telling me it's time for bed. When I tried to tug him with me one night, he shook his head.

"*Go to bed, Mia,*" was all he said.

Only when I turn my light off will Connor come in. He brushes his teeth, undresses, and then slides into bed. Connor reaches for me without hesitation, and I turn over and melt into his chest.

Then he makes love to me.

But I remind myself it's *not* love. It just feels like it.

I've never lived with a man before—not in a relationship—so what do I know. But there was one night earlier this week, after we met with the wedding planner, that keeps playing over in my mind.

I was flicking through the private website she created for us. It feels like homework. We have to pick everything: the color scheme, the dinner set, the candles, and of course, my dress.

Connor isn't allowed to see that section.

"Fake wedding," he reminded me.

"I don't care. Bad luck is bad luck. Let's not jinx things," I replied.

"I'm not superstitious...but yeah, okay," he said, and I grinned. "What?" he then asked, frowning.

"So, you *are* superstitious," I teased.

He leaned down from his standing position and put one hand on the sofa beside my head. "Not superstitious. Maybe I just want to be surprised by seeing my beautiful bride on the day."

I bit my lip.

"Maybe I'll wear black," I said, taunting him.

Testing him.

"You will wear a beautiful gown and be the bride everyone expects you to be," Connor replied and leaned closer, placing a finger under my chin. "And I'm going to remove it button by button and lick every inch of you as soon as it's over. Fuck the reception."

My body burst into flames, my nipples hardening against the cotton of my T-shirt.

But it was moments later, when my body had calmed down,

that a sudden idea popped into my head. I leaped up and grabbed a folder from one of my boxes in the guest room.

"Where's the fire?" Connor asked, pouring a whiskey across the room.

"Nothing...No...Nothing," I replied, sliding lip gloss over my lips and then scribbling ideas on my notepad. I didn't notice the big muscular man standing behind me.

"What is that?" Connor asked.

I felt a mix of embarrassment and aggravation as he invaded my privacy, so I snapped the folder shut.

"Nothing. I said it's nothing." I stood, walked back down the hall to the guest bedroom, and put the folder on the end of the bed near a pile of other things I still needed to sort.

When I turned to leave, Connor was leaning against the door-jamb, sipping his whiskey.

"Oh my God, have you not heard of personal space?" I said, crossing my arms.

"Not when it's my house," he replied, unperturbed.

"You really need to understand boundaries a little better. We may have this weird agreement in place, but that doesn't mean you own me." I pushed past him.

Connor followed me out to the living area.

"Was that a business plan?" he asked, and I huffed, flopping on the sofa, clicking the remote to turn on the TV. "Is that your grand plan to escape the clutches of your mafia family? To be a wedding planner?"

I turned up the volume.

"Project management. That's how you plan to escape the gangster life?" Connor asked, standing in front of the screen. He tossed back his whiskey and placed the crystal glass on the shelf beside him.

Then, he lifted another remote and turned the TV off.

Goddamn him.

Heat was blazing from my face.

"What do you want me to do, Connor? I've had two years'

work experience, and I've got a business degree. I don't have any money to invest, and just about my entire trust is going to you after we get married. At least I'm trying."

Despite his cruel judgement, I liked the idea of creating weddings. I'd been obsessed with them all my life, and now with my experience creating events and working with Bloom Events, the idea felt fun.

I'd been involved with some of the best events in NYC working with Donna, which accounted for something. She didn't do weddings, so she might want to expand or consider a partnership of some kind.

I had ideas.

Well, they were forming, and I had time to put things in motion.

Connor's criticism had been horribly unwelcome.

He was right about one thing, though; I wasn't sure how I was going to retain my freedom after we divorced, but I was going to try.

There wasn't an instruction manual for this.

"How about asking my advice? I might know a thing or two about creating businesses. I own twenty-fucking-five of them. I could help you," Connor growled, crossing his arms. "Ever think of that?"

No.

"That wasn't part of our deal. Just forget it. I promised I'd be out of your hair when our agreement ends. So, it's not your problem."

Connor stood glaring at me for several moments and shook his head. "Draw up your plan, and I will take a look at it."

"No," I snapped. "I want to do this on my own."

"Mia!" he yelled, and I had almost jumped. "I'm not letting you leave this house or marriage with nothing but the boxes you arrived with. If you need—want—to create a profitable business, then that's what we will do."

We?

I pressed my lips together, and we glared at one another.

"I'm not your responsibility."

He then walked over to me and pulled me to my feet. One hand brushed the hair from my forehead, the other one cupping my face. "I've decided you are."

Then he turned and walked away.

It was that night I realized I am in trouble.

I am falling for this man.

"THANK YOU FOR meeting me, Mia.

"You're my father. Of course, I'll have lunch with you," I reply, kissing him on the cheek before sitting down opposite him in the Michelin-star restaurant.

I didn't tell Connor Dad asked me to lunch, but George is standing nearby, and two other men are at the door. I'm pretty sure he knows by now, but I turned my phone to silent.

I may want to get out of the family business and all its archaic rules, but I love them. I love my father.

I don't love that I'm lying to him. He's been asking for a decision on whether I want our ceremony to be held at the Mancini Mansion on Long Island.

Your mom would've wanted you to, one of his texts said.

Ugh. Guilt is weighing heavily on me.

Not just that. Getting married at the house is something I wanted, but not for my fake wedding. Which I clearly can't tell anyone about.

I came close to telling Sienna so many times. I have no one to talk to. But I know if I did, it would be too risky, and she would talk me out of it.

"You seem happy," she said earlier this week. "Is this what being in love does? Maybe I *do* want a boyfriend, then."

"Highly recommend it." I grinned.

Love?

I'm not sure what I felt about Connor. I know my feelings aren't platonic. I know I really like him—I mean, he's Connor Barrett—but it's more than just *like*.

Despite the layers of rippling muscle, his dark, moody eyes, and the way he feels inside me, I enjoy his company.

Even when he's trying to ignore me and be all broody and dark, his eyes follow me. Or he'll throw a blanket over me. Or let me choose the TV channel.

He feels like it's something.

I just hope I'm not imagining it because I've stupidly convinced myself there's a chance this could turn into something real.

Which I know is a recipe for disaster.

I pick up the menu and focus on lunch.

"I see he has you well-protected," my father says, glancing behind me at George. Four of his own men are at different spots in the restaurant, and two are outside.

I know exactly how to spot them.

My eyes follow his to where George stands, and I nod. "Oh, yeah. You don't have to worry about me. Connor takes security very seriously."

We place our orders and watch the server fill our glasses with wine. I plan to have half a glass, as we are busy working on another big event at Bloom Events, and Donna is watching me closely.

She asked if I was going to resign now I'm engaged to Connor —something she was shocked about, just like everyone else in my life. What she didn't ask about was my roots. As in, being a Mancini. Whether she knew or is just respecting my privacy, I don't know, but I really appreciate it.

I told her I am absolutely not resigning and am fully committed. I need that job, despite Connor's billions and the two black credit cards in my purse.

"Are you sure you want to do this, Mia?" Papa asks, then holds up a large palm. "Hear me out. I love you, *mia faglia,* but have you questioned why this man wants to marry you?"

I blanch.

"Sorry?"

"We are a powerful family. I taught you to be street smart, Mia. Can you truthfully tell me this man loves you?"

No. No, I can't.

Because he doesn't.

I wave the Rock of Gibraltar at him and grin. "Exhibit A."

He frowns, and my smile dims.

"Papa, I know you don't like him—"

"I don't trust him," Joe says firmly. "There are many reasons why a man would want to marry you. He may be rich, but money is not the only thing a man might be after."

I stare at him silently as they deliver our mains.

Little does he know, it was me who asked Connor to marry me, but my father's words have planted a seed of doubt.

What would Connor want?

"Just think about it, Mia. If you believe he is the man you want to spend your life with, then I will accept it. And then we must discuss the venue. You will marry at home. It was your mother's wish. And I know it is yours."

I sigh.

I'm sure momma would be ashamed of me if she knew what I was doing, and as I take my third large gulp of my wine—there goes my plan to only drink half—I know I have to do as my father asks.

With choice comes consequences.

Perhaps by July, Connor will fall in love with me, and this will all be a funny story we never tell another soul. A crazy romantic story about how we met and fell in love.

Or I'll be nursing a broken heart, while he cashes my one-point-five-million-dollar check and waves me farewell.

I take another sip.

What am I doing?

27

CONNOR

My arms wobble as I press the bar up to the ceiling. I added an extra forty pounds of weight this morning. The twenty minutes I ran on the treadmill did nothing to appease the tension in my body.

Mia is in the shower, and all I want to do is go in there and spend hours pleasuring both of us, but I need to distance myself from her.

Not physically.

Emotionally.

My feelings for her are both a distraction and a danger. I worry about her when she's not with me, despite trusting the men protecting her. Then I worry about her and her future when she is with me.

Worse, I fucking hate she's going to despise me when this all comes to an end. Because it will, and she will.

Mia is a surprise.

A gorgeous, sexy, delicious, and addictive fucking surprise.

I want to keep her *and* get rid of her.

Last night, we attended an event. Cameras were flashing as we stepped out of the limo. Mia's long red dress showed off her slim, toned, and tanned legs. Her beautiful white smile a favorite of the American public, so my media team told me.

I prefer it wrapped around my cock, but whatever.

All night, she was the perfect date. Aside from the fact every asshole in the room tried to flirt with her, Mia stayed on my arm, said the right things, and then on the way home in the limo, I lifted her dress, pushed her thighs apart, and made her scream with my tongue.

She was under instruction to take off her panties before we left the venue and was wet as fuck by the time the car door closed.

Then she asked if we could go for a walk before going home.

Mack instructed Benson to stop at Central Park, and we climbed out, security trailing behind us discretely.

"I've got too much energy. I'll never sleep," Mia said. "One too many glasses of champagne, obviously."

Then she took off her shoes and skipped along the path, turning and dancing backward, telling me about the latest ideas she had for her business. The one I am helping her with because, apparently, I can't help myself with this woman.

"I'm useless with names, so I might get Sienna to help me, but I was thinking we could start building a website and social media channels now. I could create vision boards of weddings so people could see what to expect. Perhaps we could have some themes we already offer. Prepackaged stuff. They could be cheaper, you know. And then if they want something more custom, we will quote."

It took everything in me not to smile. I liked what she was saying, and it was clear Mia has quite the business mind. Something else that makes her sexy to me.

Everything is sexy.

Even when she brushes her damn teeth.

Mia's spirit, her unbreakable positive attitude and energy, feel like the light to my darkness. She balances me.

That night, though, with her hair twisted up, showing off her silky neck and the fresh blush from her orgasm, Mia was absolutely beautiful.

While I walked along that path, still tasting her on my mouth, I imagined the moment Mia discovers what my true objective with her is. I saw in my mind the hurt in her eyes.

It was the first time anything had even slightly given me pause. It infuriated me.

I deserve to avenge my family.

Mia doesn't deserve this.

"How about Lux-The-Knot?" she asked, while I fought my inner demons. She danced back to me, those big ice-blue eyes glittering in the moonlight. "Is it silly? You know, Lux for *luxury*. And obviously, The Knot, like tie the knot."

I smiled despite myself.

"I'm not your target market. Ask your girlfriends," I replied and tucked her arm in mine. I saw her excitement fade when I glanced down, so I added. "But your ideas are good."

Because Mia's happiness is fucking important to me.

God fucking damn it.

When she smiled again, I knew I was fucked.

As we crossed one of the bridges, I shot the men behind me a quick glance, and they retreated. Then I crowded her with my arms up against the railing.

"Put them into your plan, and we will review it this weekend. Don't leap ahead. Remember what I said..."

"Strategy first. Then action," she mocked. "Now, kiss me, Connor Barrett. I can't wait another second."

Fuck.

My mouth descended, and Mia wrapped her arms around my neck, like we were two lovers.

Were we?

The answer was so damn close to yes. I took her home and fucked her for hours. All night, I tried to think of a way to keep her. The conclusion: impossible.

So today, it is time for boundaries. To protect us both.

I need to gain Joe Mancini's trust fast because the longer I spend in this fake relationship, the harder it is to remember Mia is *not* mine and why I'm doing it.

As I realize my priorities are being manipulated by her, I drop the weights and sit, wiping my face with my towel and letting out a curse. If I don't get my shit together, Mia is going to fuck up everything. Her and her goddamn magic pussy.

Am I going to let the daughter of a gangster get in the way of me avenging my family's murders?

No.

I toss the towel on the floor and march down to the bedroom, just as Mia exits the bathroom, wearing only a towel.

I ignore her gorgeous half-naked body.

Mostly.

"We should have dinner with your father this weekend. Set it up," I snap and walk past her to the shower.

No more distractions.

TWENTY MINUTES LATER, I pack my briefcase and shove the emergency phone into the front pocket. I'm meeting the Dark Kings tonight. It's the first time I will see or speak to Nathan since the dinner in Long Island at the Mancini's two weeks ago. I know both he and Decker will have questions.

I slip on my jacket, take one last look at the photos on the wall, including Mia's, and walk out of my office.

Mia is leaning against the wall outside.

I freeze. "What are you doing here?"

"I live here. What's in the room?" she asks, swiping on her phone. "Some kind of sexy kink room?

I snort.

"You wish. It's my office. Stay out of it," I reply, not that she can get in. I let the door close behind me and then turn to punch the code in.

I could've put one of the biometric locks on it, but cutting out my eyeball is a lot easier than torturing a pin code out of me. At least, that was my thinking when I outfitted the penthouse.

"Isn't George waiting for you?" I ask as she follows me down the hall. I grab my keys and wallet from the hall table and turn when she doesn't answer.

"I'm taking a sick morning," Mia replies.

"Are you sick?" I ask, hating how concerned I am.

She shrugs.

"Just need a morning to myself. I'll be fine. Girl stuff."

I study her for a moment. She's been through a huge life change recently, and while I know she doesn't have her period, she might be premenstrual.

Things I know nothing about.

So, I nod.

"Fair enough. I'll be late tonight. Let me know when your family wants to meet," I say and stand there.

Waiting.

When she walks past me and simply says, *sure thing,* I clench my teeth. I'm used to Mia tiptoeing up, placing a hand on my chest, and kissing me goodbye with that smile of hers. Then saying, *have a good day, fake fiancé.*

Fuck.

I force myself to walk out the door and focus on my day. I even walk to the elevator and press the button, but I can hear her naked feet walking behind me across the floor, so I turn and find she's done the same. Mia's staring at me with a glass of water in her hand, her phone in the other.

She waits for me to say something, and I don't.

Mia was right all along—she's not mine, and she never will be. When this is over, she'll forget about me. I am a means to an end for her. As she is for me.

Nothing more.

"Have a good day," she says, then pads away.

The elevator opens and I curse, stepping inside. By the time

I'm in the back of the car and Mack slips into the front seat, instructing Benson of my first appointment and the address, I'm cursing more.

I upset her.

I shouldn't have been so tactless about asking to see her family. Besides being rude, it may have raised a question in her mind.

I press a button on my phone.

"Good morning, Mr. Barrett," Lilly says when she answers.

"Send a dozen white roses to Mia. She's at home today," I say. "Add chocolate."

Don't women love chocolate at that time of the month?

Mack half turns, and I lift my brows. I catch his smile before he pivots back.

"Yes, sir. Any particular kind?"

"Lilly, I pay you to know this stuff," I growl.

"Leave it with me," she says, unfazed, and I take a mental note to give her a huge bonus for putting up with me.

As I do every quarter.

I stare out the window as we drive through Manhattan and can't fight the instinct something is wrong. This is why I shouldn't have let my feelings get involved. I can't decipher whether I'm concerned about Mia's well-being or if there's something I've missed.

What I do know is, my feelings for her are far stronger than I'm admitting. After the meeting tonight with Decker and Nathan, I'm going to move her into the guest room.

Sleeping with her was the wrong decision, and while it will weaken my argument for being in this agreement, I'll find a way around that.

Falling for my enemy's daughter is a big fucking mistake.

28

MIA

We should have dinner with your father this weekend. Set it up.

Asshole.

I might not be the head of the Mancini mafia, like my father or my brother, but I grew up surrounded by some of the most powerful and influential mobsters on the planet.

And while I might not want to be a part of the mafia business, I'm not stupid.

The thoughts nagging me for the past few days since having lunch with my father start to get loud. He wants something more from me than just sex, I'm sure of it. Me or my family?

After demanding to see my father, I'm sure it has something to do with my family.

I'm hurt and angry with myself for thinking our relationship is more than it is. A contract. But I'm determined to find out what his secret is. Starting with what's inside his locked-up office.

Like I say, I'm not stupid.

Mobsters are a lot of things, including thieves, so I know a lot of ways to get inside places.

While Connor thought I was scrolling on my phone, I was

videoing him. A trick I learned while listening to two of my body-guards several years ago.

I'm not sure if it worked, or if I got the angle right, but when I press play on the video and pinch the screen to zoom in, I know it's right.

"Yes!" I whisper, despite no one being here.

George is downstairs, waiting for me. He doesn't know I'm not going into the office. Well, I am, but I'll go in a little later.

I lied to Connor. But then again, I think he's lying to me, and I'm not going to sit around any longer and let it continue. There might be nothing but boring office stuff, but I find it weird he has it so locked up when he lived by himself.

Curiosity killed the cat, and I'm about to find out.

I watch the video a few times, then punch in a combination. Nope. I try another one. Nope.

On the third try, it clicks.

Shit.

Am I doing this?

Once I cross the line, there's no turning back.

Connor may just want his privacy, or have highly commercially sensitive Barrett Enterprise information in here. No. Everything is digital these days—that's no excuse.

I don't know what I'm going to find, but I'm hoping it's not a kink room. Connor might not be my real fiancé, but knowing he's done dirty things to women in a secret sex room he hasn't invited me into somehow irks me.

Then again, maybe it's just a boring office.

I'm well aware a man like Connor wouldn't marry a woman like me. A shrewd and gorgeous businessman would marry a lawyer or some classy woman who owns an art gallery, or a duchess from England.

Not the daughter of a mobster.

So, why?

Is he the type of man who sees me as an opportunity to manipulate my family? Or plan to hurt them?

I rub my arms as the hair on them stands on end.

Would Connor do that?

Is my father right?

If there are answers behind this door, I need to know. I turn the door handle and push it open.

My mouth drops open.

It takes me a minute to realize what I am staring at as I take a few more steps.

I stand there, my eyes roaming in horror. When I see my photo, bile rises, and I throw my hand over my mouth.

Then run.

29

CONNOR

The backslapping and man hugs happen the moment I walk in the door of the Dark Kings headquarters. I had an abandoned warehouse converted into a highly secure space, with an office, kitchen area, punching bag, and pool table.

On the wall is the same CSI-type setup I have at home. Photos everywhere, with white boards where we brainstorm leads.

The biometric security allows entry to only me, Decker, Nathan, and Mack and is under twenty-four-seven surveillance by one of the best security companies in America.

Which I own.

We spent the most time here before the boys went out into the field and began infiltrating the Italian and Mexican mafias.

Damn, I miss hanging out with these assholes.

"Dude. What the fuck are you getting yourself into?" Decker asks, flopping into a chair and twisting the cap off a beer bottle.

Mack makes some, fortunately for him, indecipherable mumble from his leaning spot by the window. Nathan smirks at him.

Fuckers.

I can't decide if they think I'm insane—which is most likely—

or their attitude has something to do with Mia. Which irritates me more than I want to admit.

Especially after a long day of not hearing from her. She hasn't responded to my delivery of roses, and George says she hasn't left the apartment all day.

Maybe she really is sick.

The magnetic pull to leave and go home to her frustrates me. Tonight is important, and I'm worried her damn PMS?

She never ignores me, so I can only assume she's angry at my tone. I reacted out of frustration for my growing feelings and fucked up. Big time. Angry Mia isn't going to be organizing a family catch-up, especially when I haven't given her a reason for wanting to see them.

That could've confused her and was likely a mistake on my behalf. One I need to rectify, reasoning it out with something along the lines of needing to keep up appearances with her father and the media. Which I could've fucking said if I stopped thinking about those icy blue eyes and her sweet pussy and how they're distracting me.

I dropped her a text before climbing out of the car, and now my phone is in front of me, and I feel like a goddamn schoolboy waiting for a reply.

Wait up for me tonight. We need to talk. C

It's just sitting there with no response. Unread. I'm going to slam my cock into her so damn hard after she's ignored me all day.

Twice now.

Decker stares at me, waiting for an answer to his question.

"The opportunity fell in my lap," I say, remembering how Mia had lain *on* my lap a few nights ago as I palmed her sweet, tanned ass.

God, she was moist as fuck.

"Direct access to Joe Mancini is not something I was willing to say no to," I add.

"You couldn't just fuck her and go to family dinners?"

Decker laughs, lifting his foot onto his knee and taking a swig out of his bottle. He looks dangerous as hell in his gangster getup. Black jeans, steel-capped boots, a black shirt open and showing his vast array of tattoos—which are also visible along his forearm where his shirt is rolled up. Dark glasses on his head.

On his hands are a number of silver and black rings. One of them represents his position in the Costilla Cartel, where he's spent the last six years. Predominantly based in Sinaloa, Mexico.

"She's a sweet piece of ass," Nathan says, tossing Mack a beer.

Mack catches it and shakes his head, throwing it back. Tonight, he's driving.

Meanwhile, I'm counting to ten in my head so I don't pull out the Glock tucked into the back of my pants and shoot Nathan, the asshole.

He's taunting me. Waiting for a reaction. He won't get it. Okay, he might get it.

Fuck!

"Her brother is planning a coup. Cade Mancini is close to making a move, and it turns out Mia is one of his pawns." I explain.

Nathan flicks his cap into a trash can. "He's partnered up with Salvo 'Sly' Vitale."

Decker curses. "Let me guess, Salvo gets the sister for his help with putting Cade in the top job."

Nathan nods darkly.

"So, you what, proposed to save the mafia princess? What the hell am I missing here?" Decker asks, his humor fading. "Because you being so close to Mancini puts Nathan in a tenuous position, Barrett."

I fucking know.

"And if someone figures it out and starts talking, then starts to look at your marine buddies, I'm fucked too," he adds.

He's right, but I took the risk anyway.

These gangsters won't mess about either. They'll shoot

someone they suspect without digging deeper or waiting for an explanation.

If they did, it's only because they're playing with their food.

I curse. "Look, it's been six fucking years. I can't ask you guys to stay in there much longer. If you want to get out now, do it."

"You're not asking. I'm exactly where I need to be," Nathan growls, finishing his beer and tossing it in the same trash can as the cap. Then he crosses the room to a sofa and sits. His legs wide, his hands dropping to his hips.

The tan holster over his black shirt presses into his muscular frame, a gold chain around his neck visible over his tats. He pulls out one of his Glocks and places it on the sofa next to him. Then sighs.

We're all quiet.

Nathan's brother was a victim of the Italian mafia. Killed because he couldn't pay for the drugs one of the assholes gave him without permission.

He wants revenge as much as me.

But it's a long game, and a dangerous one.

I turn back to Decker. "Mia told her father we were engaged the night after we met. Nothing to do with me. She wants her freedom. I took the opportunity that was laid out on a silver damn platter."

"Night they fucked," Mack helpfully corrects.

Nathan snorts.

I glare at both of them.

It's becoming increasingly difficult to see her as just someone I fuck.

"Why would she do that?" Deck asks.

"She doesn't want to go into the business. She loves her family, but the shit they do doesn't sit well with her." I can hear myself from their point of view, but I don't stop talking. "She wants her freedom and has business ideas. Once I get the information I'm after, I'll help her set up a new life."

The silence is deafening.

"Jesus," Nathan says, shaking his head.

Decker stares at me.

"She'll hate you, Connor," Mack says. "If you destroy her family, especially her father, she will hate you passionately."

My jaw tightens. *I fucking know!*

"Are you in love with her?" Decker asks, rearing back like I'm the devil.

Maybe I am.

The entire plan seemed like a good idea a few weeks ago. Using her is just not sitting well with me anymore. Mia is innocent. Yet I can't turn back now.

Or can I? Maybe I should set her free. We'll end the engagement.

Would I?

"No. Fuck, no," I reply, not believing my own words. Jesus, no. *No.* "Look, I'm just saying Mia doesn't deserve to be collateral damage." I sound defensive.

"Just a pawn, like her family uses her?" Nathan says.

I stand, fisting my hands on the table and glaring across the room at him.

"Do you want to fuck her? Is that what this is?" I growl, and he slowly raises his brows, unaffected by my aggression. "Then keep your fucking eyes off her next time."

"He's in love with her," Mack says, shaking his head.

I snarl at him.

"Fuck off. I'm trying to work out how to use this situation to our advantage without hurting an innocent. We don't know if Carlos is part of the Italian mob. Until I do, we stay on script. Cade needs to be our focus right now, not where my cock is going." I sit down.

They all stare at me like I'm an idiot.

I am.

"He's right. We need to stop him," Nathan says. "He's still got plans to nab her. If our guys hadn't been in the bar that night, he would've dragged her out of there."

The hair on the back of my neck rises. I know that was his plan, but to hear Nathan speak the words sends ice through me.

"He touches her, he's dead," I say without thinking.

Decker shakes his head and stands up. "And this is why it's a fucking stupid idea. Break it off. Fuck her on the side, or whatever you need to do, but keep away from Joe and Cade, or this is going to get ugly."

I curse.

"I can't. They'll marry her off to that cunt, Vitale." I run my hand angrily through my hair.

"I'll make sure it doesn't happen," Nathan says darkly. "I'll protect her."

The fuck you will.

She's mine, I say to myself, finally accepting how damn deep I am in this now.

"No."

All three of them glare at me.

Decker shakes his head again and walks to the pool table, leaning and crossing his arms.

"We need a game plan for when Cade makes his move. First, Decker, update us on the Mexicans. Any closer to Pablo Garcia?" I ask, referring to the head of the Mexican Cartel.

He rubs his forehead.

"Fine, we'll drop it for now. But yeah, I think I have a lead. Older guy, named Carlos, living in Eldorado. There are a few rumors that indicate he could be our guy. It'll take me some time to get to him."

What?

My eyes widen.

It's rare I get excited these days. Every single lead has been a dead one. Especially in Mexico, where there are about seven trillion million Carlos'.

An exaggeration, obviously.

"Fuck man, you couldn't have led with that?" I say, laughing, and the tension in the room lifts as Mack and Nathan join me.

An hour later, there's still no reply on my phone, and my heart rate is increasing. Something's wrong. Mia is not this stubborn.

I text George, and he confirms she hasn't left, but I'm ready to go.

Decker gave us a good, detailed rundown on what's happening across the border and their plans stateside. Nathan did the same with the Mancini mob. Some of it, including my plans to marry Mia—incoming family members, including influential mobsters from Sicily and Rome next month.

"Guess we're not standing up for you, huh," Decker says, shrugging.

These two are my best friends.

I can't imagine not having them with me while I make such a huge life decision. We've killed to protect each other while serving, and now, they have put their lives on hold to help me avenge my family.

Sure, they each have their own reasons for doing it, but every day, I remind myself how grateful and fucking lucky I am to know these two men.

And Mack.

We didn't serve together. He joined a few years after us, but when we met, just before I retired, I knew he was someone I could trust. We stayed in contact, then three years ago, he contacted me and said he wanted in.

I laughed at him and said I didn't know what he was talking about. The way he stared at me across the table we were having a drink at told me all I needed to know.

"You don't know what I'm doing."

"I know whatever it is, it's a worthy cause, and I'm fucking drifting out here. I need a purpose and know you're a good man," Mack said.

"I'm not," I replied honestly. I was a man full of rage with a need to destroy the people who fucked up my life by assassinating my family. Instead of growing up with parents, I was sent away to a boarding school full of rich assholes and strict teachers.

It had been pure hell.

No one had told me it was okay to grieve or be sad. All I had were my memories of their deaths, the dead looks in their eyes as I crawled out of the space under the stairs, and a detective who gave me a new life.

Detective Scott saved my life, but I was still left with the big question I wasn't sure I wanted the answer to.

Why?

No one knew about the boxes or the key.

"Yeah, you are, Barrett. Saying you're not just proves it," Mack said.

"Give me a week," I replied, and after checking with the other Dark Kings, we invited him into the group.

I never looked back.

He might look like my personal bodyguard, but Mack does a lot more than that. He recruits men into my security, manages them, is my direct link with Nathan, and so much more.

"It's not a real wedding or marriage," I remind them. "If this lead of yours works out, it may not happen."

Decker pulls on a jacket. "Connor, you know it doesn't happen that fast. It could, but I can't make any promises. So, prepare to marry your little mafia princess."

No one is marrying anyone unless she answers my fucking messages.

I didn't miss his wording either. *Your*. And they notice I didn't correct him.

I nod at Mack, and we make to leave.

"Regular updates on Cade," I say to Nathan, and he nods.

Then we climb into the car and drive home.

When I walk into the penthouse, I know immediately.

Mia is gone.

MIA

"Okay, so let me get this straight," Sienna says, eyeing the pint of ice cream I have on my lap. "Are you going to finish that entire thing?"

I nod.

Two of them, if she has another pint. I don't ask. This is serious, but I can't tell my best friend anything. I feel like my entire life is a jumble of lies.

Not one person knows the truth about me. Except Connor. And as it turns out, he's the one person I absolutely cannot trust.

I'm hurt, angry, and feeling betrayed.

And scared.

My belongings are still at Connor's penthouse, except the small bag I was packing when I rang George and told him I was staying home sick. Then I snuck down to the garage after mentioning I'd left something in one of Connor's cars—he would've seen the elevator move—and waited for a vehicle to leave.

Then snuck out on foot.

Longest twenty minutes of my life.

"Do you have more?" I ask with the spoon in my mouth, changing my mind. These are desperate times.

I can't stay here.

Sienna jumps up and returns, sitting opposite me, and puts a pint of Ben and Jerry's vanilla on the table in front of us.

I stare at her. "Vanilla? Who has vanilla?"

"It's for smoothies. Don't judge." She laughs.

I smile back, even though it's mostly forced.

Connor just texted me to say he wants to talk, which means he's going to be home in a few hours and doesn't yet know I'm not there.

George messaged a few hours ago to ask if I needed anything. I pretended I was fine and said I was just sleeping and watching movies.

No one has any reason to believe I'm not there.

Yet.

Once he sees his office door open, he'll know. Which was my bad. I should've closed it, but I was in a state of shock when I left.

Fuck, fuck, fuck.

What am I going to do?

Connor will know to look for me at Sienna's, though not Isabelle's or Duncan's. But I'm putting both of them in danger by going there, so I'm not sure what to do.

Hence the two pints of ice cream.

"We had a fight, that's all." I don't have the brainpower to come up with yet another set of lies.

"How serious?" Sienna asks.

Very.

Connor is using me to get to my family. Fortunately, I found out today, instead of a few months into this insane fake relationship.

I spoon the last scoop of double chocolate chip into my mouth and let out a moan.

"Pretty serious," I say. "I don't think it's going to work out. We rushed in."

Sienna bites the side of her mouth and nods. I'm impressed by how diplomatic she's being.

For a moment, I realize I miss this girl-talk time, despite my current circumstances and the fact I'm eating my bodyweight in dairy. She probably thinks I'm finally coming to my senses.

Maybe I am?

Who else has to get fake engaged to...whoever Connor Barrett is? Who the hell has their office wallpapered with images of mob families? Many of whom are *my* family members.

And me.

That is the cherry on top.

A big part of me wants to run home and confront him, but the images terrify me. There are a lot of people who would want to destroy my family. Apparently, Connor Barrett is one of them.

And I have feelings for him.

Did.

Right now, I hate him.

"You can stay here a few days, and perhaps whatever you fought about will start looking different by then," Sienna says. "But yeah, you've rushed in, so maybe this is a good thing."

Oh, it's definitely *not* a good thing.

"I can't stay here. He'll find me," I say, then realize what I just said.

Shit.

"Mia! Has he hurt you?" she asks, sitting bolt upright.

"No, no, I just...Connor is protective and bossy." And probably dangerous. I never once before today thought he'd hurt me, and it makes me want to burst into tears.

Sienna sees the look in my eyes and flies around the table, pulling me into her arms. I let the tears fall and sob. The hurt, the betrayal, and my fear all come rushing to the surface.

I thought he was going to help me build a business. I thought we were going to stand at the altar and promise each other forever. Or at least six months.

Instead, I made a deal with the devil.

"Oh, babe. I'm so sorry this has happened. Do you want to talk about it? Tell me?"

I shake my head.

My phone texts again, and I ignore it. Then Sienna releases me.

"Maybe you should talk to him. I've never seen you this upset."

Sniffing, I grab a tissue and wipe my eyes.

When I pull my phone out, I see it's from Cade.

Mia, I'm sorry I've been a dick. Can you stop ignoring my calls and talk to me?

I sniff.

Maybe I should go home.

It's not like they'll marry me off to Vitale overnight. I can speak to my father and make a new plan. I need to tell them about Connor. I can't keep this to myself. If something happens to them, I could never live with myself.

I make a decision.

You were a dick. I reply.

He sends a smiley face emoji. Then, *Meet me for a drink... 7pm.*

I frown.

It's probably my best choice. I can be home in Long Island tonight if I get Cade to take me. Father is currently in Manhattan, so I'd have a few days to think about things.

Plus, Connor can't touch me there.

The Silver Ring, Cade adds, and I reply, saying I will see him then.

I'll take a few days off, apologize to Donna, and then decide where to go with my life. My plan failed.

My stupid heart is broken.

"It's Cade." When I see her face, I smile. "Don't worry. He's apologized for the other night. He won't hurt me." I lift the phone to show her the message. "He's a self-confessed dick, but he loves me."

She flops back into the cushions. "Man, mafia families. It's so complex."

"You got that, all right," I say, flopping back with her. Then I sigh. "I wish my mom was alive. I miss her so much."

Sienna turns her head. "You can share my mom. You know she loves you."

I smile, my eyes tearing up again. "She's the best. Tell her I'm coming over soon for more of her brownies."

Then I sit up because I need to fix my life. "Can I have a shower and borrow a dress?"

"Of course."

"I'm going home to Long Island. Tell Donna I won't be in tomorrow, but I will call her and explain." I won't be telling her anything, but it buys me time to come up with lie number seven hundred and something.

"She won't be happy after you took today off," Sienna says, "but I'll tell her you're still sick for now."

I nod, then shower and dress for one of the nicest bars in NYC.

Why Cade wanted to meet there, I have no idea.

31

CADE

I drop my phone and smile. I knew Mia wouldn't stay mad at me for long. She's always been far too soft to be a Mancini.

Well, she won't be for much longer.

Soon, she'll be Mrs. Vitale.

I lift my head and glance around my penthouse. I see a handful of my men milling about, smoking, on their phones, feet kicked up, talking shit.

"Game on, boys," I say, and everyone turns to me.

"Tonight?" Dean asks.

"Yes, and where the fuck is Nathan?" I look around.

"He went out with a chick," Freddie says. "Which is a relief. I thought the guy was gay. Never fucks any of our broads."

Fuck's sakes.

"He can fuck a cow, for all I care. I need him here. I need all of you here. No one is to leave," I growl.

I type out a text, telling Nathan to get his ass back here. He's one of my top three guys right now. I handpicked them all because of their loyalty and skills. He's a hard ass motherfucker.

But I don't pay him—or rather, my father doesn't pay him—to get his dick sucked.

Is it urgent? This chick has skills, my man.

I'm not your fucking man, and yes, it's go time.

I'm going to kick his ass for questioning me, but I appreciate a woman with a good mouth, so I let it go for now. I'm too fucking excited it's finally happening.

Mia's engagement threw a spanner in the works, but she won't get away from me tonight. It's as good as done.

After tonight, I will be in charge of this city.

I will be the Don.

Nathan is still replying and taking his damn time.

...

...

The big move?

Yes. Ten minutes. Get your ass back here. Fucking now.

Next, I ring Vitale and let him know we're ready to go tonight. Mia will be his by the end of the night and not my problem.

"Good. I'll arrange the priest and expect you in a few hours," Salvo replies.

"Eight thirty at the latest," I add. "Get your men ready. When we move, we move fast."

Tonight, I kill my father.

32

CONNOR

"Goddamn it. Mia told me she was in bed, sick." George wipes his face with his palm over and over. "She never left."

Mack walks back in.

"She went out via the parking garage," he advises, thrusting the phone in my face, and I watch as Mia hid in the corner of the garage and then ran when the roller door began to close, after the car exited.

"Jesus Christ," I curse. It's been five minutes since I got home, or maybe six now, and every minute counts.

Mia knows my secret and could've exposed me.

Does Joe Mancini know? Is Nathan walking back into a trap?

There's nothing in my office which connects Decker or Nathan visually, but there are names.

How close did she look?

"Pull the video footage from inside my office. See what she did. What she looked at. Work out what she could've been focused on and thinking," I say to Mack, asking the impossible.

But this is what they trained us to do as marines, and it's better than standing around, flapping our lips.

He grabs a laptop off a nearby table and starts tapping. The

233

data is accessible from the cloud, and I know why he wants a bigger screen rather than his phone. He wants to watch her eyes.

"Fuck, I'm sorry, Connor," George says, even though he has no idea what's really going on.

Aside from my three Kings, no one knows my other venture or my true identity. Which is why I need him to leave, before he sees or hears anything more.

Usually, there would be no excuse for this type of oversight, and while part of me wants to throttle him and take out my anger at losing Mia on someone, I know George did nothing wrong.

I'm not willing to lose him over this.

"She's the daughter of a gangster. I underestimated her. This is on me," I growl.

It absolutely is.

I ignored my instincts, which I'll never do again.

I toss him a set of keys. "Go pull the Maserati around. Park out front. I'll be down in five."

"Yes, sir," he says.

Next minute, Mack has the video casting on the huge screen on the wall in the living room. We stand shoulder to shoulder, watching Mia walk into my office.

God, I feel sick seeing her in there.

I cross my arms, then run a hand over my chin nervously.

She freezes, and while the video isn't good enough quality to see, I imagine the blood draining from her face. Then she's looking at the section where her family is displayed.

Her hand flies to her mouth.

I curse.

Then she runs out.

Mack pauses the video and turns to me. "How the hell did she get in?"

"I don't know," I say, shaking my head. Then I work it out and curse again, sharing what I think happened. "She videoed me punching in the keys while pretending to be a sassy little bitch."

Jesus, I'm impressed.

He smirks. "Sorry, but that's quite badass."

I afford myself a smile. "Yeah, it is."

But now, everything has changed. She knows enough to hate me, to fuck up everything I've worked for my entire life, and to probably put a hit out on me by two mobs.

If she talks.

Mia's smart, but I know she has feelings for me. Genuine feelings. I've been trying to fight hers and mine. Now I need to acknowledge them because it could be the one thing that saves my life.

I've got the best security team in the damn world, but if two of the most dangerous mafias want me dead, they'll eventually succeed.

I have a backup plan. Of course, I do. You don't fuck with the mafia without having one. But if I'm going to activate it, I need to make a call very soon.

It will mean leaving behind my entire life and business.

"What are we doing?" Mack asks.

He knows I'm contemplating Plan B and is thinking the same things I am, but I doubt he's worried about how Mia is feeling. Despite the risk to my life, I hate she's hurting right now.

She feels betrayed and confused.

I know that woman. She want answers and feels alone, feels like she can't trust anyone.

Which is true.

She shouldn't trust me.

But she can.

With her life. Not her family.

I walk to the floor-to-ceiling glass window overlooking Manhattan and go through several scenarios in my head. It's likely she went to Sienna's. She won't go home. Not immediately.

"Ask George where Sienna lives," I say to Mack. "Meet me downstairs."

He nods as I go change. I quickly remove my suit and pull on a pair of blue Prada denim jeans and a black T-shirt. Then add a black leather jacket. It's not cold, but if things turn ugly, I want some protection.

I open my vault and pull out a handful of weapons, checking them with a click or two, then slide them into my pockets and into the back of my jeans.

I add a black Yankee's cap at the last minute, then grab my phone and head downstairs.

"Got the address. Who's driving?" Mack asks, as George waves farewell for the night and walks off down the sidewalk. Likely heading to the subway to go home.

Or a bar, after the night he's had.

"You." I move to the passenger door. "Whatever happens in the next few hours, I want you to make sure Nathan is protected," I tell him. "Forget me. I have a Plan B. I will contact you when it's safe. Nathan is your priority."

He pulls away from the curb with a *fuck this*.

I pull my phone out of my pocket as we drive through the NYC streets and text Nathan. He needs to know what's happening, and I'm giving him the same instructions but to protect Mia.

Despite whatever decision she has made in the past few hours, she *is* still innocent.

My phone beeps as I'm unlocking it.

CODE RED. Nathan texts before I can even start typing.

Mack's phone goes off beside me.

Fuck.

None of us have used that code before.

I dial.

"He has her," Nathan says at once. "I'm on my way there now. They have a priest."

What the fuck?

He's talking about Cade and taking an enormous risk by telling me. If he gets caught breaking omertà, the mob's sacred code of silence, he'll be dead the next second.

Adrenaline bursts through my body, and I start to piece everything together, my heart pounding in my chest.

"No more contact," Nathan says before I can speak.

"Stop. Nathan!" I yell, and when there is only silence, I keep talking, hoping like hell he's still on the phone. "She knows. She saw my office."

"Fuck," I hear him curse, then he hangs up.

Mack slows for the red light, and we share a dark look.

"Get to Sienna's, fast." We need to find her, and Sienna is the only one who may know where they went and where she might be.

Fuckkkkkk.

I stare out in the night as we drive, my jaw tense and trigger finger itching. It feels like my entire life has brought me to this point. To this woman. I'm getting Mia back and saving her from Salvo Vitale.

Nobody is marrying her or touching her but me.

The rest, we will sort out.

33

MIA

I walk into The Silver Ring and glance around the luxury bar. It's busy, but I spot Cade quickly. He's sitting at the bar, looking all kinds of mafia royalty.

He's wearing one of his best suits—Armani, by the looks—and is drinking a martini. On his wrist sits a huge timepiece, and his hair is slicked back.

Cade slides a cosmopolitan cocktail a few inches along the marble bar when he sees me. Standing, he kisses both my cheeks. "Mia, thank you for forgiving me. Sit, please."

"You didn't need to get dressed up for me," I say, running my hands along the green dress Sienna loaned me. We're the same size but with different shaped bodies. The material is cheap, but I don't care. It's the cowlneck which is bothering me—it shows off way too much boob than I would like. Especially for a drink with my brother.

Connor would growl.

Fuck Connor.

Cade studies me. "Sister, you look a little pale. Are you unwell?"

May as well stick to one set of lies. "Yes, I've been feeling off today."

"Not pregnant, I hope," he says, staring at me closer.

God, I hope not. I take my birth control religiously. But I can't help the twinge of emotion flickering at the edges of my consciousness when I imagine having Connor's baby.

Imagine him holding my hand as I birth it and the joy on his face.

The fucking traitor.

"I know you don't like Connor," I say, thinking he saw something when I didn't. Just as my father had. "But please, don't bash him tonight. I'm not in the mood."

He raises both his hands.

"Hey, fine. The fiancé is off the menu," Cade says, dropping them. "How's work, then?"

I narrow my eyes. He's trying too hard. I glance around and then ask, "What do you want, Cade? Is this really about apologizing?"

He laughs. "I'm trying to be a good brother."

Taking a sip of my cosmo, I sigh.

I need to chill out and stop mistrusting everyone. I'm losing my mind—can't even have a drink with my brother without thinking the worst.

"Sorry, I'm just not feeling that well." I take another big sip because damn, I need this alcohol right now. Ice cream didn't help at all, except for making me all bloated.

As the liquor takes hold, I relax and remind myself I need Cade's help to get home. If I use my cards, Connor will track me.

"Can I ask you a favor without you making a big deal out of it?"

Cade nods once. "What is it? Anything."

I relax further, feeling safe for the first time in hours. I should've known I could rely on my family. They're the only people you can really trust.

Even if they are mafia.

"I need to go home. To Long Island," I tell him. "Tonight. Can you arrange transport for me? Or drive me?"

He glances around the room, and his brows drop.

"Mia, where is your security?" Cade asks. "Don't you have a driver?"

Oh, that.

"Gave them the night off," I mumble, taking another sip.

He knows I'm lying.

"Sure. Wherever you want to go, Mia. I'll take you."

"Thanks," I reply with a smile and finish my drink. I decide I can have another one before leaving the city. Now, I'm safe, so I slide my glass toward the bartender, hoping to catch his eye.

Then the room wobbles.

"You okay there, sis?" Cade stands, and his hand lands on my hip.

I stare up at him and find a cold, dark expression that looks nothing like my brother.

Oh God.

No!

"What have you done?" I ask, my words coming out drunk.

"Sorry, Mia. Things are about to change." Cade lifts his head and nods to someone.

The world is a fuzz. I hear *she's had too much to drink,* and I'm led out of the bar, then feel myself being placed into a vehicle.

He drugged me.

My fucking brother drugged me.

I feel my body tremble as I go in and out of consciousness.

Where are they taking me?

Despite what I saw today, the only person I want suddenly is Connor. I know without a shred of doubt he would kill my brother and every single man responsible for this abduction.

And I know I will never see his face again.

34

CONNOR

Sienna visibly reacts when she opens the door to her apartment, which is how I know Mia was there.

"What—"

"Someone has kidnapped Mia. You can either let me in and answer my questions so I can find her before she's seriously harmed, or I can call the police," I growl in my most intimidating voice.

I'm not going to call the police. It won't help, and I don't have time to fuck around here.

Sienna steps aside and I walk in, followed by Mack.

"Oh my God, do you know where she is?" Sienna cries, her hand still gripping the door.

Mack peels it off and closes it behind him.

"No, but you might. Where did she go when she left here?" I ask.

Sienna blinks at us, and I guess we're probably intimidating, filling up the small apartment she lives in. This is the first time we've met, but I don't have time for niceties.

"Sienna," I press.

"Umm, ahh, she went to meet her brother. She said you had a

fight." Sienna's eyes dart around the room. "That she was going to go home to Long Island."

And her brother said he'd take her?

"Where was she meeting her brother?" Mack asks.

Sienna rubs her forehead. "Shit, um, she didn't tell me. In Manhattan. Obviously. Oh God, this isn't helping."

I lead her to the sofa to sit down and spot Mia's T-shirt lying over a cushion.

Fuck. The need to find her is making me lose focus. Who knows what that psycho Vitale will do to her. If his cock goes anywhere near her, I'll slice the fucking thing off before I slit his throat.

"Sit. Take a breath and try to think about what she might have said," I reply.

Mack picks up the T-shirt. He recognizes it, just as I have.

"She got changed. Why?" he asks. Like me, he's trained to think critically and guide witnesses or hostages to remember information.

Sienna stares at the T-shirt. "Ummm, shit, where. Think, Sienna. Think.

"Take your time," I tell her, meaning the opposite.

"Yes. Yes, she, ahhh, she changed into my dress because it's fancy—" She begins clicking her fingers and pointing at Mack. "The Silver...Silver."

I know at once where she means. I've been there a handful of times.

"The Silver Ring. It's a bar in midtown. When did she leave?" I glance at Mack, and he's pulling up the address on his phone.

"Ten minutes away," he says.

"When did she leave?" I ask Sienna again as I stand.

"Twenty minutes ago." Sienna wraps her arms around her middle. "Is she going to be all right? Oh my God, Mia. You will find her, won't you?"

Absolutely, and anyone trying to stop me will wish they hadn't.

"Yes. Mia belongs to me. I'm going to bring her home," I say, then nod to Mack. "Let's go."

As we race down the stairs, relieved we have a lead, I know this is just the beginning of a long night. Finding Mia is just one piece of the puzzle.

I've been toying with an idea since we left my penthouse. It's insane, but it might work.

Or it'll backfire.

First, because I have no idea if Mia has told anyone about what she saw. Sienna didn't mention it, but that doesn't mean anything. It's unlikely she would compromise her friend.

Mia loves Sienna. I know that.

But she may have told her brother and her father.

So, this is a risk I need to decide if I'm willing to take. My heart is slamming into my chest every moment I don't have her in my arms, and I know my priorities have shifted in the past hour.

I'm about to make a life-changing decision.

One that could mean the end of my life.

Or win the trust of the one man who could give me the answers I've been searching for.

The power, ironically, will lie in the hands of the woman I love. The daughter of my enemy.

Mia Mancini.

We pull up outside The Silver Ring, and I turn to Mack. "Get hold of Nathan, while I go in and see if they are still here. Find out where he is."

"Got it," he says.

He doesn't say anything about the call he just heard me make, except for a handful of curses and shakes of his head as I was talking.

"And Mack, don't tell him about the conversation I just had. He needs to be in the dark on this."

Mack nods.

Not because I don't trust Nathan, but if someone tapped his phone, this is far too important to risk. Nathan is trained to adapt, and he'll figure it out.

I climb out and pull my cap down as I walk into the bar. I glance around at the well-dressed patrons, looking for Mia. Her long hair, her beautiful ice-blue eyes. That smile.

She's not here.

"Mr. Barrett." The manager greets me with a handshake, and I see the question in his eyes at my attire. It's Friday night in Manhattan, and they're used to seeing me in a Tom Ford suit or tuxedo, not jeans.

"Evening. I'm looking for my fiancé. I was hoping to surprise her this evening," I say, knowing she's as recognizable as me right now.

He nods.

"Yes, Ms. Mancini was in here earlier with another gentleman."

"Her brother," the bartender says, wiping his towel along the bar, having overheard our conversation. "He took her home."

No, he fucking didn't. But he's taken Mia somewhere, and I will find him.

"This early?" I ask, playing along.

The bartender smiles. "She had a little too much to drink, sir." Then his smile disappears. "Not here. She only had the one cosmo."

The asshole. Her brother fucking drugged her. Urgency races down my spine like a sharp knife.

I force a smile. "What a shame I missed her. People are so hard to surprise these days."

"Let us know when you next want to visit, and we will organize you a good table, Mr. Barrett."

"Thank you."

I'm one hundred percent sure Mia will never want to come

back here. And I'm only one percent sure she will ever want to see me again after today.

But I'm going to fight for her.

First, I have to find her.

35

MIA

The world is made of marshmallows. I never knew that.

You're drugged.

My head sways back and forth, like one of those bobble guys people stick on the dashboard of a car. Am I a bobble person?

Stay awake.

"Bring Mia inside and take her out the back," Cade says, but it sounds more like *bwiiing hurrrr emsideee…*

Wait.

Where are we?

I try to blink and draw in some deep breaths as my arms are gripped and someone half drags me somewhere.

"Cwade," I try to call out but can barely speak.

No one replies.

Suddenly, there are loud voices all around me, and I'm shoved onto a soft surface. A sofa. Oh, yes, I can curl up and go to sleep.

Don't sleep, Mia. Run.

"So, this is my bride," a man says. But it doesn't sound right.

I'm Connor's bride.

That's not Connor's voice.

I start to panic. Where is he? He needs to help me.

"Cwonner, cwona," I moan, trying to lift my hand.

"Jesus, did you have to drug her so much? Talk about a hit to my ego." The man laughs.

"You want to marry my sister, then here she is," Cade says.

No, no, I'm marrying Connor.

"Of course, I want to marry her. Hot piece of ass, she is," the man replies, and I feel him cup my breast. Then he grunts. "Put your fist away, Mancini. In less than twenty minutes, she'll be my wife and mine to do with as I please."

No.

I try to lift my head, but it keeps flopping onto my chest.

"Cwadeee." My voice is barely audible, even to me.

"Shut her up," Cade says to someone, and they put their hand over my mouth.

Oh God.

No. This can't be happening. Why is he doing this?

Where is my father?

Tears slide down my face as I wriggle and try to move, but I'm held in place. Then there's a door opening, and the hand over my mouth is removed.

"About fucking time," the man who I now suspect is Salvo Vitale says. "Father Michael, this is Cade Mancini. His sister, Mia. You will marry us tonight."

Like hell.

"Father," Cade says. "Excuse my sister's appearance. She doesn't hold her liquor well. Let's call it a bachelorette party."

"She looks drugged," the priest says. "She needs to be able to at least speak, for goodness sakes."

"You will marry her or get a bullet in your forehead. You decide," Cade growls.

Oh God, oh God, oh God. This cannot be happening.

He's handing me over to Salvo, and they are going to force me to marry him. My freedom, my life, my...fake marriage. It's all gone.

"Fine, but by law, she needs to give consent," the priest says, less sure, and he should be. Nothing about this is my choice.

Chairs drag on the ground as Cade growls.

"She will give consent."

We all know I will. I have no choice.

Blurry figures move around me when I open my eyes, but my eyes fall closed. I'm no longer fighting—I know how this works. There's no getting away from here. The priest won't help me, or Cade will kill him.

He's killed before.

"Get her up and hold her," Cade says. "Remember the deal, Salvo. You marry my sister, and then you get ten minutes with her before we leave."

I let out a moan, my stomach lurching, as two men pull me to my feet and prop me up.

Tears pour down my face.

Connor.

I know he's betrayed me, but my heart still wants him. I want it to be his face I see as the priest speaks his words. His hands holding me as I say my vows. His eyes on mine as I promise to love him forever.

I think I will anyway.

Despite everything.

"I'm ready. My men are ready," Salvo says. "First my bride, then our empire."

"Enough with the dramatics, Vitale. Just make sure I'm covered when I step into the restaurant and tell my father his time has come, and I am taking over," Cade says, and it hits me like a ton of bricks.

He's going to assassinate our father.

I begin to wriggle, but I'm dropped to the ground as a dark familiar voice speaks behind us.

"You can tell me yourself now, son," my father says.

36

CONNOR

I stand inches behind a man I never thought I would be stepping into battle with.

Joe Mancini.

But my war strategy changed the moment I knew Mia was in danger. Funny how that happens.

My eyes find her lying on the floor, and I fight every damn instinct in my body telling me to push past the mafia leader and go to her. But there are about fifteen guns pointed in the air in all directions, and no one is moving anywhere.

One of them is Nathan, who is pointing a Glock at me.

A scenario we've always considered.

I stare at him, and he doesn't even blink. He's calculating the situation and working out why I didn't tell him we were coming.

Behind him and the others, Joe Mancini's soldiers move in, after taking out the men outside.

They're surrounded.

"Lower your weapons," Joe says to Cade's men. Who are actually Joe's soldiers. "Remember who you work for. My son is not in charge here, nor will he be." He waits for a beat, then growls in a menacing tone. "Drop your fucking weapons or lose your life."

Nathan obeys.

Thank fucking God.

I let out a slow breath and almost feel Mack do the same beside me.

"Fucking disloyal motherfuckers," Cade starts shouting, and all hell breaks loose.

My eyes remain on Mia as Gabrielle—a man we have been watching for many years, Joe's second-in-command—begins screaming at them, waving his guns.

"I knew I shouldn't have trusted you," Vitale shouts, trying to make a run for it.

Boom.

Jimmy "Fingers", Joe's head enforcer, fire's his weapon, and Salvo goes down. Bodies start dropping as bullets fly. I push past Joe and throw my body over Mia's.

She's trembling and making little noises I can't decipher as the room explodes around us.

"Mia, it's me. I've got you," I growl into her hair.

"Cwonner," she cries, clawing at me.

"I've got you," I say, twisting as I scoop her up.

Mack's on my six and nudging me out the door. I take a last look in Nathan's direction as we go. He's against the wall with his hands in surrender mode.

He gives me a small, near indecipherable shake of the head.

Fuck that. I'm sending Mack back for him. We can get him out.

Nathan looks away.

"Go," Mack says, even as my head is screaming, *never leave a man behind.* "He's got this."

Shit.

"Barrett," Joe calls out.

Mia is still in my arms, drugged, feeling no heavier than a ragdoll.

He walks over to me.

"This doesn't mean I trust you. I know you're not going to tell me how you knew Mia was here, but it only strengthens that mistrust."

I nod.

It was what I had to take to get Mia home safely.

"But I *do* trust you with my daughter because I know you've taken a significant risk to save her, and that means something to me."

"She's all that matters here," I reply darkly.

"And if it wasn't for you, I may be dead tonight."

We stare at each other. Two powerful men with our own agendas and desire for complete control.

He nods at me. "You have my blessing. To marry her."

I want to reply *fuck you, I never needed it*, but for some reason, it does matter. Maybe because I know it will matter to Mia.

Because I *am* marrying her.

I am not letting her go.

Not now.

Not ever.

"Take her home," he says, running his fingers across her forehead, which is flopped on my shoulder.

Mack and I walk out the door, leaving the Italian mafia to clean up their shit. I got what I came for.

I've left with much more.

I've gained a small amount of Joe's trust, whether he wants to admit it or not. Saving the Don's life is no small feat, and his code of honor will force him to acknowledge it as he did. But I've also left behind a seed of doubt.

He will never learn the truth from me.

The rest is up to the princess lying in my arms.

37

CONNOR

I stand over the bed, watching the doctor as he cares for Mia. He's my personal doctor and came as soon as Mack called him.

"The drugs will take another few hours to wear off. Twenty-four hours and they'll be out of her system." He takes his stethoscope out of his ears. "Otherwise, she's fine."

"Okay," I say numbly.

"Give her some electrolytes when she wakes. Lots of water. She'll be nauseous, but if she wants to eat, that's fine."

I nod.

"No alcohol for a few days. Tell her to take it easy." He packs up his things. "Connor, you need to report this. The police should be here. I know publicity is harmful, but…"

I shake my head. "Thanks, doc. I need you to keep this confidential. The people who harmed her are being taken care of."

He holds my stare for a long moment. "I'm not going to ask."

"Don't," I say with a hint of darkness. Nobody else needs to get involved.

Mack waits by the door and escorts the doctor out. When he returns, I am still standing in the same position, staring down at her.

"Call Sienna and let her know Mia is home safe."

"Already done," Mack replies. "Decker is updated as well."

"Any news on Nathan?" I ask, and Mack shakes his head.

Fuck, I hated leaving him.

"He would've indicated if he needed us," Mack said. "You know that."

I nod.

But it doesn't lessen the guilt.

We both stand there staring at Mia. Mack slides his hands into his pockets and lets out a quiet sigh.

"She's growing on me," he says, and my lips stretch into a small smile.

Same.

She's stolen my heart—the one I thought was dead.

"You're going to marry her, aren't you? Legit now," Mack asks.

"Yup." I nod. "If she'll have me. But that's a really fucking big *if,* my friend. Otherwise, I go to ground."

He nods.

"I'll prepare for the latter because, honestly, I think your chances are pretty fucking low."

I glance at him, wanting to tell him he's wrong. But he's not. Unless this woman loves me, there's no way she is going to compromise her father. Not unless I tell her everything, and even then, it might not be enough.

And that's a risk I'm not sure I can take.

I CLIMB INTO bed with Mia once Mack leaves. I've changed her into one of my T-shirts and sponged her as much as I can. It was therapeutic in a way. I tug the covers over her and slide my arm under her head, listening to her breathing.

Thank God I found her.

The moonlight falls across the floor as I go over the millions of scenarios that could happen once she wakes. It's the most powerless I've ever felt.

If only she hadn't gone into my office.

Except, even if it took me months to acknowledge I've fallen in love with her, I still would've needed to tell her, eventually.

Wouldn't I?

Lying to Mia forever? No. I respect her too much for that. She's been used her entire life.

I'm a man who gets what he wants, but this time, the power is in her hands. If she can't forgive me, if she can't accept who I am, then I will need to let her walk away.

But I'm not stupid enough to think she will keep my secret forever, which is why Mack is preparing for our exit.

Plan B.

A separate set of IDs for all the Dark Kings, money, and accommodation in case we need to exit fast.

While I knew this day could come, I never thought I'd be doing it and leaving my heart behind.

Mia stirs beside me, and I close my eyes, taking in her warmth and her familiar cinnamon and honey scent.

This could be the last time I hold her, so I'm basking in her softness for as long as I can.

38

MIA

"Ah, fuck," I cry. Consciousness hits me like a sledgehammer.

A body beside me stiffens.

Where am I? Memories, foggy memories, come racing back, and I let out a cry.

"Mia, it's okay. You're safe," Connor says.

Connor?

I blink my eyes open, and he's leaning on an elbow, that gorgeous muscular chest and his sexy tattoo, in all its glory, on display.

"My brother...," I try to say, but my voice is a croak.

"I know. It's okay. We got you out," he tells me, and I'm flooded with relief.

My mouth is clammy, and as I start coughing, Connor hands me a glass of water. Pink water.

"Electrolytes. Drink."

I accept it, and he helps me sit up. I take a sip, and it's heaven. And sweet. With another sip, more memories return.

Sienna.

Salvo Vitale.

"Wedding. God, Connor," I say, being sparse with my words until my throat starts working properly.

But he just nudges at my glass, encouraging me to drink more. There's a tension in his eyes I've never seen before.

"You didn't. We stopped it," he replies, and as I take another drink, I see the way he's clenching his jaw.

"You saved me. Papa, he...OMG, Cade. He was going to kill him," I gasp out.

"All stopped, Mia. Relax. You are home safe," he says, running his hand over my hair affectionately.

I finish my drink, and immediately, I feel better. The electrolytes are working their way into my system.

I lean into him.

"I was so scared," I say, and Connor pulls me into his arms, planting a kiss on my head.

"I know."

"I should've known. I was at Sienna's—"

Oh fuck.

The rest of the black gaps in my memory fill, causing me to stiffen.

"Mia," Connor says, low and dark.

He knows I've remembered, and it's all I can do not to scream into his chest as I realize I'm still not safe.

I've gone from one enemy into the arms of another.

I PUSH AWAY from him after the initial panic subsides. Connor lets me go, and I clamber off the bed.

Then collapse.

"Just take it easy. You're still recovering," he says, tossing back the sheets.

I wave at the air in front of me. "Put something on."

He's naked.

His brows shoot up.

Ugh.

Grabbing the bed, I stand and glance down at my own body to make sure I'm clothed. I'm wearing one of his NAVY T-shirts. He must have dressed me.

"Who are you?" I croak out.

"Connor Barrett," he replies, taking a step toward me. "Your fiancé, and the man you are going to marry."

I snort angrily.

"Is that a threat? Why the fuck does everyone want to marry me?"

"Because you are mine, Mia. I am not letting you go. I know you feel the same way."

I fish-mouth it for a second, not believing my ears. Then, I point toward his office. "You know I saw that shit, right? I know you know."

He nods.

"I don't belong to you. Whatever you had planned is now over." I glance around for my belongings, but I have no idea where my phone or my purse are. "You can't keep me here," I add and can't help but glance at the heavy member hanging between his legs.

Stupid penis.

Connor walks into the wardrobe, and I stand there, staring at the doorway. He walks out in a pair of shorts and a T-shirt.

Well, at least I can now concentrate.

Which doesn't last long because he walks right up to me and cups my face.

"I won't keep you here. If you want to leave, you can, but I ask that you give me a few minutes to tell you what you saw. To explain."

Why do I want him to kiss me, and at the same time run?

"Why would I?"

His thumb brushes over my cheek, and those damn chocolate eyes bear down on me so intensely, they nearly knock me over.

They don't, but his next words do.

"Because, Mia Mancini, I am in love with you."

CONNOR

NOW THAT I have her attention.

"You...Don't lie to me, Connor." She pushes me in the chest, and I smile. "And don't laugh at me. I'm not some stupid woman you can trick."

"I know that now," I say, stepping away to give her space. "Get dressed and let me feed you. Then I will tell you what I can."

She narrows her eyes at me.

"You will tell me everything."

I haven't decided whether I will or not, but I nod.

Mia glares at me, and I realize she's questioning if she should trust me. After what she's been through, I am asking a lot of her.

A better man would've taken her home to her father and then waited for her to be ready. That wasn't and isn't an option.

Obviously.

I have this one chance to save my life and see if I can convince Mia to be a part of it. Because I do fucking love her. It's ruined everything, but I do.

"I swear on my life, you're safe. Mia, I love you. I risked every-thing last night to get you back."

She blinks. "My father."

Mia's so damn smart.

"Yes," I say. "I had to tell him what was happening, as no one wants Cade to take over, and I wasn't letting anyone else marry you. You belong here with me."

I'm throwing it all at her.

"You saved his life."

I nod.

"Why? I saw..." She points down the hall. "What is it? Why, Connor?"

Emotions boil up, and tears fill her eyes.

"I never wanted you to find that."

"Clearly."

She wipes her eyes, and I can't help it. I go to her and pull her into my arms.

"Ugh, why am I letting you hug me?"

"Because I think you might love me too," I say, but even I can hear the heavy hope in my voice.

I've never been so unsure.

39

CONNOR

Mia showers while I make us breakfast. It gives me time to consider what I will tell her. By the time she walks downstairs, I've changed my mind about five times.

"Not going to lie. The need to run out that door is overwhelming." She sits on one of the kitchen stools. "But you saved my father's life, and I know he wouldn't have let you take me home if he didn't trust you a little."

Honestly, no one could've stopped me.

I had enough of my own weapons and men around me, including Mack, if it came to that. Which it didn't because I was still in control of what was happening.

However, if it makes Mia feel safe right now, then I'll take it. So, I nod.

"Why do you have all those photos of my family on your wall? The truth," she asks as I slide pancakes in front of her.

I lean against the kitchen bench, facing her, and sip my coffee. I'm about to tell the fifth person in my life my story, and this time, it feels even more important.

I never thought I'd fall in love.

Caring for my Dark Kings is different. I know they can protect

267

themselves. The likelihood of them dying on me is slim, despite the risks they are taking each and every day.

Mia is vulnerable.

Which means I'm now vulnerable.

"Because I think they may have murdered my family," I tell her. "Correction, slaughtered."

Her face pales.

She drops the fork she's holding and swallows.

"I thought they died in an accident?" she whispers, and I shake my head.

"It may not be anyone in your family, but I've been investigating for a long time, Mia." I put the coffee down on the bench and slide my hands into my pockets. "If I tell you anymore than I have, it will put you in danger."

I let that sink in.

She's a mafia princess. I don't have to spell it out. Mia knows exactly what that means.

She stares down at her plate, then slowly, she lifts her eyes and meets mine. "I want to know."

"You sure?"

I need her to be sure.

"Connor, you just told me you love me. You're insisting I marry you," Mia says, and a tinge of hope springs to life in my chest.

"Yup," I reply, forcing myself to stay where I am.

"Then I deserve to know everything," she adds.

I stand there, staring at her, my brain misfiring. I'm trying to work out what she is saying.

"Mia," I finally get out, my hands sliding out of my pockets.

My feet are moving.

She slides off the stool as I pull her into my arms and my mouth claims hers. I don't know what this means, but it's been this way between us from the start. We're like fucking magnets, unable to stay away from one another.

My mouth takes from her, sweeping through her sweetness

and reminding her she's all mine. I know it's not that simple, but right now, I need her. I need to make her mine.

She pulls her lips from me, and I groan. "Mia."

"I need to know everything first." Her eyes close for a moment. When they open, they lock with mine. "Because if you make love to me one more time, Connor Barrett, and then break my heart, I won't survive."

"The only way this ends badly, Mia, is if you leave me. Then we'll both be fucking broken."

I gently kiss her lips one more time, then lead her down to my office.

Where do I begin?

40

MIA

Tears pour down my face as Connor tells me his story. He's right—it's dangerous that I know. Possibly more than anyone else because Joe Mancini is my father.

I know he's done terrible things. I also know he's responsible for the deaths of many people. Fathers and even mothers.

But children?

I feel equal parts shame, hatred, and nausea at the fact it could be my father who was responsible.

God, my heart is tearing apart imagining what Connor saw that day as a scared little boy under his parents' stairs, watching this Carlos person shoot his family one by one.

His sister, Rebecca. A tiny child.

Then, thinking they might hunt him as he withheld his screams and tears, hoping not to be found.

It's horrific.

Connor believes it might be my father who ordered this Carlos to do these horrific things. I want to deny it, but we both know it's possible.

I brush away my tears with my arm, and more begin falling just as quickly. I don't know how I'm able to departmentalize how

I feel about my family. Perhaps it's a coping mechanism. How can I love my father while still being aware he does these things?

It's for this exact reason I don't want to be part of the mafia world.

From drugs to people trafficking and worse, I cannot and won't work in my family's business. Yet, to turn a blind eye and let Connor actively search for proof that my father ordered the slaughter of his family?

To marry him and not warn my father...To sit back and let him kill my father?

Because I know he will.

Can I do that?

Can I stay silent and carry on with my life, knowing this is going on? While loving the man who could kill him?

It's asking too much.

"It may not be him, Mia," Connor says, sitting on the edge of his desk as I stand between his legs and stare into space over his shoulder.

He wipes a couple of tears from my cheek.

"If it is, you will kill him," I say, sniffing.

He's silent.

When he doesn't reply after a long minute, I meet his eyes. The pain on his face mirrors how I feel. This is an impossible situation.

"You belong to me, Mia," Connor says, his voice thick as he grips my face almost painfully. "You are mine, and I'm going to fucking marry you."

A sound escapes me as he takes my mouth, and I let him.

He doesn't want to lose me; I don't want to lose him, but if I marry him and he destroys my family, I'm as responsible for their deaths as Connor.

I make another guttural sound against his lips, and he stops and gazes down at me. Then with a *fuck this,* he swipes at whatever is on his desk—papers, a monitor, a mobile phone—and lifts me onto it.

Thank God.

I claw at his T-shirt, needing him as much as he needs me. I haven't said it out loud, but I am deeply and madly in love with Connor Barrett.

There's just no way we can ever be together.

So, while he rips my clothes from me and tosses his own across the floor, I let him make love to me for the last time.

41

CONNOR

Mia's insane if she thinks I'm letting her go.

Not because I've told her all my secrets. Not because she's the greatest fuck of my life—although, that's a fantastic bonus. It's because I love her with all of my dark, crumbled heart.

Because she needs my protection.

Because without me, she'll be handed over to a gangster who would never love, honor, cherish, or pleasure her like I can.

Like I will.

I tug her to the edge of the desk and take in her complete, glistening nakedness. My body feels pumped, anxious, and in need of claiming this woman in ways I've never experienced before.

I feel hungry, raw, primal.

"Hurry," Mia pleads as my eyes slide over her breasts, my fingers following their path.

I let out a low moan when she reacts to my touch. When she arches and those pink mounds rise up, I grip my cock, stroking it, teasing it between her wet folds.

"More," she groans, trying to control this, but she knows she can't.

I palm the wall above her head and sweep my lips over hers.

Mia wraps her legs around me, and I nudge my cock in a small inch, licking my lips as she reacts with a sexy damn gasp.

As her pussy clamps over the head, my patience dissolves in a flash. In a growl, I thrust inside her, hard and fast.

"There's no going back, Mia Luna Mancini."

"Connor," she cries.

"You're mine." I press my eyes closed as I pull out, then slam into her again, then again, then again.

God, fucking hell, she feels like heaven. Feels like mine.

When I open my eyes, I see tears falling down her cheeks, and I know Mia believes this is the end, and she's leaving me, but she's wrong.

I won't fucking let her.

We will find a way.

I will find a way.

I reach between us, find her clit, and rub harshly as I speed up the friction, claiming her pleasure and demanding her soul.

"Harder, Connor. God, take me, own me," Mia cries.

"That's it, good girl. Give me all of you," I cry with her, almost there.

Her pussy tightens, and those eyes lock on me as she begins to pant, showing me she's close. Her eyes flicker and slide back in her head, and she begins to tremble.

"Connorrrrr, I need..."

She doesn't finish her sentence because she knows I know what she needs and that I am the only man alive who can give it to her.

I lift Mia's hips, taking my cock deeper, and pound until scorching heat travels down my spine, and I'm filling her with my seed.

Every last drop.

✦

AN HOUR LATER, we're soaking in my hot tub, holding each other. Mia sits between my legs, running her fingers through mine, up my forearm. Touching every inch of me she can reach.

She still thinks she's saying goodbye.

I'm still trying to work out how to keep her. I kiss her neck and move her long, dark hair aside. She lets out a little moan.

I harden.

I reach and slide my fingers into her pussy, feeling the cream, so I lift her, and she easily takes my cock again.

God, I want this every day for the rest of my life.

The question is, what am I willing to give up?

Mia might be a mafia princess who knows how these things work, but she won't tolerate me killing her father if he's ultimately the one responsible for my family.

And how can I not?

As she rides me and I throw my head back, letting out a moan, I realize it's not just her who has to take a step toward a fucking uncomfortable choice. It's both of us.

I'm not letting her go. Not fucking ever.

And she's here, alive, with me, fucking me, and while she hasn't said it, I know Mia is in love with me.

But my family is gone.

Nothing can change that. Nothing will bring them back.

If I let her go, what will that achieve?

That's not to say I won't destroy Joe Mancini if he's the one, but for Mia, to have her and love her for the rest of my life... Perhaps I can spare her father's life.

After all, I have taken the asshole's daughter instead.

"Fuck my cock, Mia," I growl, taking her hips. "That's it."

"Oh God, oh God," she cries.

"Come for me again, like a good fucking girl," I say, my own orgasm teasing.

Then I feel her rubbing her clit, and I'm gone.

"Yes, motherfucking, yes, fuck!" I cry.

Mia collapses, and when I catch my breath, I pull her off my cock, lift her into my arms, and climb out of the hot tub.

We shower, just staring at each other, kissing and saying nothing. Then I turn the water off and wrap a towel around her.

She pads out of the bathroom, and I lean my hands on the bench, looking at myself in the mirror.

I was nine when I saw my family slaughtered. Now, at thirty-three years of age, after all this time seeking revenge, can I really promise Mia I won't kill her father?

If I prove his guilt?

Will the Dark Kings respect my decision after committing six years of their lives, despite their own motivations, to this cause?

I brush my teeth, shave, then slap some moisturizer on my face before walking out into the bedroom.

"Mia?"

My heart tightens in my chest.

Fuck.

42

MIA

I need to take another look on my own.

Without the panic. Although, that's debatable. Seeing all the photos on the walls, with so many of them recognizable, it still creates so many different emotions within me. Fear, sadness, terror to a degree, and responsibility.

I need to warn them.

The air is colder in here, and I shiver as I turn and take in the desk where we made love. It's a total mess, and a small smile hits my lips.

Connor is an incredible lover. Today was different from before. I felt his love in every touch. Did he feel mine?

I want to say it, but who would I be if I agreed to the murder of my own father?

I was born into a mafia family. One of the most powerful. All of them have done terrible things. Should I have to live my life protecting them, paying the price for their sins?

Have to walk away from the man I love because of it?

Everyone has a choice. There are consequences for every action in life.

If I walk away from Connor, I let them win.

I will have to return home and eventually be married off "in the family."

I know what it means to be loved and adored and protected by a powerful man who will do anything for me. I'm not enough of a gambling woman to give him up and hope it happens a second time.

So, if I do, I need to know love won't be in my future.

If I choose him, there's a price to pay. My father's life.

Possibly.

My eyes cast around the room, and I realize it's not about whether I can accept that price. It's about whether I can live without Connor.

The answer is yes. I can.

I will be miserable, but I can live without him.

But for what? To protect a man who is a dark shadow on society. I shouldn't have to pay the price for his choices.

But I'm not Joe Mancini.

I may be his daughter, but I'm not a killer.

If I marry Connor and sit back and let him kill my father, *should* Papa be responsible, then I'm no better than him.

I can't live with that.

I lift my hand and stare at the Rock of Gibraltar, twirling it between my fingers. I belong to Connor. I always have. From the moment I spilled whiskey on him.

My eyes fill with tears.

God, I love him so damn much.

I'm not surprised when enormous arms come around me and tighten.

"Mia," he purrs like a lion. "Mia Luna Mancini,"

We stand there for a long moment, until suddenly, Connor reaches in front of me and pulls my photo off the wall, scrunching it and tossing it.

What did he just do?

I spin in his arms, and our eyes connect.

"I love you," I say, tears prickling in my eyes. I need to tell him I can't be responsible for a man's death, but the words are struck.

"I know." Connor cups my face, then he drops to his knees.

Oh my God.

"Mia. My love. Marry me. Be my wife. Forever," Connor says as my mouth stays gaping. "I promise to spare your father's life, regardless of what I discover, but I refuse to spend *my* life without you."

Oh God.

My hand flies to my mouth. "You would do that?"

"Mia, I would do fucking anything for you. Now, please say yes," he growls, and there's a glint in his eyes.

I nod, smiling as I cry.

"Words, Mia."

"Yes, yessss!" I let out a wet laugh and fall to my knees in front of him, throwing my arms around his neck. "Yes, I will marry you. Forever."

"Great. This is so much easier than having to kidnap you for the next sixty years." Connor grins as he scoops me up.

Then he takes me to bed.

EPILOGUE
CONNOR

The helicopter begins its descent onto the front lawn of the Long Island Mancini Mansion, and I squeeze Mia's hand.

We'll be here for the next five days.

I'm still grappling with the fact I'm marrying into a fucking mafia family—for real—but then those crystal blue eyes meet mine, and I don't give a shit.

I have the woman I love.

The rest, I will deal with.

The Dark Kings were unsurprised and said we'd deal with it. God, I love those assholes. Mack has a new respect for Mia, and now there are no secrets. They get along like a house on fire.

In fact, he's very protective of her.

George kicked her ass, and she apologized, then said she wanted to keep him as her security detail. He was trying to hide his pleasure, but it was written all over his face.

Protecting a mafia princess isn't easy. She's not as innocent as she makes out. Every day is an adventure with her, and I'm totally up for the challenge.

"Jesus, Mia." Sienna is staring at the vast estate with her mouth open. "This place is enormous."

Mia grins and then smiles up at me.

I can't wait to show her some of the homes I have around the U.S. and the world. Mia has much to learn about my life, and I've already begun preparing what we need for her if we ever have to activate Plan B. As my wife, she will always be protected and by my side.

"It's just a house, babe," Mia says as the chopper hits the grass. "I can't wait to show you around. Your room is right next to mine. Ours."

Her hand lands on my leg affectionately.

"Now I can show you my dress!" She wiggles, then glances at me. "Not you. We're doing things properly now."

"Now?" Sienna asks, and Mia waves her comment away.

I smirk.

Things changed fast once I proposed for real. Mia said she wanted to keep her ring when I offered to buy her a new one.

"The Rock of Gibraltar is part of our journey to falling in love with each other," she had said.

"The Rock of what?" I'd asked but got waved off.

Ignoring whatever that meant, when I reflected back to the moment I chose her engagement ring, I realized there was a part of me that *was* selecting it for her, not the agreement, and perhaps even then, I knew it was forever.

And it is.

Mia Mancini, soon-to-be Barrett, is mine.

For fucking ever.

Her happiness and safety are my priority. Everything else comes second. Joe can ask us again about babies, if he wants. We've agreed we want three. Or four. A big family.

First, we need to get this enormous Italian wedding over with.

Five long days.

Deliveries have been arriving for weeks, with one thing or another. A second helicopter will follow us shortly with more Barrett security. Some arrived by car ten minutes ago.

I'm not taking any risks.

I glance outside. There's a light drizzle, and I see two men running across the lawn with their umbrellas up. Joe is standing under the awning, smoking a cigar.

One day, you will learn that your daughter saved your life.

I'm still dedicated to finding Carlos, or whoever destroyed my family. When we're married and arrive back home, I will open my father's boxes and solve the mystery of the key and what it unlocks.

It's nearly time.

Right now, I am clear about what's important to me. Mia. Our marriage and the family we create together.

My revenge will resume in five days.

What can go wrong in the meantime?

THE TWO MEN drop the umbrellas as they get closer to the chopper blades, and one opens the door.

Shit. Nathan.

I don't have the details yet, but he's been able to gain back the trust of the senior Mancini and, it appears, to get even closer to the guy.

So apparently, he's attending my wedding after all.

He's looking gangster as fuck, with all his tatts on show and gun holster over his black shirt. That same smirk on his dial.

The blades slow to a stop, and we can all finally hear and stop shouting.

"Ladies," Nathan says with a grin, completely ignoring me, then reaches out a hand to Sienna.

She blushes and gives him her hand, shooting Mia a look which speaks to all kinds of trouble.

Hell no.

Mia's friend is off limits, Nate.

Sienna starts to climb out, slips and lets out a squeal as the umbrella goes flying.

"Sen!" Mia cries.

Nathan simply scoops her up. "I've got you, little lady."

"Oh my God." Sienna gasps like some eighteenth-century madam as I roll my eyes.

"I think it's better if I just carry you," Nathan says, winking at her.

"Oh, umm," Sienna starts, but it's too late. Nathan is already walking across the lawn with her in his arms.

"What is your name, my fair maidan?" I hear Nate ask.

For the love of God.

"Sienna," she says, with another little laugh and a glance back at us.

I gave her some instructions on how to behave and stay safe during our five days. Falling into the arms of a Mancini gangster was not on the damn list.

Lucky it was Nathan.

Mia glances at me with a mix of concern but grins, biting her lip. "We need to keep her away from these men. They're dangerous."

One thing I haven't done yet is introduce her to Nathan and Decker. That's their decision to make. A risk they need to take. However, she's aware Mack knows the truth.

"I'll make sure no one touches her. Now, let's go," I say, taking her hand and helping her out. I take the umbrella from the second guy. "You going to carry us?"

"No, sir." The guy shakes his head and takes off.

"Bully." Mia nudges me.

"You know how this works, princess. It's a pecking order." I take her hand again. "Let's go save Sienna and get married. Then get the hell out of here."

She slaps my chest, and I smile down at her.

"You're lucky I love you."

"I am. I'm the luckiest fucking man on earth." Then I stop, pull her against me despite the rain, and kiss her hard.

She's breathless when she says, "You just did that to upset my father."

I grin and start walking.

Yes. Yes, I did.

He's still my enemy, and this is not over.

Want to read Nathan and Sienna's dark romance in THE RUTHLESS KING?
Go to www.books2read.com/theruthlessking
Turn the page to read the book description.

If you love steamy romances with dark tones, then check out **SINFUL DUTY!** The eBook is **FREE** to download! Turn the page to read chapter one or go to www.books2read.com/sinfulduty-dufort now to get your copy.

It's also available in paperback!

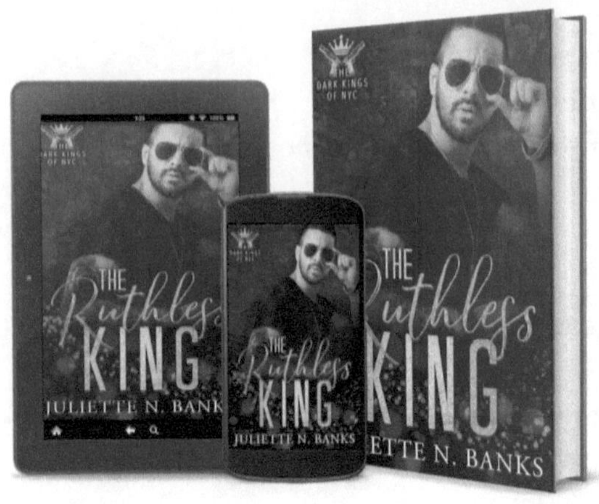

THE RUTHLESS KING

NATHAN

A fellow former marine of mine has fallen in love and is marrying the fucking mafia princess. For the next five days, I have to pretend I don't know him while being undercover inside the Mancini mob. Except I do. We're both members of the Dark Kings —former military dedicated to avenging those we love.

When the wedding party arrives and bridesmaid, Sienna, falls into my arms—*literally*—green eyes lift to mine with an invitation my body says *hell yes* to.

I know I should stay away, but I have two choices: corrupt her or protect her. Both come with deadly consequences.

SIENNA

I've just learned my best friend's father is a mobster. When we fly to his mansion IN. A. HELICOPTER, it's clear I'm out of my depth.

It's both thrilling and terrifying.

There are gorgeous armed gangsters everywhere, but it's Nathan who watches me behind his dark sunglasses, who's captivated me.

I crave his touch and the white-hot lust between us. Despite the danger it poses.

When I find myself thrust into a web of lies and vengeance, I'm not sure if I will get out of here alive. Or with my heart intact.

The Ruthless King is the second book in The Dark Kings of NYC, a dark billionaire mafia romance, by bestselling author Juliette N. Banks. If you enjoy dark spicy romances with twists, revenge, and dominant, protective heroes, then you'll love this book. Expect a happy ever after in every book.

Get your copy at www.books2read.com/theruthlessking

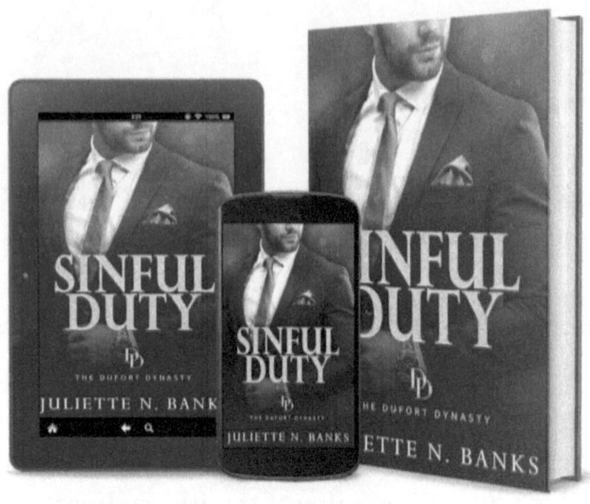

SINFUL DUTY
Chapter 1

Daniel Dufort lifted his whisky to his lips and nodded at the blonde who was regaling him with an apparently *hilarious* story of her father at their recent New Year's party.

Daniel knew who the man was. The fact he'd actually spent time with his wife and family was a small Christmas miracle. He'd heard rumors—and his source was pretty reliable—that her father, Senator Johnson, had two girlfriends. Neither of which knew about the other. With Valentine's Day approaching, it would be an expensive one for the politician.

Three women. *Ugh.*

Daniel shivered at the thought. He preferred his women in and out in an evening, not sticking around for breakfast or a ring on their fingers.

He glanced around *Bar Hugo*, one of Manhattan's most exclusive bars, and saw most of his key connections had now left. The only reason he was still nursing his Macallan was, to put it bluntly, his cock. The blonde, who wouldn't stop talking, was going to have her mouth around it within the next hour.

Beep, beep.

Daniel, we need to speak. Meet me in your office in an hour.

After reading his father's message, he mentally rearranged his plans. Dropping his crystal glass onto the polished wooden bar, he replied to confirm he'd see him there, and then took the petite blonde's arm. "Shall we go?"

Her face lit up.

"Your place or mine?" she purred.

"I have a meeting in my office tonight, so let's head there," he replied, leading her to the private exit. The last thing he wanted was to be photographed with her and more gossip spread about his relationship status.

When would the media give up? He was never getting married.

She hesitated slightly as his offer sank in. There would be no breakfast in bed. Daniel held her gaze. The decision was hers—she could take it or leave it.

He knew she'd take it.

They all did.

A billionaire in a suit was an aphrodisiac to these types of women.

Like his brothers, he had inherited their father's good looks. At six foot three with a muscular frame—which he worked hard to maintain in his gym—and a square jaw, Daniel was confident and powerful.

Some of it learned. Some of it was natural.

In the United States, and other places around the world, Daniel Dufort was frequently quoted in business and economic media, and unfortunately in less respected publications for the women he took to events. Rarely, if ever, was it the same women, and yet they insisted on discussing his marital status.

The gossip columns had a few cringeworthy nicknames for

him. Try as he may, Daniel struggled to keep his sex life private. He only had a few rules.

No promises.

Nothing overnight.

No, do overs.

Okay, fine—he occasionally slept with the same woman twice, but not in the same quarter or it gave the wrong impression.

Daniel Dufort wasn't interested in a relationship. Of any kind. He didn't believe in true love, nor was he going to settle for something vanilla. However, he did enjoy female company, and the activities at the end of the evening, so he took dates to the events he had to attend, or to meet some social obligation.

And he wasn't lacking in options.

But a relationship was not for him.

Settling down with a *best friend* and having missionary-style sex three times a week? No thanks.

As predicted, she'd walked through the door, so they head to Dufort Towers. Daniel hung his dark gray Tom Ford jacket on the hanger and turned.

Miss Johnson—*fuck, he'd forgotten her name*—lingered, taking in the valuable 57th Avenue view that overlooked Central Park. It was one of the best along Billionaire Row.

"Stunning," she said, stepping up to the full-length glass.

Daniel removed his cufflinks, and they pinged as he dropped them on his custom-made oak wood desk. He rolled his shirt sleeves to his elbows and checked the time on his Piguet watch.

They had thirty-five minutes.

Daniel moved to stand beside Miss Johnson and dug his hands in his pockets. "I'm going to assume you give head."

She turned, her mouth opening.

A good start.

Daniel leaned in and ran his finger through her hair. "Or I can bend you over my desk and fuck you. You decide."

Her mouth closed and acceptance settled over her features.

She was too proud to storm out, and he knew she was wet for him.

She reached for his fly and slid to her knees. "Both." Her eyes lifted to his as she gripped his cock.

Daniel didn't answer. He simply watched her tongue swirl around his swollen head and take him deeper, inch by inch.

Daniel let out a low moan. He gripped her hair and pressed in further while she moved skillfully over and around him. It wasn't long before he was fucking her throat as she milked him dry. He groaned out his orgasm while she swallowed.

That was a bonus—he thought she'd be a spitter.

She sat back on her Manolo Blahnik heels and licked her lips. She was a beautiful woman, more natural than many in this town, but like all those before her, Daniel suddenly lost interest.

Most of them were here for his last name. They often had trust funds or money of their own, but he had power and they falsely believed by marrying him, they would also have power.

They were wrong. Power was something one either had or didn't have. It came from within, as much as a bank balance.

Dufort Hotels, which made up most of the Dufort Dynasty, had properties all over the world. It had been built by his father and went public five years ago. Two years ago, his father had stepped away—though remained the majority shareholder—and Daniel had taken on the position he'd been groomed for all his life.

CEO of Dufort Hotels.

"Thank you for being my date tonight," he said, zipping his pants. God, why could he not remember her name? Megan. Shit. "Give your father my regards, Megan."

She stood and smiled at him, all sultry. "I think you've forgotten about part two."

No. He hadn't.

Fortunately, his father was always early and at any moment he'd be interrupted if things got tense. Occasionally, claws came out when they felt rejected.

"Looks like we are out of time. I need to prepare for my meeting," he replied with no pretense of disappointment, then stepped away. "Please make use of the facilities before you leave if you need to."

Daniel stepped behind his large desk and lifted his laptop open.

Megan cleared her throat and picked up her purse. "No, thank you. I will gargle the sperm from my throat with a glass of *Cristal* champagne when I get home," she replied, then spun and walked out of the office with her head held high.

Despite himself, Daniel smiled.

Good for her.

A moment later, his father stepped into his office, thumbing his finger over his shoulder. "Was that Senator Johnson's daughter I saw leaving?"

"Yes. She accompanied me to the *Glass Towers* rebrand launch this evening," Daniel said.

Glass Towers were a friendly competitor in New York City, but a competitor, nevertheless. He'd chosen the senator's daughter as a political statement because of some government lobbying he was doing regarding the water system in Manhattan. The CEO, David Glass, disagreed with Dufort, which could cost *Glass Towers* a small fortune if it went ahead. But it was the right thing to do, and they both knew it.

Daniel smiled. He loved the game, and he was good at it.

Johnathan Dufort walked over to the same spot Megan had *performed* in and rocked on his feet. It wasn't unusual for them to meet in the evenings, but Daniel knew what this was about. It had been a hot topic for weeks and was his least favorite subject right now.

"I don't have good news, son," he said. "The agreement is still missing and now Senator Mackenzie is trying to extort us."

He looked up.

"With what?" Daniel asked loudly. "He's already doing that by claiming we owe him more interest on the initial loan than was originally agreed to."

Nearly two decades ago his father had entered an agreement with his then friend, Bill Mackenzie. The amount had been substantial—in the high six figures—and was paramount in Dufort Hotels growing into what it was today. The loan was to be repaid in twenty years with three percent interest.

It was no secret. Their finance team had been putting the money aside over the years and were preparing to pay it out in this financial year.

A few weeks ago, they'd received a letter from the *now* senator requesting payment for a much larger sum. Attached was a copy of the agreement.

Except it wasn't the original—it had been doctored.

The three percent interest had ballooned to *fifteen* percent. A rate no one in their right mind would agree to.

Very few people were aware of the situation, outside his father, his brothers Fletcher and Hunter, their financial advisor and lawyer. The latter had advised they hunt down a copy of the agreement before going to the authorities.

Johnathan Dufort had thought he had a copy at home in his own files, along with the one kept in the vault at Dufort Dynasty.

Apparently not.

His father ran a hand over his face.

Shit.

"Father. Tell me."

Johnathan slammed his fist down onto the arm of the sofa next to him. "He has said we have thirty days to pay, or he wants his daughter married into the Dufort family. The prenup cannot exclude her from the Dynasty shares."

"You have got to be fucking kidding me," Daniel growled.

He knew what was coming next.

"She has asked for you."

Get Harper and Daniels steamy billionaire romance, **Sinful Duty** **eBook FREE** right now!

www.books2read.com/sinfulduty-dufort

It is also available in paperback.

ALSO BY JULIETTE N. BANKS

Go to www.juliettebanks.com to buy or download

The Dark Kings of NYC

The Darkest King

The Ruthless King

COMING SOON

COMING SOON

THE DUFORT DYNASTY

Sinful Duty (**FREE**)

Forbidden Touch

Total Possession

Desire Unbound

Dark Surrender

THE MORETTI BLOOD BROTHERS

The Vampire Prince (**FREE**)

The Vampire Protector

The Vampire Spy

The Vampire's Christmas

The Vampire Assassin

The Vampire Awoken

The Vampire Lover

The Vampire Wolf

The Vampire Warrior

The Vampire's Oath

The Vampire's Fate

THE MORETTI BLOOD WOLVES

Steamy paranormal shifter romance

The Alpha Wolf

The Unbound Wolf

The Protector Wolf

REALM OF THE IMMORTALS

The Archangels Battle

The Archangel's Heart

The Archangel's Star

LET'S STAY IN TOUCH

JOIN MY PRIVATE READERS GROUP!
www.facebook.com/groups/authorjuliettebanksreaders

Official Juliette N. Banks website:
www.juliettebanks.com

Instagram:
www.instagram.com/juliettebanksauthor
Facebook:
www.facebook.com/juliettenbanks
TikTok:
@juliettebanksauthor

Want to know when I have a free book or something on promotion? Here's two great ways:

Follow me on BookBub
www.bookbub.com/authors/juliette-n-banks

Or join my BookClub
https://bit.ly/JNB_VIP_BOOKCLUB